GW01466067

SO LONG AS THEY'RE CHEERING

SO LONG
AS THEY'RE
CHEERING

Sue Krisman

WEIDENFELD AND NICOLSON
LONDON

£
‾
100

Published in Great Britain in 1986 by
George Weidenfeld & Nicolson Limited
91 Clapham High Street, London SW4 7TA

ISBN 0 297 78803 5

Typeset at The Spartan Press Ltd,
Lymington, Hants
Printed in Great Britain by Butler & Tanner Ltd
Frome and London

This book is dedicated with love to my sisters

And in loving memory of L. E. Jacobson

ACKNOWLEDGEMENTS

It is with real gratitude that I acknowledge the help and encouragement with research matters that was given with such cheerful willingness by:

Professor William Fishman of Queen Mary's College, London University; Dr Harold Silver, Principal of Bulmershe College of Higher Education; Dr Clem Adelman, Reader in Educational Research, Bulmershe College of Higher Education; Danny Friedman of the Victoria and Albert Theatre Museum; Colleagues and library staff of Bulmershe College of Higher Education; Celia and Michael Press.

PROLOGUE

1   And from the twelve tribes of Israel *came* leaders and warriors. There came good men and women of worth. There came those who would oppress and men of violence. There came the sick and after them the healers, the evildoers and after them the lawmakers and *those* too simple to know right from wrong. There came the musicmakers and the scribes, the *poets who* with their womenfolk, their children and their children's children in every generation told and retold the tales of the nation.

2   And the people *listened* and the people *were* wondrous glad.

3   And lo, in the *fullness* of time, though many elders of the tribe spoke ill *of* the poets in their midst who laboured not, the storytellers came *unto* the people and *told* their mysteries and their wonders with tongues of silver *and* apparel of gold.

4   They *travelled* far from the cities of their birth to *bring word* each to another of peace and of bloodshed, of joys and of sorrows, of darkness and of light.

5   And the people *hearkened well* to the tales the strangers brought *and* learned the ways of foreign lands *and* the manners of many nations.

6   So the people listened *and* the people learned.

7   And in the time of Elisha, *from* the tribe of Reuben, from the loins *of* Joab the Tishbite, came a great leader of men, strong in sinew and tall of bearing. He were a comely man, light of hair about him and *his* voice was the voice of the lyre. When he spake silence came upon the market place.

8   And the people listened *and* the people were moved.

9   Thus they *spread* the words of the man of the tribe of Reuben and called him *even* son of Reuben. And he gathered about him not men of valour nor men of the sword, but men and womenfolk and *their* children and *their* children's children who had the gift of tongues.

10   And they went forth *and* they multiplied.

ACT I

SCENE I
Wisherodik, 1891

Bubba Rubenovska had been dying on the Yiddish stage for as long as she had been alive.

Back at the beginning of the nineteenth century, in the light of a kerosene lamp, in rough tenting, her cheeks artificially whitened, she had lain motionless on couches, on floors, in arms, until she grew too big to be carried and was succeeded by her younger sister. There is a right and wrong way to be dead and in this, Bubba's final death scene, she could be relied upon to die like a professional.

On a particularly ordinary day in 1891, when she was as old as the century itself – or thereabouts, for in those days who kept records? – Bubba decided that enough was enough.

She washed her sheitl and made quite sure it was dry before putting it neatly over her thinning hair. You could catch your death in a damp wig. She dressed in her finest, most embroidered nightclothes, slipped neatly into the bed that had seen her through a good marriage and the bearing of nine children, then, for all anyone knows and nobody would be surprised, sold tickets to the best-acted public death witnessed in the long histrionic record of the ancient family of the son of Reuben.

She holds a growing audience in her overfurnished, over-flounced bedroom, daguerreotypes of herself in her roles and costumes on every surface and every inch of wall. Despite being of the Rubenovska family only by marrying into it, she is passionate about their future and as the family gathers she urges them never to stray from the family tradition. To uphold their theatrical standards to the best of their individual abilities and to marry wisely so as to breed year by decade better performers. Randomly amongst these wisdoms she strews parts of plays she has loved, tells stories of Rubenovska triumph and failure, of sagacity and foolishness. She sings half sentences of songs even the older members of the family can barely remember.

She alternately harangues and entertains the family, happily aware that this time for once no one will interrupt, interfere or argue with her. She does not notice that except for me, Zelda Shergold, no one is listening. My sister, Leah, is getting above herself as usual. All the children have stopped being good. Now that Bubba is still talking and not dying as they'd been promised, they see no need to keep still and not fidget. On top of that, Uncle Sol goes nowhere, not even into a sickroom, without his pipe and Great Aunt Mimmie wafts her camphor smell as if it came from her pores.

It's so oppressive in there it can't hurt if I tiptoe out a minute to give you a little look around.

Here, in the now-Polish, now-Russian village of Wisherodik live many of the branches of the Rubenovska family who are content to make a living anyhow by day just so long as they can act by night.

But quite a few families prefer to live in Vilna. That's a busy, bustling place ripe for business if you have the head for it, and not too long a ride away from Wisherodik if you have a horse and plenty of time. Only Cousin Avrom the hochum, the cleversticks, had to go all the way to London (London's also a busy place they say) to make his own theatre and writes home letters of such success you can believe him or not as you please.

But in Wisherodik the Rubenovskas seem to be everywhere. If there's a committee formed they are bound to be on it. In the synagogue they are good doers, giving a bit here and there for charity, making up a minyan, a quorum; taking home to a meal any stranger to the village. And of course they sing. The bimah, from which prayers are led in the synagogue, is also a

4

raised platform and to a Rubenovska a stage is a stage. But pray? Well, it's nobody's business but the Almighty's whether they do or they don't.

Scholars of the Torah they're not, except for the bits with the stories, but they are mostly wise and generous with their time, willing to find a few zloties for the Rabbi, bless his soul, or a few planks and the thumps to nail them for a neighbour's house when it has been pushed about a bit by a pogrom here and there. In fact in Wisherodik no one has a bad word to say about the Rubenovskas. (With such a large family a bad word could get in the wrong ear, you understand.)

No matter what job they conscientiously do in order to put dumplings in the family soup and dimples in the family cheeks, when they've finished the tilling or tailoring, shoeing the horses or birthing a calf, when even the committee meetings are adjourned for lack of breath, there is miraculously always time enough left over for the Rubenovskas and the families Shergold (that's my father, called Tata or Tata Dovid by everyone), Littman, Preiska and Weissen, who had the sense to marry themselves into glory, to go secretly, in twos and threes, to the bare and basic little playhouse they built with their own unskilled skilful hands and give there the performances Wisherodik and all the surrounding districts live for.

And you're asking me why did they have to go there in secret? And why does the theatre from the outside look for all the world like a cowshed in constant use?

Ah. That's because now we're talking about Poland in the 1890s and in those days to be Jewish was not the simple straightforward privilege that it is today.

When the tsars – a fire in their guts, though the curse sounds better and more painful in Yiddish – had finished forbidding the Jews this trade and that trade and had driven them out of enough towns to make the barren permitted areas so over-crowded that even the Jews' own brethren started to get mad, the authorities, not finished yet, found a few more uncomfort-able decrees to decree.

There were times when the Jews wondered whether the tsars wouldn't have preferred them gone altogether.

One of the minor irritations was that they were forbibben to assemble in groups. Then the Jewish Theatre was closed down; 1883 that was, ask any Rubenovska child. Finally, any performance in Yiddish was banned outright. Now are you beginning to understand the sense of building a theatre that looks like a barn yet has never seen a cow? – unless a plot should call for one especially, that is.

Perhaps it is puzzling you that with such problems on their heads as not being allowed to do the work they were capable of, not being allowed to live decently, that with such tsorus as seeing the family you loved hungry and sometimes ill in the ways that poverty and repression bring, how anyone has the head or the time to worry about a little bit of acting, a little bit of pretend.

But think. Last time you went to a theatre and the show was good, what did you do? You forgot. You forgot your troubles, forgot your husband never appreciated you, forgot your wife always kicks you when you're down, even that decision you'll have to make sooner or later you forgot.

That's why, in every community, after the well and the pump, the synagogue and the school – and I'm not saying in what order – comes a raised platform, rows of seats and a curtain's also nice.

And make no mistake about it, the standards of Yiddish Theatre are always fastidiously high. The more there is to be forgotten in the real world, the better the show must be in every detail. Not just the play itself or even the acting – though for the Rubenovskas anything less than perfect simply won't do. Though the materials necessary to build ambitious sets are impossible to come by, when the curtains draw back, there they are for all to see. The gasps that greet the wonders of the designs and the novelties of a new play are as much in appreciation of the ingenuity in getting them there at all as for any intrinsic merit.

Another mistake you shouldn't make is that because it is secret theatre, none of the Cossacks know about it. Stupid they aren't. But in such fripperish foolishness and defiance, even a black-booted Cossack can see no harm.

They are sent, now and then, to creep in at the back of a performance unnoticed – except by everyone in the building – just to make sure nothing against the Tsar is being said and that the strictly forbidden Yiddish is not being used. They notice, as they enter, a certain calling-out and they observe that no matter what the scenery and the costumes it is customary for the whole cast to come to the front of the stage to sing loyal and rousing songs in Russian and they sing so well and it is so moving that the Cossacks themselves almost join in. When they leave, however, they compare the Jews' lack of originality ill with the wonderful theatre of Moscow where they were posted in the good old days.

And when they are gone, the Yiddish play resumes and the Tsar, his hair would turn white and drop out if he knew the curses they spit and the fool they make of him. (His own back he also gets, this being the third cowshed in four years, and this one only saved by Uncle Preiska's emergency buckets the rest of the family had laughed at.)

So, you've seen the theatre, passed the wooden houses full of clean shabbiness, waved to several horse-drawn carts, marvelled at the size of the potato fields and trudged a few miles of the dusty roads. You can say you've seen Wisherodik, more or less, and dozens of villages just like it nearby.

Back at the house, Bubba Rubenovska is still with us though it is lunchtime and she has refused the lovingly prepared chicken soup with its tiny golden whirlpools of fat. This ritual soup smiles its sabbath smell on ordinary weekdays only in extreme contingency and if Bubba is already refusing this cure-all, then her time must be nearly over. But until the way ahead is more settled she is going nowhere.

When the children had all been fed and we were assembled once more in the used-up air, Bubba began to organize.

'Rosa, Dovid, bring here the girls close to me.'

My Mama fussed quickly with our stockings, pulled bows too tightly on our hair and pushed me and Leah ahead of her through the ranks of relations around the bed.

'My Bubba is watching you,' Mama snapped. 'Walk nicely,

Zelda.' She was unable to stop herself glancing a look of triumph at Betra Rubenovska, her second cousin by marriage, as she pushed past her politely. She regarded Betra's Benjamin as an insufferable show-off for ten and his sister, Drushki, had, let alone a mean, sullen sulkiness, a heavy, dumpy body.

Passing Benjamin, my face burned with the burdening love I had for him even then. He crossed his eyes and stuck out his tongue. On him it looked good.

Mama arranged me and Leah around the bed and stood behind us as if staging a tableau vivant and Tata stood by Mama's Bubba holding her tiny hand.

I'm older than Leah. Everyone petted me when I was little. I've dramatic red Shergold hair and I can learn anything by heart no matter how long. But Leah came. She's naughty and she's difficult, Tata says, but she can mimic anyone she hears, she can sing, she can dance, she can charm the leg off a chicken and she's as pretty to dress as Mama could wish for and – well it would be bad enough in a normal family but, well . . . 'And only five, yet,' cooed the Rubenovskas admiringly, and me already a seven-year-old nothing.

Bubba held out her hands for us and Mama dutifully put one each of our hands into those unnervingly soft fragments Bubba had left.

'Zelda,' Bubba said, 'has a head on her.' She paused. 'But Leah – Leah can do anything. Leah has a great future ahead of her, haven't you choochele?'

Leah nodded. Parents of children all over the room cleared their throats and waited for their turn by the bedside for the blessing.

'Things can get bad,' Bubba sighed. 'You know they say there is to be famine this year?'

The room muttered and nudged. How come Bubba always listened to no one and knew everything?

'When there is a famine, the Jews starve,' she said philosophically, 'but the Rubenovskas will survive and it will be Leah who shall take them to the Goldene Medina.'

The family gasped. To go across so much land and so many

seas to Americhky the Golden, where, it was said, even Jews were welcomed, was a dream talked about in every home and on every street but contemplated seriously by very few. Who wanted to leave a house furnished so laboriously from a living so ingeniously carved out? To give up a certain crust for uncertain cake was only for gamblers – or those with nothing to lose – like Cousin Avrom.

'Why not?' Bubba queried, her voice not half as weak as it should have been. 'Must the Rubenovskas leave the stage to the Adlers, the Kesslers, the Thomashevskys?'

We Rubenovskas sat up straighter. How many times had we dreamt of seeing those three great families act, knowing secretly that we were better? And Bubba was right. They had made the journey and done all right for themselves. Avrom had worked with them all.

'Of course the whole world should know the Rubenovskas. What, stay here? Leah, you and the other children,' she gestured vaguely to all those in the room, 'and certainly Benjamin – one day, who knows. Zelda you're a sensible girl and you remember all Bubba's stories, don't you? Well listen, when I was your age . . .'

The room shifted to make their comfort more permanent as they settled to one of Bubba's longer narratives.

'How old are you now, Zeldele? Really – well, when I was eleven, a few years older than you are now, I was only your size, if that. So tiny I was. I still am, I suppose,' she teased herself, stretching her wrinkled neck up high as if to improve at last on her four feet eleven.

Uncle Sol snorted a vicious puff from his pipe as though this might hurry her through the preliminaries but he could save his breath. She would take her own time. The room coughed and fanned the air and prepared to listen again.

'When I was eleven, my parents, rest their souls, could scarcely make enough to feed my sister and me. They were only tingle-tangle players, just like the old couple Thomashevsky. That was the thing in those days; it was all they knew. You know what tingle-tangle is, don't you Zeldele?'

I nodded, pleased to have remembered and delighted to be

singled out for Bubba's old story. But Leah had her head on the counterpane saying 'tingle-tangle, tingle-tangle' in a pretty sing-song way and Bubba stroked her hair tenderly.

'Yes, they would both dress up like men who'd been drinking too much and they would dance and sing and fall down quite a bit and you know what, Leah choochele? They weren't very good. Not like us at all. After they finished it was my job to shake the tambourine and with my smiles I had to make the people watching unlock their pockets and their baytln and fill it with groats and zloties. And the money tingle-tangled in the tambourine – sometimes full as full so we could eat again and maybe have even a bit of herring with the potatoes.' She sighed, perhaps remembering what it was to be young and always hungry like us.

'But one night,' she went on, aware as any actress of the room shifting and glancing, an eye caught here and there in delight and despair, 'your great gran'pa, may he rest in peace, Zaider Yaacov, was at the show. What a fine young man of twenty from such a fine family as the Rubenovskas was doing in that miserable tent I still don't know to this day, but there he was. And when I came to him with my tambourine a-tangling he asked me my name and how old I was and said, "One day I shall marry you and make you a great actress." And when I was seventeen he did marry me.'

'But Bubba, how did . . . ?' I began to ask. Now I was seven, the difficulties and impossibilities that marriage must have had to overcome seemed too easily passed over to me with my own worries about how to get my Benjamin to marry me.

'Ssh,' hissed the room, grateful to be getting the shortened version of this well-known family tale.

'And when Zaider Yaacov married me and brought me here as his bride to Wisherodik, the Rubenovskas took me to their hearts. And from the family I learned. Since a baby I'd been on the stage but the Rubenovskas had class, they had style, chein. They could act like angels. I used to curse my own parents, rest their souls, who had taught me nothing – them and all the foolish tingle-tangle players who had to fall down to make them laugh or sing of the bad times to make them cry. My

Yaacov – with a glance he could do both.

'Did you see him in – aach, no – you're a baby yet. That was years ago, years ago. Such a young man he was, but when he walked you believed he had been very ill and was oh *so* old. Something in his shoulders, you know what I mean?'

Everywhere in the room young shoulders tried to look old; old shoulders shrugged themselves. The Rubenovskas were always in rehearsal.

'But here in Wisherodik is not the world,' Bubba concluded, sitting up a little and shaking a tiny finger at me. 'My Yaacov and I were wasted here. In Americhky is Yiddish Theatre on every corner. Even in London L. E. Jacobson is like a king. You think the Rubenovskas can't do better than anyone? Cousin Avrom can't do it all on his own. And you, little Leah, small as you are, I see you taking the Rubenovskas across the water.'

Bubba was watchful as her soothsaying caught and blazed amongst the family, but Tata, thinking her exhausted, went to her side. She leaned forward, ready to lecture on.

'The children must go to Americhky, Dovid; Sarah Siddons, Sarah Bernhardt, you Leah. And Benjamin too. And Zelda, in that neat little writing you do you'll write down the stories I've told you, then my Yaacov and I won't be forgotten. And every day you'll write about your Mama and Tata and then over in Americhky you'll write about Leah and Benjamin – the Rubenovskas will always be – today you'll start, Zeldele?'

Mama pressed my hand and I nodded. She pressed it again. 'Yes, Bubba.'

'Write this, Zeldele. In all the world there wasn't a better husband than my Yaacov. Good? Like Moses. Wise? Like Solomon. As red-headed and blue-eyed as you, Zelda. Write that down, Zelda. For the Rubenovska family there will be journeys,' she foretold sternly, sitting up a little to include everyone in the room. 'But to Americhky I won't go. On a boat you wouldn't get me, just the same. The only travelling I'm doing is to join my Yaacov.' She fell silent as if waiting for someone to argue with her.

Too late to listen to any more of Bubba's stories. Too late to ask her any more questions. From Bubba Rubenovska's throat came the echo from the tingle-tangle of her last tambourine.

INTERLUDE

1891
Mama's Bubba's dead. I'm writing about the family. I said I would. There is Tata, Mama, me and Leah. Mama's having a baby. She wants a boy. She's got enough girls.

1892
Our baby's dead. It wasn't alive, Mama says. So it's not dead, Mama says.

1893
Tata's much older than Mama. I don't know why. They burned our theatre. No more dressing up.

1894
Tata smacked Leah because she was rude. She took my pencils so I smacked her then Tata smacked me. It isn't fair. The new place is ready so we'll have plays again. I bake the biscuits for Shabbos sometimes. Leah can't cook at all. After his barmitzvah, Benjamin let me borrow his books.

1895
I don't mind being Gretel because Benjamin's going to be Hansel and I asked Mama ages ago but she says Leah's old enough and she's doing it. I hate Leah sometimes and I hate Mama. And I hate Pinchas Rottman who has to have his meals with us every day. He's thin. He's silly.

1897
I haven't been writing about the family because it's just plays, plays, plays and I'm growing into a woman, Mama said when it happened, and gave me some zloties for my dowry box.

1898

I could leave school if I wanted to but I'm clever so I'm staying. It's nearly all boys now. I don't think Leah would go at all if it wasn't that she's allowed to sit next to Pinchas. It's awful he nearly lives with us now. I know we're supposed to be sorry for him but why can't we have our house to ourselves? They broke all the windows of the synagogue last Shabbos. But people were only hurt, no one was killed at all because G-d was looking after us, Tata says. Tata said G-d was also looking after Levi the glass-cutter. G-d's funny sometimes.

June 1899

Leah told me she loves Pinchas and he loves her. How does she know? He never speaks when I hear him. She says he's different with her. Well, he certainly can't be any fatter with her. Or pinker. His face is like the inside of an empty flour bag. He isn't – cheerful. He draws and paints all our posters and programmes now. That he's really good at but Leah's face on just everything makes me cross. She's a baby yet and I told her there's no law that says you have to marry the nearest person and that's a great big world out there we'll please G-d see one day and she said I was a fine one to talk – what about Benjamin? She doesn't understand. Benjamin is different. If the other side of the world he'd been born I would have waited and found him.

November 1899

There's going to be a new country only for Jews soon, Pinchas says. That's silly. The Cossacks will find it and burn it. Benjamin's spots have nearly all gone. He's beautiful. Leah must be blind not to see how handsome and talented he is. She says he overacts. She can talk.

It was so funny at the theatre last night. I made up a play about Nero so Mama and Tata let us do it all by ourselves as a surprise for them and they left us alone and they were so pleased when they saw it they said we could do it at the theatre and let the seats be half the price and everyone came and it was full. (Sometimes I think they'll watch anything rather than stay

14

home and the Rubenovskas make too much fuss about being perfect.) I was only Agrippina so I died quite soon and didn't have to be on the stage for long, thank goodness. As Octavia, Drushki didn't have anything to say at all – which is my idea of the right part for her – and the sheet covered most of her; another blessing. It was so funny – when Nero said 'Octavia go and be killed!' they all cheered, so Drushki forgot she was meant to scream and kneel and beg Nero to save her. She just nodded and waddled off. We nearly had to bring her back for an encore.

Afterwards Aunt Preiska pinched my cheek and said I was a pretty kleine Shakespearele but Uncle Preiska shook his head and said it wasn't Nero who destroyed Jerusalem because he'd killed himself long before that happened. Well I knew that. Everyone knows that. But doesn't my way make a better play?

1900
The whole village had a celebration for the twentieth century. The men put boards up over the shul windows this time to keep out the vodka drinkers and the Cossacks, but Tata took us all in the cart to the market square to join in the dancing. Mama should have come. Most people didn't mind us being there. Isn't life wonderful? Benjamin has had to come to live with us. Right in our house. And he's shaving! I don't think Pinchas will ever grow a single whisker. Mama says it's not so hard to make the food from the cooking-pot go around a few more mouths. You just add a bit of this and a bit of that, she says, and put more water with it. But she's crosser than she used to be. It's Drushki being here, I suppose. Drushki's horrible. If my parents were killed (G-d forbid) in a pogrom and I had to live with cousins, quiet and kind I'd be and not get in the way and my opinions I'd keep to myself. 'Help your Mama more,' she says to Leah and me. Mama doesn't need help. And Benjamin's started saying how beautiful Leah is getting. It's worrying. But Leah only sees pale Pinchas and his endless Hebrew books and his paint-box. He makes hand bills to deliver round the neighbouring houses and we take them to the stalls on market days so always our theatre keeps full.

Pinchas teaches boys their barmitzvahs now and gives all the money to Mama. Drushki and Benjamin dig potatoes for their money and complain about it quite a bit. To keep Leah's mind off Benjamin, I praise Pinchas and his goodness to her all day long – she never tires of it. I've promised to write her a play for her to be the biggest part but she nags she wants it to end with a wedding, and me, I like crying at the end of a play. They clap louder.

1901

They've taken Pinchas for the army. They just burst in and took him. They didn't knock over anyone or even break anything. Leah and Benjamin were rehearsing. Would they have taken my Benjamin if he'd been home? Oh my G-d. I thought Leah would die when Mama told her. Please G-d don't let them come back for Benjamin. Mama says Leah's only fifteen and boys will be falling over themselves for her but we all know Leah – once she's set her mind on something. She won't go anywhere on her own but I don't mind because she's changed so much. She never argues now. It's funny how everyone loves Pinchas now he's gone. He'll never come back, whatever Leah says. He was always kind and thoughtful and put everything straight somehow with his truthfulness. Poor Pinchas. They killed all his brothers and sisters quickly. It'll be slower for him in Siberia. And he's so thin already. I wish Benjamin wouldn't keep on saying it's his turn next.

Benjamin will look fine as Dreyfus. Drushki and I are making the uniform for him. Leah won't act at all; she didn't even speak to Benjamin's friend Josh when he was invited for meals so he soon stopped coming, and she will only talk to me because Mama says we mustn't mention Pinchas (as though he's already dead) but it's all Leah wants to talk about. I love Leah. I wish I could help her. But I wish she wouldn't take my things and leave them anyhow. She tried to read my journal without asking me. I'm going to have to lock it up. I'm not allowed to tell her off yet.

England's Queen Victoria died and they have a king again. Tata says kings must be better than tsars.

1902

I told Leah all about Trotsky's escape from Siberia because it will be something new for her to hope about. Mama said I ought to start telling her it's a pity Pinchas is dead but that seems a bit unkind to me. She is back on the stage, at least; she was wonderful as a disguised police officer in *Wrongly Accused*. When Benjamin and I took her to the Purim-Spiel she danced all evening with Josh and his friends. She'll be all right. What about me? I don't think Benjamin really likes Josh's sister. She isn't a bit witty and I think he just talks about her so much to make me jealous. That isn't difficult. I'd like to tie him up in a box and never let him out.

Drushki's terrible; she's joined the Bund now. 'In labour there lies freedom for all,' she says in her bossy way. (Mama says she labours all day long and has no freedom at all.) I know what Drushki means but you never really make a revolution work, because most people would prefer things to stay as they are no matter how bad they may be.

It's a regular thing now for the family to ask me for a new idea for a play. I pretend it's very easy but usually I've been reading and reading all the papers and books and have already got it all planned out by the time I'm asked. I think Mama ought to stop playing young girls. Even if she married at twenty she must be nearly forty. There are plenty of Shergold and Preiska and Littman and Weissen girls but they all end up being dancing girls or maids or schoolchildren.

Cousin Avrom wrote from London that his own little theatre was burned down. Mama said 'See? Bubba's wrong, all over the world things are the same. Anything Jewish they want to burn.' She simply won't read the rest of the letter where he explains it was an accident and that his English friends are trying to help him find somewhere else. He's lost all his money. 'Stolen, of course,' Mama wails. 'Everywhere they hate us.'

1903

If it was just up to the Jewish people there would perhaps be a revolution after all. The only word you hear is pogrom. We're hardly allowed out at all. There are look-outs all round and above the barn if we're doing a show, and we only do short playlets now so that not too many of us need stay backstage, and an escort sees us home after every performance. It's awful. Josh's sister hasn't said a single word since – since they brought her back from the market. It's awful. When I ask Mama why we can't go to Americhky the Golden like the Weissens, she says we're making a nice living here and Americhky will also have pogroms so you can't run away from them. I asked Leah once if she believed Bubba could see into the future when she said Leah would go and Leah said she can't leave Poland ever because Pinchas might come back. I thought she'd forgotten about him the way she flirts around with Josh the whole time. I almost preferred her glum; our room is a mess of her clothes and hair-ribbons and she never listens to a word I say. I started writing about us because I promised Bubba I would; now, I couldn't do without writing. This is the twelfth year I've been writing my journal. Next year will be its barmitzvah – I'll have to make it a party. Tata had some wood over from that wreck he made for *Storm at Sea*, and I asked him to make me two boxes with hinges and little locks for my papers. Mama calls them my scribbles but Tata calls it the Rubenovska Bible and tells me stories Mama mustn't know that I know. He understands how I feel about Benjamin too. The boxes, when they came, were a bit too short and much, much too deep, but I cut off the margins at the top and kissed Tata and said they were just right because Mama tells him off all the time.

Aunt Beila Littman and her eldest, Yankel, died from the fever. It's all over the village. Mama went mad when Leah seemed a bit hot for a few days but it passed over. I loved Yankel. He was going to make a fine actor. Benjamin spent a lot of time with him and was so upset that for once we closed the theatre until the shiva was over. Everyone's talking about moving pictures. Practically the whole world's seen them except Wisherodik. But I don't care because remember how we all rushed to see the stereoscopic pictures in those metal frames down at the hall? That didn't last. Nor will moving pictures because it's just mime and mime is tiring to watch. I told Mama why people come to see plays is because if they can't talk themselves at least they like to come to a theatre and overhear people saying all the things they feel and dare not say. Still, if they came to Wisherodik, these moving pictures, I'd be first in the rush to say I'd seen them.

Nothing happens here except pogroms and plays. And Josh, Josh. Leah and Josh. Josh and Leah. Amazing how he knocks at the door at mealtimes; his parents must save a lot of money that way. Benjamin said to me, 'Your young sister will be married before you. Two suitors she's had already and you've not even had one.' Blind, stupid Benjamin. Tata came after me where I was crying and said that one day Benjamin will notice me, just as soon as he can take his eyes away from himself. Tata doesn't always like Benjamin because he isn't the obliging wood-chopping, flour sack-carrying, chicken-plucking sort that Josh tries to be and poor Pinchas was (olev hashalom). But as there isn't an actor to touch him in the whole family (in the whole of Poland, I think) he's really Mama's favourite. She loves him better than me. 'He's a real born Rubenovska like me,' she often says. But Leah's a Shergold like Tata yet she has the Rubenovska gift. If I can ever get Benjamin to marry me, I'll be a real Rubenovska, too.

That's if it is possible to be 'a real Rubenovska' yet to be dying never to have to act again. Making up ideas for plays is fine but the stage is just a place to come home from so I can put my feet up, take out my box and my pencil and watch Benjamin sip his tea and Drushki spill hers down yet another grey blouse. (We'll know who to ask for material for some prison scene in a play I suggested called *Betrayed*.) I could watch Benjamin for ever. And it is my duty to record the fine whiteness of his teeth as they bite down on the grey-brown lumps of rough-cut sugar as the sweet-sour taste of the strong tea and the bitter lemon gush through them. His dark hair and skin, the trademark of the family, rest my loving eyes, which are weary of my own freckles and white-paleness.

As I fitted the little key into the lock of my journal box tonight, Bubba came into my mind. She wanted me to write the history of the Rubenovskas and I certainly started by doing so – even being persuaded to read bits of it aloud at family gatherings, but I couldn't now. Over this last couple of years it's becoming secret and all mine. Benjamin, Benjamin on every page. But there's so much I wouldn't want everyone to read any more. I wouldn't want everyone to know things – not only about me but, say, Tata isn't a very good actor. That's hard to write down because I love Tata, but on stage he's only Tata with a job to do. Mama, Leah, Benjamin, they all take you to some other place. And Mama – although I don't argue with her like Leah does, she could drive you crazy with her bossiness and even if she is right more than she's wrong she needs to calm down a bit. She livens everything up when she's around but sometimes – all I know is, when I'm a mother, surrounded by dark-eyed, dark-haired little Benjamins, I shall always be in the kitchen or by the fire when they come home, reading a book or writing a little piece about their school progress for the third or fourth journal box. And if any of them show signs of being 'a real Rubenovska' G-d will perhaps give me the strength to knock it out of them. A scholar, a physician would be surely no disgrace, even for a family impressed only by a clear top A or a new way with an old joke.

When Josh came in just now Leah stopped slumping over her endless needlework and sat up pink and pretty. I just get more awkward when I'm being looked at. I'm nineteen already and Benjamin still hasn't married me though I was ready when I was seven. It's only having awful Drushki to compare myself favourably with that keeps me from fretting more so I generously smile over at her. No good; she's writing something for the local labour underground newspaper – they won't print it. She scoffs that they're scared to – so would I be. 'Just say what injustice is taking place, Drushki,' I tell her. But she must accuse and offend when she writes; it's her way.

Speaking of writing, Cousin Avrom sends no more letters from England. Mama cries sometimes, and says he must be dead and who is there to sit shiva for him? Tata says Avrom must be fifty and it's too late for him to start again after his disasters but I think he went on to Americhky with the last of his money, as he said he might in the last letter, and now has no job, no money and is, like any Rubenovska, too proud to write. And if Bubba had been right and we had gone to the Goldene Medina we could have found him and looked after him. About one hundred and three, Mama's Bubba would be now but I wish she was here so I could ask her about my future and whether I'm doing things right and whether she minds that my journal doesn't always detail all the theatre doings. (Did I say last year that Mama decreed that every one of the family over four years old must play some instrument. The tears, the wails must have been heard high above the reluctant twanging and the laboured blowing. And, of course, again Mama was right because here and there a little talent peeked out, sparking more. 'Soon an orchestra we'll have,' she bragged, clucking out a warning to a tiny passing Littman to repeat over and over again his scales.) And here it is 1903 and Leah will never cross the waters now. Twelve years gone since then and it's impossible to get Leah to leave Josh and his family to come on our overnight trips to the market at Vilna to stay with the family let alone hankering for the great shlep to Americhky the Free. So it isn't true what Mama always says; her Bubba didn't know everything.

ACT I

SCENE II
August 1904

Despite the August heat the theatre-barn was packed right through the first week of my newly-baked play, *Ticket to an Unknown Destination*. It's easy to fool yourself into believing that these Wisherodniks puffed in fanning themselves to sit uncomfortably on benches in front of a stiff wire from which sacking hung stiffly down because Zelda Shergold baked something good. The truth is that if you're forbidden assembly, assembly is all you crave.

Work was over for another intolerable day, and where else but this playhouse could people gather to meet so many friends? Here, picnics and gossip could be brought and shared. The undisciplined audience visited from row to row, aisles full of wandering Jews and their unruly children. And why not? Better they should stay up a little late than, Heaven forbid, be left at home unattended and in danger.

That last week there had been thick, blue satin curtains and small, gilted chairs was a matter of little conversation and less concern to these mayvans of the arts. A raid is a raid. Meanwhile the feet of the Rubenovskas worked on visibly behind the sacking that fell short of the boards. Ankles flexed, sandals flapped, arches arched. The few oil lamps that had been unsmashed were being used at the taking of the entrance money and to show people to their seats. In a while there would be chairs again and curtains and lamps for those few who care about such things.

Many came assured that the play would be witty, others

certain of at least one soaking wet handkerchief to stuff in the pockets or up the sleeves. With a bit of luck everyone could go home satisfied as stories aren't Yiddish stories unless things are so bad that they're funny. Life for the Jew is always serious – but solemn, no.

The oil lamps were now taken backstage. In the sudden dark, the audience groped for their lost places, there was a gradual lessening of the eating, laughing, shouting until a silence rippled, prickled, stilled.

My hands were wet with worry and my swallowing seemed to be too loud. Round at the back of the stage, where Mama was fussing her way through from panic to disaster and back again, my legs felt like lockshen in gravy. Throughout the whole theatre I was the only one who knew for sure that Mama's disaster was actually about to come true this time. There was a cast change she knew nothing about and trouble coming that made trouble past seem like festival. I'd tell Tata first; I'd do it now.

'The bow for Ena's hair. Where is it? Where is it? And where's Leah? She should be dressing. Zelda, take that ribbon from your collar – don't stare, girl. Take it off! If it wasn't for me the lot of you would . . .'

Later. Let the play finish. Soon enough for bad news. I tied the wrong-coloured bow on the little girl's hair, gave her a kiss and pushed her towards the stage.

Ena, one of the Preiska-Rubenovskas, a kugel-faced child, with a voice gifted to her through the angels and her Uncle Krauz, the cantor, carried a single lamp with her, placed it on a table set outside the sacking and sang.

Unaccompanied, except by three-quarters of the audience, she sang of her Yiddishe Mama. With brilliant clarity she told of this paragon, this saint. A beauty and a delight, her phrasing said. None like her Mama for sweetness, her trills insisted. Not a dry eye in the house and cheering rose from everywhere.

'You hit the top C sharp,' I heard Ena's dear Yiddishe Mama scold her, flattening her for fear of spoiling. (Just in time or my Mama would have told Ena's mother off for not noticing.)

Twin cousins of Ena's, a boy and a girl but, as their father

23

always said, identical apart from that, juggled competently, interminably, stiffly and without a smile, with old cartwheel rims while picnics were resumed, conversations finished and deals proposed. Look, even in the shul you can never keep a congregation quiet; why expect it to be different here?

The jugglers juggled on unperturbed by the restlessness they must have been able to hear. The cheering that greeted the finale of their act was mistakenly interpreted and they doggedly juggled through an unasked-for encore. As they bowed, the last piece of scenery crashed into place behind them. Time to run off to enthusiastic applause – whatever it was for.

Young Shmuel, the shining success of the music lessons, came through the curtains, handing the little table back through the sacking. Standing over to one side he put his quarter-size violin under his baby-chubby chin and played a tune that hurt in its awful simplicity. Stilled, the audience, aware that this was going to be some play if it lived up to the hopeful helplessness of the tear-jerking melody, shushed each other crossly making the more noise doing so.

Bowing obediently but impatiently he slipped off the stage. 'Come on, Shmuel,' his cousins urged him. 'It's nearly dark.'

He tore off his lacy collar, eased off the tight black jacket that would soon be handed down to his younger brother and sat in the wings unbuckling his shoes.

In everyone's way and cursed by us all, Shmuel laced his skates and the other children dashed after him in theirs – shushed angrily by Mama, furiously by Uncle Preiska – and were gone.

As the sacking parted, private conversation stopped as the front of the house gave noisy approval for the realism of the setting. Hadn't their own rooms looked like this not so long ago? Drawers pulled out just like that and emptied on the floor, furniture broken, food wasted. And hadn't they scrubbed and mended and triumphed in the end? But tonight they sat secure in the knowledge that I would not be allowed to end my story in suffering; no Rubenovska would dare. Life would be seen to go on even in an apprentice play.

24

On stage, at a table, on the only whole chair on the set, Mama sat with her head in her hands.

Off stage, in front of a mirror I sat in a chair with a broken back with my head in my hands.

On stage, Tata, in a beard tonight, playing her stern brother, was scrubbing hopelessly at slogans scrawled across the walls.

Off stage, I scrubbed at my tears and drew a piece of curtain behind me. I should have been changing into Leah's costume. I should have been making up. I sobbed on.

'Now perhaps you will listen to sense,' the stern brother said dominantly through his beard as the play warmed up. 'Your husband must come with me to the Goldene Medina and there he will earn much gold and send for you and the children.'

'Don't do it,' called a stout woman who always sat in the front row because her eyes were poor. 'Look what happened to me. He never wrote. Never sent a zloty. Alone, oy, I'm all alone in the world.'

Mrs Feingold thought the story I had made up was real; her outcry moved half the audience to sympathize, the rest to curse her interference and for me, her tears made me hopeful enough to dry my face and smooth on some of the disgusting sallow cream, then the sticky rouge, the tiny red dots in the corners of the eyes, the deep colour on the eyelids and the blackening on my ginger eyelashes. They would all, soon enough, be washed off by the tears after the show tonight and for many nights.

Leah's clothes fitted me only with much breathing in and heaving and a quick removal of a hook or two at the tiny waist. The wig helped to disguise me and a lacy shawl Leah never used was a cover for my freckles. So long as I got on stage before I was found out, Tata and Mama could do nothing until the curtain came across – if we'd had a curtain to come across, that is.

When Bubba told me to write down everything that happened to the Rubenovskas did she dream that their history might end this way in 1904?

On stage the arguments raged on. Wasn't leaving Poland, after all, the main topic of conversation in every persecuted village in the land? Those who were doing well enough felt there was too much to lose and those who had nothing swore that to stay in a country where they were despised was simply disgusting. It was simply, for those who had made up their minds to leave, a question of where. Americhky the Golden, first choice for most. And England, plenty of opportunities there – plenty of work. And the promised land – Palestine – for some the obvious historic answer; for others too much like hard labour with a good chance of malaria thrown in. As the discussions on stage swayed backwards and forwards like the pious at prayer, with joy I heard the audience calling, 'That's right!' and 'Don't be foolish!' and I cursed Leah for spoiling my first good play.

The first comic scene in which I had given Benjamin, the ticket-seller, the best lines, of course, was nearly over. My Benjamin, pacing his lines perfectly through the maze of the howls of laughter, was making the absolute best of my plot, which set out to cheat the cheater, reunite the family and make everything come out like a successful game of pisha-pasha in the end.

Wonderful if I could make things come just as right for Leah – for all of us. Deftly wiping each tear as it came before it could streak a line through the make-up, I put on my pointed shoes and stood up. Mama and Tata would be frowning into the wings, seeing Leah not there and clucking tch, tch, children today, they aren't what they were.

Ah. They could see the back of her now. She'd better be earlier tomorrow night, they would be thinking. Enough to worry about without thoughtless children.

In a flurry of pretty dress and with the natural comedy of a young girl simply not perceiving the chaos of the room nor being sensitive to the atmosphere of despair, the audience greeted my every innocent phrase with laughter. The play was going wonderfully.

On stage Mama was like a bad winter in Moscow. Tata frowned and pulled his beard faster than the script required and Benjamin missed three important speeches which I had to quickly summarize or the whole scene would have been incomprehensible. The other thing I did was keep my eyes firmly off everyone's disapproval, especially Mama's.

The sacking jerked across at the end of the first act and the applause was so prolonged and generous a tiny flash of foolish confidence warmed me for a moment.

I smiled at Mama. 'Too fast I took the last speech, Mama?'

'Whose idea? Leah wants a night off, she can ask. You want to take a part, you can also ask. Where is she? Well?'

'Rosa, she's ill maybe.' Tata said, unwilling to accuse Leah yet.

'Better she's ill than lazy. Well, Zelda?'

For bad news, I was finding, the mouth takes longer to open. 'Zelda . . .'

Tata coughed and put his arm round me. 'Ssh, Rosa. She's a good girl. You're a good girl, Zelda, stepping in like that. An actress you're not but you weren't too bad tonight. Wherever Leah is, it's Leah you should be screaming at. Where would we have been without Zelda? Would it have been better that no one had come on to do the part at all?'

'You're right,' Mama said, her anger working itself further up her neck. 'Nobody could have come on at all. The play would have been ruined. A disaster. What's Leah thinking of? A fire in her guts, a plague on her . . .'

'Stop it, Mama. Listen, in Leah's shoes you would have done the same thing.'

'Me? What are you saying, Zelda? I would abandon my family? Leave the theatre without permission? Rosa? A born Rubenovska? Why even the night you were born . . .'

'Mama, Pinchas is – Pinchas has deserted. Leah's hiding him, Mama.'

People witness to the second act of my play that night in which the family are in mourning and the mood is of hopeless despair, tell how the great Rosa Shergold, Dovid, her husband, and even the elder daughter in her first big part were so brilliantly grief-stricken that their own tears splashed in harmony.

That's because the grief was indeed real.

It is possible that you don't know what the desertion of a Jew from the pressed service of the Tsar's army meant for the

27

deserter's neighbourhood. If they sheltered him the village would automatically be razed, so this made for a less enthusiastic welcome than he might otherwise have expected.

Who knows how the authorities knew that Pinchas had been left alive after the pogrom that killed off his brothers, his older sister, parents, grandparents? He had been left – could it be deliberately? – to grow into a slender brooding young Jew with a scholar's brain and young muscles ripe for conditioning in the service of the Tsar. Was his life spared so Siberia could benefit from his labours for the usual period of fourteen devastating years, no argument?

And if he did survive there was little fear of sending him back still useful to his own people. Those few who got back were nicely broken. Disease, exhaustion, exposure, malnutrition usually dealt with any unfortunate tendencies to stubbornness. The only alternative was desertion. But the vast desperate distances they would have to travel without food, shelter or support would cause massive physical breakdowns first, then the madness of desolation.

So before that knock came at the door when they seized Pinchas for compulsory death, the orphaned boy had been educated in the Torah, provided for by his own villagers, sheltered and given more collective caring than perhaps anyone can expect from his own family. There is an old and profound Yiddish proverb (no coincidence; trouble through five thousand years can't help bringing with it a little wisdom so there is an old and profound Yiddish proverb about almost everything and if there isn't, most of us are capable of writing our own) that says: 'Your own you try to love; your adopted you have to love.' So there is no need to be too sorry for Pinchas.

Not until now, that is.

With the destruction of the village on their minds you can see for yourself that Pinchas's return was not filling the Rubenovska family with loving delight. The whole community, you're thinking, would be rightly fearful, understandably anxious to save themselves by delivering him up to the Tsarist troops.

Ah, but you're wrong.

Miracles like the survival of Pinchas were a local reminder of the larger, better documented wonders of the last five thousand years. Who but the Holy One could have kept such a stick of a boy alive? Who but the Holy One could have made such puny legs run faster than those of his pursuers? Through the journeying in the Siberian blankness, through the despair and constant fear of discovery, there must have been those who sheltered him, fed him, refused to return him to the militia despite the certain favour they could claim. This is two thousand unappetizing miles we're talking about through the spring and summer pogroms of 1904. He must have endured months of scrabbling over the Urals – a miracle all by itself – then where: the river beds, Perm, Kirov, Gorky, Moscow? How did he even find his way, this untravelled mole? Something he must have learned, his head stuck always in a book or gazing at Leah. And when he was nearly back home to us, his only family, the signpost for Vilnyus striking with terror rather than joy, so near to home. In the places where he was known, he might be recognized and betrayed by anyone. And still for him there was shelter and compassion. And finally Wisherodik – the Holy One, blessed be He, had allowed Pinchas to reach this season.

Mind you, there was still Mama to fear.

My play strode wonderfully through the tears of the second act to the laughing solutions of the third despite us and our dreadful preoccupations.

'If they knew what we knew,' Mama muttered, radiantly beaming to acknowledge her ovation, 'cheering they wouldn't be.'

'We all leave together tonight,' Tata whispered, bowing from the waist and raising his arm to include the whole cast.

'Good baking, Zelda,' Benjamin said, taking the largest applause and stamping for himself.

Benjamin had praised me! I dizzied, curtseying happily, nearly forgetting Leah for a second.

Uncle Preiska lifted a finger to Mama. 'Again, Rosa?'

Tata shook his head at Mama. 'Not tonight. To Leah we

must go.'

Mama waved us back into our positions. 'Again bow,' she said, 'so long as they're cheering.'

So Uncle Preiska parted the sacking once more and there we were, dipping, smiling, giving our famous Rubenovska imitation of happy serenity until the audience were content to let us go. Soon non-acting members of the family took the oil lamps to light everyone from the building, pick up the orange peelings and the screwed-up greaseproof papers; to be a Rubenovska is not always a glamorous thing.

Into the hot night at the end of this Polish summer, children close by them for safety and affection, the audience forgot their discretion in the excitement of the evening, calling out one to another, going again through the play as they hastened home.

Backstage the cream-pot lids banged grimly and if Tata hadn't hugged me and told me I was wonderful, my acting would have had to do without praise altogether.

'In the last act, where I have to look twenty years older, tomorrow night I won't even need any make-up,' Mama moaned dramatically. 'Didn't I beg Leah not to wait fourteen years for someone who's never coming back . . . ?'

'But he is back, Aunt Rosa,' Benjamin said.

'Back in one piece? Ill, he'll be. Mad, perhaps. Who needs him? A lame duck. A celebration you're asking me to make?'

'A lame duck he isn't, Mama. Look what he must have survived to get here and go through all for love of Leah.' Even just saying it brought tears to my throat. Would anyone ever want to go through so much for me?

'Love!' Mama tensed every muscle. 'At eighteen in and out of love you should be every day. If it has to be this – cripple, this – Pinchas, why couldn't she start to love him when the audience had gone home?'

Ah. Of course. The fact that Pinchas's return might bring destruction to this area of Poland was as nothing compared with Leah's non-appearance on stage. We were, after all, the Rubenovskas.

'You know what they say, Aunt Rosa,' Benjamin said,

picking pieces of glue from his hair-line where the bald wig had been, not looking at me at all as I gazed at his wonderful face in the speckled mirror we all used. 'When love flies in, sense flies out.'

Please G-d, by Benjamin.

That fine intelligence of his deep, dark eyes under those endless lashes. Never mind what Mama said about him being too young to take the leading part yet, I'd bake a play with only one person in it. He'd be – well, never mind the plot for now – but the last curtain would fall on him dying – he was nearly as good as Bubba – pathetically calling my name over and over. 'It was Zelda I always loved – Zeldele.'

'Zelda. Zelda! Tata's waiting for you. What's Leah thinking of to bring us such worry. For this we had children? A fine home and family and Josh falling in love with her more every day. Pinchas Rottman crawls in with maybe some disease they only give out in Siberia – a disease that's catching, G-d forbid, and my Leah, she . . . A moment. Zelda? What happened? She's maybe hiding him until Tata can give him some money and then we're to wave him a long goodbye? How did she seem?' Mama looked hopefully at me.

I pictured Drushki turning astonished from the door and Leah screaming once and running to Pinchas. Not Pinchas-the-orphan and my-little-sister. Two adults, lifelong love. Leah bringing tea, his sudden lying – I thought dying – on the sofa, sleeping, his hand still in Leah's as I promised to wear her grease-paint for her tonight. Wave goodbye? She'd be happier in Siberia.

'She won't leave Pinchas, Mama. If you send him away, Leah will go with him.'

I suppose Mama didn't know what to do next so she lost her temper. Tata kept quiet – what he always said was 'a married man's trick.' Uncle Preiska came running at the noise and reacted to the news by covering his head with his hand and uttering a prayer for our deliverance. Adding that he would organize a senior family council in the early morning, he pushed us out, locking and bolting the barn door, hugging Mama, his sister, and Dovid with serious compassion.

'Why did we have to tell Uncle Preiska, Mama?' I said, hurrying to keep up with them. 'Surely the fewer who know about Pinchas . . .'

'Secret? You want to try to keep a secret in Wisherodik? No, Zelda; we need the family. To take it in turns to hide him, perhaps. Ach, trouble he's brought us, that's no secret.'

Mama and Tata were walking so fast. Benjamin, who'd stopped to help put the bar across the door was a long way behind. I remembered something that Leah said once and stooped to check that the top button of my summer boot was firmly clasped.

Benjamin waited politely till I'd finished and helping me up kept hold of my hand, wrapping it tightly round his arm.

Thank you Leah, the boot-button trick does always work. I will hand the knowledge of it on to my daughters and to their daughters too.

The shock of his rare closeness kept me plastered tightly to his side so I could make the most of his tautness against my rib-cage; soon enough he would move away and all I would have left would be this entry in my journal.

'I felt really good in the play tonight. Did you notice we've sorted out that coin-counting at last? Did you hear the laughter? A good part, I suppose.'

(22 August 1904. Dear Journal, at last Benjamin has held me close to him and then he flattered my baking. He'll maybe love me one day? Drushki read in my palm that I will have three husbands. It's time to get started on the first.)

How the moonlight whitened his black hair. Through our lifetime together I would watch him until he looked like that without the moon. Drushki had it wrong; she meant my Benjamin was worth three husbands.

'Your Mama's going to be dreadful to Leah at home,' Benjamin said. 'We ought to have an idea to offer. Anything to make it easier. Something.'

Leah. There was darkness and terror ahead for Leah and me with a head full of fluffy veiling and the seven priestly blessings.

'So, Zelda? You're the one with the plots.'

32

'Only for plays.'

'So pretend it's a play.'

'I'd been thinking already that we could maybe – Look, if we say that he did come back here but it was too late – that he died as soon as he got here, (G-d forbid).'

Benjamin looked round so admiringly at me, it took concentration to remember who Leah was.

'When you see him for yourself, you'll know why I thought of that. He's nearly dead, Ben. I'm sure that if he hadn't been so in love, he couldn't . . .'

'That's good, Zelda. If he's dead, he's safe and we're safe. Or are we? Do you remember what they did in Pinsk?'

Pinsk? How could you remember which atrocity fitted which place? What difference did it make? Though the rain falling on one Jew should be but a single drop, the whole nation must run for shelter.

'I think it was in Pinsk,' Benjamin frowned. 'They said the village would be left intact if into the street they sent the other young men and the boys came out, expecting to be taken to Siberia and the swine got off their horses, fixed their bayonets and . . .'

'Stop! I remember, I remember.'

'They'll maybe call me out, Zelda. Who knows why I've been overlooked so long.'

Hadn't I gone over and over that fear with the family at home? Hadn't I pictured myself at the knees of a Cossack begging him to take me instead?

'I'm sure if we made a very public funeral – of an empty box – and if the whole village could seem angry with Pinchas for returning here, it might save us. Then Pinchas could disguise himself and in time, marry Leah secretly?'

I thought of something.

Was it in Lvov or nearer – over in Smolensk – that the annual number of marriages had been restricted, driving even urgent weddings underground? I imagined the porches of all the wooden houses that stretched between here and the shul busy with flowers for Leah's wedding procession. Children running behind them with flowers in their hair, everyone smiling, shouting the blessing, 'Muzeltov, Muzeltov.' And as they round the last bend of the road in their finery they can see the rabbi in his best robes, his best hat, a big fur streimel, smiling at them in the gateway to the shul. But what could I see behind him? A hundred, a thousand Cossacks – on horseback – shrieking.

'She's younger, Zelda. First you have to marry.'

I've tried and tried to remember the words he said to me as he kissed me for the first and fifteenth time, held back under a cherry tree, murmuring my name. Amazing. It actually felt so much more vividly exciting than all the hundreds of times that I'd imagined it. I didn't know until then that each person has their own flavour and taste nor that when you're being kissed it makes you beautiful even if you maybe aren't.

As we walked together, turning into the wide dusty street, I felt lonely for him already. Why did he stop kissing me so soon? Was I, perhaps, no good at kissing? Who could I ask? Down we went through the market place and up into the road opposite the fields where at daylight Benjamin and Drushki would be digging potatoes and holding their backs. At the end of this next short street we'd turn left to where we lived some twenty houses down. Did a man have to marry you after he'd kissed you, or did he try you out and if you weren't good at kissing . . . ?

'Something temporary won't do, Zee-Zee.'

Oh my Benjamin. Than marriage there is nothing more permanent. Ask me. Ask me.

'The mumsers won't be satisfied with anything less than Pinchas's grave. The militer will come and . . .'

Since I learned to do up the buttons of my own bodice, I have loved Benjamin. Here I stand, dazzled, twenty in a few weeks' time, kissed at last, just as the whole strength of the Russian Army gathered to overrun and destroy us and Wisherodik. Is that fair? I kicked the rocking-chair into motion and watched it rock itself in the still summer night.

'Pinchas is so thin and frail they could save their boot-leather,' I said, miserable to have to talk about Pinchas again.

'With a small shmaltz herring fillet you could knock him about.'

'In that case,' Benjamin frowned, 'perhaps a good disguise for him after the funeral might be girls' clothes?'

Too much in one night. Silly laughter bubbled loudly out before I could stop it. Three times I tried before I could speak.

'Oh, Benjamin, he's got this little fluffy beard . . .'

As we fell on each other to laugh together, the door shot open and Benjamin's warm arms disappeared instantly.

'Our life is in ruins and you're laughing? Your sister hasn't brought enough pain and suffering to the family for you to . . .'

'Oh Mama – she's done no such thing. Pinchas is the one who . . .'

'On the doorstep you're arguing with me? And where were you dawdling so long?'

Any other night and I could have confided in Leah. Told her every detail for once, running my fingers lovingly over every tiny crease of this new love-fabric. Such a waste.

Tata bent to kiss me, then bolted and barred the wide-planked door behind us. Inside I saw the family grouped like the death scene in my play. Half sorry for my selfish laughter and half sorry for myself, I felt large tears fall down the sides of my nose. I wiped them away but so many came to follow these that I just leaned my forearm against the inside of the door and wept. Someone was stroking my head and whilst I hoped it was Benjamin I was too subdued to look up and find out.

Wiping my face with the end of the shawl that Drushki had woven for me in the lull of the last big snow, I saw Leah standing, red-eyed, chin wobbling ready to join me and when I hugged her, aware of the hugeness of her sorrows, both of us were weeping.

'Where's Pinchas? The troublemaker?' Benjamin said, nodding to his sister, Drushki, who sat quietly, not even reading her Bund pamphlets tonight, watching everything, saying nothing.

'You should have seen him, Benjamin,' Leah said fiercely. 'He's so weak and so brave.'

'If you hadn't taken your time getting here you could have seen him for yourself,' Mama snapped. 'Like dead, he was. Josh was here when he came and we decided he should go there to Josh's family better than to any of our family when they start searching . . .'

Each of us in our heads could see that massacred room on stage tonight, each of us picking up treasured books, momentos, oy, my journal. If they destroyed that they would destroy me more than killing me: I'd protect those writings with my life.

'And you, Benjamin, and Tata are going to Josh's family as well. To protect them, in case . . . well, they helped us . . .' she trailed off.

'Of course, of course.'

Tata opened a drawer and packed his pockets with something I couldn't see, then Mama turned her back and gave him some money from a belt around her waist. (A Jew is always expecting trouble, you might say, and is often prepared beyond reason.)

'Herring you'll take, Benjamin,' Mama said, calling to him as he went to the cupboard. 'And some goat cheese. And half that loaf. Empty-handed you shouldn't be. And a bag of plums take from the box under the sink. Leah said he was like a wolf. You know how he used to be, pick, pick, pick. Not now. You'll rest, Dovidel, and you, Benjamin – turns you'll take to guard Josh's family, yes? Trouble you shouldn't bring on their heads too. And in the morning the Holy One will help us to decide what to do.'

The door shut behind them; my lovely Benjamin was taken away from me before I'd had time to count his eyelashes. We women stared uneasily at each other as if unanchored outside a harbour.

'Much sleep', Mama said quickly, before we could burst into tears again uselessly, 'we're not going to get. Sit, everyone. I'll bring something to eat.'

I held Leah's hand and sat her on the cane chair next to the stove, Drushki alone on the double bench and the chair with arms ready for Mama as usual.

She bustled in with a small three-tier cake-stand of apple strudel and almond kichlech; then supervised the right tea for each of us, effortlessly remembering. Very strong for Leah, mine very pale, Mama's so-so but with plenty of lemon and Drushki's? Just as it comes.

Mama set her own glass of tea at her place with care. It was the only one left from her Bubba's original dowry set and was taken care of like an ancestor.

Placing the rough sugar lumps between our teeth, we sipped the hotness, hands around the glasses, savouring the temporary silent warmth of each other's company before the inevitable wrangling would begin.

'So, Leah, a shock it's been?' Mama said softly, a flake of strudel pastry at the corner of her mouth. 'When from the theatre I arrived, I know I was angry but, darling . . .'

'Mama, I just love Pinchas so much,' Leah said, fidgeting with the oilcloth on the table and looking at no one. 'Nothing else I can think about but Pinchas. Wasn't it the same with you and Tata?'

'About loving I understand, Leah, don't you worry. But I'll tell you the truth – since I was a little girl the theatre meant more to me than breathing. I was, after all, a Rubenovska. For Tata it was a great privilege to marry into the family . . .'

Drushki shook her head in a moment's disbelief and Mama, catching the gesture just as we had, took it out on us.

'Sit up straight, you girls, you want to grow up round-shouldered?'

Like Drushki, Leah and I spoke to each other with our eyes, straightening our backs, pulling our chairs closer to the table, lifting our chins. Poor Drushki, as single-minded as her brother, but in her case theatre-deaf, revolution crazy. Everyone to their own obsession. Drushki and her secret meetings everyone knew about. Still, she has only us, I thought, pushing towards her the stand of biscuits with almonds set vaguely towards the middle of each, in Mama's domestically absent-minded fashion.

'And now with Pinchas how can you live? If all the time he's hiding, how can he work? If all the time they're searching, how can we . . . ?'

'Pinchas says there is only one thing we can do,' Leah started then faltered as we all turned towards her, surprised. She pushed the spoon bowl against the pudgy slice of lemon sunk in the bottom of her tea nervously. 'Pinchas thinks . . .'

'Oh? A brain he's developed as well as leg muscles on that long walk? Exercise is good for the mind they say.'

'Mama, Pinchas was always clever. He's just not – not full of himself like – some.'

This brought a jealous smile even to Drushki's blank face, this unfair criticism of my wonderful Benjamin. Benjamin, Benjamin, how I wished I could go to bed taking with me all the new words Benjamin had said to me, all the touching, the kissing. I burned with this old accusation but couldn't defend him just now when it was Leah who needed the support.

'So. Pinchas the great brain, what's his solution? Convert the Cossacks to Judaism?'

'He says – that he'll have to leave Poland altogether. Forever.'

Mama sat back heavily in her chair, shut her eyes and sighed. She t, t, t-d through her teeth and pulled angrily at the lacy mats on the table, spilling some tea. Leah looked at me fearfully and I took her hand to try and help her through her own personal thicket.

'For that he came all this way, putting the whole village in dred? So I was right – he came to say goodbye to you. A letter he couldn't have sent, a scholar like him? Doesn't this smart fellow know where the border is? The other way? The way he came?'

'He came to – he's taking me with him, Mama.'

One more cross fidget from Mama at this blind mulishness and Bubba's last glass fell onto the blood-coloured flagstones, smashing, just as the others had.

'You're not a married woman to go anywhere with Pinchas

Rottman,' shrieked Mama, crushing more of the broken glass as she stood over Leah. 'And is this any time for a wedding? And what about Zelda? And what about Wisherodik? As you run off you won't mind seeing the flames of Wisherodik rising behind you?'

In the sobbing, shushing, arguing, shouting, jabbering that followed I made a small experiment learned from Tata. I kept out of it.

Leah's happiness and the safety of the family – even the whole area – was in my hands. As the elder daughter I must marry first, before Leah could join with Pinchas. No sacrifice is too large for your own sister. Benjamin hadn't actually asked me yet but – he would see that it was the only decent thing to do. From a swatch of colourful maybes I pulled out a stout quality serge and rosy argument. Leah had merely added a refinement to my suggestion. Yes, the mock funeral of Pinchas must indeed take place and a headstone set for any Cossack to read (if Cossacks read Yiddish). Then Leah and Pinchas must marry and leave Poland to live at peace together. Ah, but they could only marry after me – and Benjamin. Leah always turned to me in times of trouble and this time I was not just willing to help her, I insisted.

'Listen, Mama,' I said, loud enough so that they all stopped talking at once. Despite the weariness, the running nose, the swollen eyes, Leah still looked beautiful. Lucky Pinchas.

'Mama, this may all be a blessing in disguise.'

'Such a disguise I'd like to use at the theatre, so good it is. And such a blessing I can do without.'

'Mama, I think Leah has to leave Poland. She must be with Pinchas and he can't stay here – so you see? Bubba's last wish has come true. Leah will take the Rubenovskas to the Goldene Medina just like Bubba saw.'

The room was still. Weren't all Jews superstitious? Wasn't Benjamin more so than most? (May the Evil Eye never fall on him, p, p, p.) And hadn't we indeed received a sign?

'Look at the glass, Mama,' I said, bending down amongst it. 'It's maybe Bubba speaking to us.'

Mama looked down to me at the floor, holding her fists to

her collar bones. She spoke quietly as if carrying the avalanche of events.

'You think that's the miracle my Bubba wanted? That such a tragedy must come to break up a family and force Leah over the oceans?'

'In a way, Mama. Life doesn't stay the same all the time.' Was this me, Zelda Shergold, speaking? Me who only wanted every day to be the same as the one before?

'Bubba knew that better than us. Bubba's family came from Austria, didn't they? How many generations have lived here in Poland? We all came from somewhere else. Now it's time to move on again.'

Then everyone was having their say again. Leah weeping it was all her fault, Mama agreeing with her. Me begging them to wait for the family council to put our ideas to the men for agreement, Drushki passionately reminding me that women have intellect enough to make good decisions and should stick by them.

Out of weariness and despair Mama listened to my ideas about funerals and weddings without screaming much, and when I insisted that we must all get some sleep to face the difficulties tomorrow, she even meekly agreed and rose sighing, patting Leah's shoulder and giving her a kiss by her wet eyelashes.

'Don't worry,' I said as Leah knelt to wipe the floor where the tea had spilt, 'I'll do it.'

'Don't worry,' I said, kissing Mama, 'of course I'll snuff the lamp.'

'Don't worry, Drushki,' I said as she brought a broom to sweep up the glass. 'Leave it here and I'll do it. Go to sleep, all of you.'

In the silence I swept up the pieces and splinters of glass and reached for an empty sugar bag to wrap them in. Sitting for a moment with the bag in my hand I dreamed of Benjamin with his arms round me again, lifting my veil, putting the ring on the fourth finger of my right hand as it beseemeth a Jewish husband to do.

Before I snuffed the light I reached inside that bag of glass and removed a large piece engraved with the over-elaborate R that so impressed Mama and propped it on the mantel between the photograph of Bubba as an angel in a Golfaden play and one of the heavy brass candle-sticks.

Signs and miracles are easily forgotten.

ACT I

SCENE III
On the Road, 1904

The sway-backed, pot-bellied horse, whose better days were so far behind him as to seem merely legendary, good-naturedly trotted, only just ahead of the cart he pulled.

The leave-taking had been prolonged and dreadful; the lamenting could have been heard two turnip fields away, such a well-kept secret it was. The sounds of the wailing, the warnings, the promises, the sights of the loving faces, the waving arms of Mama, Tata, uncles, cousins, aunts, had been left behind three villages ago but still there was silence in the cart, each of us looking behind, as if straining to catch some last essential wisdom.

Except my Benjamin, of course. He sat at the reins as if in a Roman chariot, declaiming some of his favourite tablecloth speeches from the ends of many plays – even some of mine. (Why tablecloths? Because they covered everything, that's why.)

Pinchas had been publicly buried. Leah had enjoyed the party following his 'funeral' more than anyone. She sat next to him now, covering him tenderly with a blanket if other carts approached, if Cossack horsemen rode past, when larger villages were reached. How appropriate for him to play dead whilst Malachi, the undertaker's horse, pulled the cart we were travelling in. No one could die in Wisherodik until it was returned.

So it had all happened just as I had wildly suggested. Drushki was right; women could think for themselves a little.

And to prove it, here Drushki sat in the cart with us. Who asked her to come? Not me. And certainly not her brother, my Benjamin. I do remember a passionate speech about a New World in Americhky Where Workers Would Be Free – what then? Pinchas probably nodded politely and here she was. Just as well; with us gone, who would she have to lecture at in Wisherodik?

I sat twisting my golden ring round one way on my finger then round the other, staring at the wonderfully straight, broad back of my husband.

Benjamin rushed over the cobbles of another main village street and glanced back to see that Pinchas was once more under cover. I smiled encouragingly at Leah and wondered if Mama's sobbing still sounded in her ears too. Tata turned away in pain over and over again whenever I shut my eyes. Drushki held a small book closer to her eyes saying a few words over and over looking at the page, then holding it to her chest and repeating, repeating.

She didn't join in when Benjamin began to sing as he drove. But us, one after another now Pinchas was sitting up again, we joined in the song gradually taken up by the excitement of getting away, of being free, of starting again. Drushki tutted at our childishness and squeezed her eyes tight, muttering again.

'What part are you learning?' Leah asked, waiting for the next chorus and stroking the hand Pinchas had around her waist, her own ring shining in the late morning light.

'That's all you know: parts, plays,' she scoffed. 'American I'm learning.'

'Say some, Drushki.'

'Pliss. T'ank you. Ha much? Pliss. T'ank you. Ha much? Is good, Pinchas? Like a real American?'

Pinchas sat up straighter, his teacher's voice on. 'Say th, th. We don't have that sound. In Americhky it's all th, th, yes, now stick your tongue out a bit, like this. Try it, everyone, th, th, thank you.'

'T'ank you, T'ank you,' we all repeated.

'Good,' Pinchas said kindly.

Malachi drank gustily at the trough in the main street of

Oshmyany and at once we seemed to remember we hadn't yet eaten. I knelt to help hand out the food that Mama had prepared in such haste the night before when we finally knew the tickets had arrived and that the cart could be spared. I handed the first packet up to Benjamin and he thanked me with a private look that made me hope again that things – married things – would sort themselves out between us in time. One for Leah, one for Drushki, my own – we laughed till we cried when we found the note from Mama saying we should eat slowly and chew twenty times. I smoothed out the creases of the note and folded it into the deep pocket of my long brown skirt vowing to keep it for ever – until Mama and Tata came to join us in Americhky that is, I corrected myself sharply, not allowing my fears room in the cart.

'I'm going to learn American too, Drushki,' I said, throwing my peach stone far into the forest and trying to believe that even if that pip rooted and grew I'd never be back here in Poland to see it. 'Show me the book.'

'What for?' Leah frowned. 'It's Yiddish theatre we're going to do. And when we're there the odd word we'll also pick up.'

'Maybe, but I don't want my – plays only to be in Yiddish,' I said weakly, unable to say that what I really didn't want was for my children to think I was a foreigner. But with a terrible week of our marriage already gone, tears fell down my face at the thought of Leah a grandmother before I should finally bear a child.

If only we weren't all cooped up together perhaps I could talk to Leah. I knew she'd help. But she'd know, then, and she'd tell Pinchas and it would shame Benjamin and – no, I'd keep it to myself.

And I could learn American twice as quickly as Drushki, surely – pictures of myself standing at the back of an American theatre listening to my play in American and understanding every word smoothed the hardness of the cart and the juddering of the movement. In life, Mama used to say, for nothing you get nothing. So – I'd get started. 'Pliss, t'ank you, ha much,' I stumbled out wondering what these words meant and startled by cheering from Pinchas and Drushki.

44

The villages and towns came and went, Drushki taking the reins several times whilst Benjamin rested near me, bragging, joking but never touching. Pinchas marked the passing hours with the appropriate prayers for the time of day, Benjamin joining in only to lead the tuneful passages.

All the money the family had collected for our journey had been entrusted to me. As I dug for a little of it to buy some black bread and jumped down from the cart, pleased to be shopping again, it pained me to remember that from here onwards to Kovno we must trust no one. Carefully answering no questions at the bakery, I walked back to my family with Pinchas Rottman ridiculously hiding under a cloth. With the lonely fear of a grown-up keeping my moods from the others, I kept my miserable thoughts to myself.

Squeezing a wet muslin cloth very dry by the next pump, I wrapped it tightly round the second fat loaf to keep it fresh for the next day. So many sabbaths had Mama done this – one of the silly skills you pick up just by being around. Shame you couldn't learn marriage like that. But Leah must have learned it somewhere – Pinchas clung as close to her as a skull-cap to a skull. Benjamin was to me more like a streimel, a fur hat you only unpacked for high and holy days.

At Kovno, where our cousins Annie and Lev were supposed to be expecting us, perhaps things would be different. Annie had lots of children; her I could talk to.

Leah bought goat cheese at a place further on and we chose some fruit at another town, fearful of being remembered if we bought too much at any one stall. Benjamin made us stop and buy some absolutely unnecessary but irresistible carrot candy from some children selling it from their own front porch and the chewy gingery ingber somehow cheered us and put into focus my penny-pinching ways with our new money matters. Fun you also have to have.

In the worst heat of the day, we stopped at every pump, washing and greedily taking as much water as we could hold before filling our leather bottles and the big can. The samovar, which was secured to the bag of books by an old leather belt of Tata's, would have to wait its turn to be filled and heated in

Americhky. It was surprising that Uncle Preiska had insisted we take this; it had been his pride and treasure.

Pinchas quietly delivered the evening prayers as Malachi's hooves more and more reluctantly followed each other into the dusk, then into the dark. We had to stop for the night. Easy. Just stop. But not too close to that small farm with the chicken runs because of the possibility of wolves, not under a tree because of the birds, not here because Pinchas thought it was too exposed, not there because the noise of the stream might mask any sudden approach – we're agreed, yes? Except for Drushki? Well, with Drushki nobody can agree, so Benjamin reined Malachi in, (if you can call it reining in when it's an exhausted animal without an ounce of koyach left) unhitched him, fed him, carried him to the water and petted him down in his grandest manner.

Leah put her arm through mine as we walked away to the stream. 'I wonder if Mama's thinking about us,' she said, unpinning her long dark hair and shaking it loose. 'I keep saying to myself, "My sister and me, we are married women and we're going to live in Americhky", but all the same it doesn't make sense and it doesn't seem real. For you, too, Zeldele? Isn't marriage wonderful? I never dreamed, I can't believe . . .'

My sister, my oldest friend, dazzled with love, came back from behind a tree still sparkling words of miraculous marital delight, anxious to share the fidgets of her rapture with someone she was sure to be bound up in the same Eve-before-the-fall ecstasy. Smile? You should have seen me. How I nodded, how I agreed that men were the best thing God ever did. And I wiped my tears away unseen with my palm, feeling the coolness of my wedding ring on my cheek. An actress is an actress and Leah reached up to pick a fine piece of night-blooming jasmine for her hair before kissing me goodnight tenderly, running off to her new irresistible husband.

Oy. That poor feeble Pinchas could ring up such a curtain. Or was it, dreadful thought, that lovely Leah could inspire any man to, you should pardon the expression, great heights, but me . . . I hesitated then walked on without a flower in my hair. A whole bush of jasmine wouldn't help if Benjamin simply couldn't love me. I hated marriage; it had spoiled our lifelong friendship. It was a whole week since our hastily improvised double-wedding day and a whole week since that awful night – it's no good, I can't write down about it yet. Yet? Never. In all my plays, where there's a happy ending, there used to be a wedding-chupa in there somewhere. No more.

'Zeldele? Zeldele?'

That voice. Like the back of your neck stroked with loving fingers. Like morello cherries soaked in vodka. My Benjamin. I'd maybe give our togethering a little longer.

'Kruonis' – we read the signpost with relief through a midday heat-haze shimmer. It had become silent in the cart as each of us became tired of the side-so-side slowness of the journeying. I could see Benjamin's strong forearms tensed as if he were carrying Malachi down towards sea-level. Poor Malachi, with his look of a prisoner expecting at any moment the hangman and the rope.

'Kovno' – even better. Another midday, flatter ground and Drushki driving Malachi now as we called out in delight seeing the chalk-marks we had been told to expect on the trees of these avenues. We freshened up at a trough, tidied our bundles – not long now. The chalk turns led us to a narrow overgrown lane and a crossroads.

Against the signpost two young boys sat, their caps pulled firmly back over the vulnerable napes of their necks. We pulled in, suddenly out of chalk marks. Having decided on a three to two vote to go straight on, Malachi picked up a reluctant foot or two and began.

'Shalom aleichem,' the boys called doubtfully after us. 'Aleichem shalom,' we all waved back cautiously. Maybe. But then again there was a good price on the head of a turned-in deserter.

One word drifted back to us.

'Rubenovska?'

We were all down from the cart and running. 'Annie's boys,

yes?' We embraced and helped them up for a ride. As Drushki drove on, the boys squeezed tightly to us, I gazed at them, trying to fit their faces to our family. Our young cousins were fine boys – one perhaps a little like Tata? No, don't think about Tata. Too painful.

'I'll take the reins,' the younger boy said. 'I'm good,' he said poking Drushki in the back and climbing all over her insistently. 'Then I won't have to tell you "left" and "right" – it's better, yes?'

Even Drushki didn't argue with him.

'Straight on, straight on for a long way, I'm Hersch and he's Manny and he can't see very well, what are you called?' He chattered on talking now to us, now to the horse, now to his brother in some private code that made them both giggle and shout. Hersch was lively and lovely and the whole cart came to life with him there. Manny just sat still admiring him. It was a bit like Benjamin and me.

Pinchas solemnly folded away the blanket under which he had been hiding, lifted Manny kindly to his side and took out from his canvas bag his pad and one of his typically shortened pencils. I watched him draw the two boys as highway robbers holding up our cart. Manny held it very close to his eyes, then suddenly laughed out loud. 'That's clever,' he said seriously. 'But Mama said all the Rubenovskas of Wisherodik are actors. You're an artist.'

'No I'm not. I'm not an artist or an actor or even a Rubenovska. Me, I'm going to be a rebbe.'

'Draw something else.'

Pinchas tore off the first page and drew a rabbi thin as himself with a full beard (only wispily growing still) dancing around the Americhky landmark, the Statue of Liberty, the scrolls of the law in his arms, the two boys dancing beside him, the Torah clutched to their chests as well. 'I'm not a Rubenovska,' he said, 'but I'm going to look after your family like they did me. It's my duty. It's my pleasure,' he said, allowing himself the briefest of immodest glances at Leah. The leaping jealousy I felt would keep me busy during the repentance and fasting of the next three Yom Kippurs.

48

'If I could draw like that,' Manny sighed. 'I'd be a rebbe too. I wish I could go with you. They can make my eyes better in Americhky. I heard Tatele say so from his newspaper.'

The cart brackled onto the cobbles of the main street. Left again. Right again. A wide low house with no porch stood very far from the road, fields all around it, chickens scratching, a cow miserable in the shade. The one green-frilled tree that stood by the broken slatted fence brushed its foliage against the glass of the attic room – surely cutting out all light inside. The shutters on the front windows were closed, promising cool rooms to rest in, a small stream beckoning a welcome bathe.

'Mama! Tatele!' the boys called jumping down and running towards the back door.

I sighed, staying where I was in the jumble and fuss of the exodus from the cart, wondering what our own Mama and Tatele could be thinking about us. Were they weeping still? Was Mama maybe taking a singing lesson and giving one of the little Preiskas a begrub because he took the chorus too fast?

Annie, Lev and the younger children came out to kiss and greet us. How they marvelled at our arrival. How warm they were. They gave us their best comforts and their whole attention. They were prepared to spend and waste several good market days returning Malachi and the cart and heaven knows how many days of discomfort and danger returning home. All this for nothing but a thank you.

That this saintly family happens to be related to us is just a coincidence; you shouldn't go away with the idea that they were the only ones.

Emigrant aid committees and groups had glued themselves together passing people like the Rubenovskas from hand to hand right across the Baltic routes, always in force at the borders, even on the trains, it was said. Without the help of such angels many more of those who set out on these perilous journeys would have been robbed, murdered, or, as Mama put it, worse. Information, health care, language translations and interpretations, kosher food, even money – all were dispensed where necessary with objective kindliness and democracy. For the persecuted Jews with not a lot to lose, streaming across the East Prussian borders, from the intolerant Ukraine, from far down south in White Russia, they knew as they plodded and rumbled their baggage and their children that even after all the travelling and the dangers, things were still not going to be cinnamon and sugar – not even in the Goldene Medina. A little freedom was all we wanted, just like everyone else.

So it wasn't just for curiosity that the family made Pinchas tell over and over again the story of his escape and survival; to explain what he ate and where he hid, who hid him and what he carried. Annie and Lev were at the centre of many secret things. True, the area around Kovno had not been attacked lately – all the more likely it would soon be Kovno's turn.

'And in every generation,' we still remind each other at the Pesech table, 'they shall rise against us.' Passover in Kishinev last year had stuck out the tongue of truth at this saying again. The shockingness of the pogrom in Kishinev in 1903 was shaken from head to head through the four hundred miles that news rose from the south. Lev had caught the stories from Gomel in the east, too, where hundreds of Jews rose success-fully against the rampage in untypically violent self-defence that must have reddened some Tsarist faces. Lev, a compas-sionate man, ready to turn any number of cheeks, listened to the evidence from Kishinev, considered deeply, then quietly raised and trained troops of his own who could, if called, battle to their last bagel to keep Kovno's Jewry from the eliminating tick on the Tsarist lists.

Whilst we rested at an impromptu concert, Hersch was allowed to show off to us playing tunes on the piano to order (you-hum-it-he-played-it), singing his heart out like a real Rubenovska, his brothers and sisters lined up in teasing pride around him. Pinchas spent the hours sketching out for Lev everything he had unwillingly learned at conscription. Uni-forms, insignia, formations, hierarchy. Russian commands and random pieces of intelligence he wrote phonetically in Yiddish. I stayed to listen in awe that quiet Pinchas could say so much. Benjamin, wildly enthusiastic about Hersch's talent, stayed there with the children, clowning, singing, dancing –

any audience who could cheer would do.

'Lev, don't you think maybe you and Annie should take the children and come with us to freedom?' said Pinchas, man of peace. 'Maybe one day even to the Promised Land?'

'If I spend my life running,' Lev shrugged, putting the new information under a loose flagstone by the stove, 'trouble can still catch me up.'

More pious than us, though less than Pinchas, of course, Lev had faith not only in the Almighty but also in the Bund.

Drushki nodded till her head nearly fell off. Hadn't she said this all along? Hadn't she distributed leaflets? Hadn't she written them in the first place? This labour movement would sweep the country, it would revolutionize Russia and Poland, it would free the downtrodden workers, it would . . .

Well, it must have been quite a shock for Drushki. Look at Annie and Lev, nodding, agreeing, disagreeing a little, speech-making. Drushki hesitated, uneasy as an honoured guest at a cannibal's party. For years we had infuriated her by sitting restless, shtumm, waiting for the Bund-talk to be over so we could go back to talking about the quick changes of the current play or the problems with the next. It was what she was used to.

'And the attic, Drushki – the one so darkened by the tree outside – is the meeting-place of the Bund, secret even to the people of this village. Up there we . . .' voices were lowered, Drushki never looked happier, notebooks were written in.

What did talking revolution that would never happen have to do with us and our life in the theatres of Americhky? With saving a single Jew from hatred? Workers would always be slaves to masters and Jews would stay slaves to the lowliest of Ukrainian peasants. I shrugged at Leah and Benjamin and they shrugged back.

When we were finally scattered to our beds – Benjamin and I mercifully parted – Drushki was still up in the secret attic with Lev.

Stepping over the three little girls I was sharing a room with, I swung still dressed into bed, too tired to start worrying, too unhappy to stay awake.

Had there been a sound? Something had woken me. A cobweb? A tiny girl was trailing a knitted shawl over my face.

'Katya? It's dark yet, choochele. A bad dream you've had.'

'No. Get up.'

'It's too early, choochele. Unless – Katya, your Mama sent you to wake me, yes?'

'No. Get up. Cousin Zelda – '

'Yes?'

'That's my bed,' she said, 'Mine and Tilly's.'

Poor babies. I lifted her and put her beside me, tucking her own shawl round her, watching her thumb go to her mouth, her lovely eyes close. How many times did cousins, uncles, strangers come and there Annie's children were, back on the floor.

And if I didn't find some way of speaking to Annie about Benjamin and me tomorrow, I'd never have a floor full of lovely girls – just empty beds and empty days ahead.

My pillow had dried and Katya had breathed many hundreds of deep murmuring breaths before Benjamin walked out of my mind long enough to let me sleep.

Before it became too hot for work, we began, Leah singing as she washed and ironed everything for us – for Annie as well, and quite right too – Benjamin repacking the cart in his methodical way to give the extra room that we'd need for Lev to drive us, Pinchas grooming Malachi and praying for us. Drushki? Where's Drushki?

'Secrets in the attic,' Annie smiled as she handed me a second apron and opened all the windows in the kitchen. 'A very intelligent woman, your sister-in-law,' she added as she pulled forward a flour sack for me and began peeling the potatoes herself into a big basin, sitting like Mama, her knees wide apart, the basin resting in the lap this made.

'Where's Drushki?' Leah asked on her way through the kitchen for a cake of soap.

'Working for the people,' I said raising my chin to the attic scornfully, making Leah laugh to be heard after her footsteps had died away. Annie shook her head, meaning that we weren't right or even fair but said nothing.

Such a lot to do – we were too busy to look at each other. The right time to question loving gentle Annie about love, about being married.

Sifting and beating; Cousin Annie, when you were first married? Slicing and chopping; did you and Lev immediately? Basting and tasting; was it a long time before you? Baking and frying; did you ever worry?

Wonderful woman – a mensch. By the time the house was full of the arguing smells of gefilte fish, lutkas and strudel, she had kneaded the leaden 'duty' of marriage Mama had droned into us, into the tender lip-smacking delicacy it was worth waiting for and that Leah looked like she had just tasted.

I felt like a woman again – but knowing I must smell like a dead haddock I begged a huge towel from Annie and ran down to the stream to wash me and my hair.

'It's too hot out here, Zeldele,' Benjamin called to me as I came up past the cart. 'A cold drink, I'd really like. The cooking you've finished? Come inside with me.'

Looking at him with Annie's knowledge stored in its own special little box, I marvelled. How had I known at seven that there would be no one as wonderful as this ever? His skin, his eyes, his voice. I leaned up and kissed him.

'Come with me to the stream?'

Benjamin looked behind him, looked at the house and frowned. 'No, Zelda. Not now. I want to talk to Lev – before it gets too late.'

It was madness to stand there bawling – there weren't that many hours before we left and Lev was full of advice and knowledge that we needed but – tucking my dress up and splashing in the wonderful cold of the stream I called evil curses on Benjamin's head and body that would, if answered, have finished him off as a husband right away.

I dried myself off with Annie's best towel and stepped out across the pebbles, screwing up my mouth as if that made it less painful, and lay flat down on my stomach in the grass, unwilling to go back to the house yet.

Birds hopped and pecked at the dry bushes, the goat raised

his beard to watch me but found me uninteresting, near the house Katya and Hersch played turning round and round, their arms outstretched until it made them dizzy enough to stagger and fall shrieking with laughter. Up again, round again, down again. Like Benjamin and me when we were children, I thought angrily, biting a long grass as I rested on one elbow. It was so easy, then.

Katya ran to a box on wheels with strings tied to it for reins and ordered Hersch to pull her. He waved to me and Katya whined to him again to pull her, pull her.

'It's too hot,' Hersch said, running over to me and cart-wheeling neatly to my side, lying next to me chewing another grass in imitation and friendship. We chewed on together companionably for a moment or two like two old men studying some joyous passage of Rashi.

'Did you hear me sing? Did you hear me play? Why are you shutting your eyes? Are you going to sleep?'

'When I think about something special,' I said, dismissing my vision of myself in Benjamin's arms, 'I always shut my eyes. Sometimes it comes true, then, like a wish.'

Hersch sat up and screwed his eyes shut. 'I wish I could go with you to Americhky and be famous,' he said. 'Cousin Benjamin says I'm not as good as him but better than Boris Thomashevsky. Now you've closed your eyes again. Is it Americhky you're thinking about?'

Opening them so that inside my eyelids I wouldn't have to remember the despair on Benjamin's features, I nodded. 'Sort of.'

'If I could go I could take Manny,' he said. 'He can't sing or anything but Tatele said they could make his eyes better in Americhky; he read it from the papers.'

'Yes, Manny told me. Perhaps we'll go to Americhky first. Then when we've lots of money we'll send you the tickets and we'll all be together . . .'

'People come here all the time to us on the way to the trains. Tatele gives *them* money. I see him. And I always say, "Can I go with them?" because I could look after Manny and his eyes could be got better and he says, "We'll have to see; this is your home." But when I asked him today he says family is different but he didn't say no and I can play piano for money and get money for Manny's eyes and then for tickets for Mama and Tatele and Katya and the little ones and they'll come on a boat and I'll be the first one to see them and I'll wave . . .'

'One day, Herschele,' I said, not to hurt him. 'But what would all your brothers and sisters do without you? You're like a whole theatre of your own for them, you're so good. And your Mama – how could she part with you. And in three years it'll be your barmitzvah and . . .'

'So,' Hersch said, throwing away the piece of grass that had linked us in friendship, 'you don't want to take me.' He gave me an adult look of hatred, and tightening his lips he shouted, 'You wouldn't care if I died. Everyone except us goes to Americhky.'

He ran unsteadily into the house leaving me wet-faced in the shadow of his unhappiness.

So now I had time to lie in the sun and forgive myself not only for being no good to Benjamin but no good to anyone else either. Too restless to stay, and disregarding Mama's echoing voice about making aches in my bones, I flung the wet towel over my shoulder and went into the house past all the children playing, defiantly humming a love song and hoping that Benjamin would know it was for him.

And in the house what was happening?

Nothing. There was no one around. All the windows were open in the kitchen but it was still hot from the morning's baking. Squeezing lemon juice into a glass I added some cloudy barleywater from an enormous stone jug of it and took it to look for somewhere cool to drink, feeling somewhat between a thief and a trespasser in the silent house.

'Ssh,' my Benjamin whispered, making me spill some of the drink over the stone floor of the passage. 'I've been waiting for you. Hersch was crying and crying – why not take him to Americhky? He'd be more of a star than me, almost. He could send home all his money and one day . . . I love you, Zeldele. Much comfort the next few days we won't have. Come up with me, we'll rest a bissel. It's so hot. I'll rest and you stand and fan

me.'
    When am I ever without words?
    'Everyone's dozing, Zee-Zee.'
    How comes a pet name can mean so much?
    Katya's empty room was cool, the shutters firmly down and
a heavy chair soon wedged under the handle of the door.

Wait till I see Leah.
    Wait till I tell Leah.
    She sparkles, but me, I'm a whole sky at night.
    Pinchas? Compared with my Binyomin?

I don't need to tell you how sick I am to hear days later that it is
Pinchas, the mumser, who tells my Benjamin what to do.

• ·

ACT II

SCENE I

London, 7 September 1904

Oy, were we sick. Singly, together, all the time. Leah recovered first and with her horror of low standards was soon chivvying us all, washing everything, smoothing it with her fingers as it dried in the sea breeze until I was well enough to help her. She resewed any holes and made more than a little effort to pull the family back into the orderly cleanliness Mama would have demanded.

'England must be glad to see us,' she said primly, so like Mama in that mood. 'They'll wish we were staying longer,' she fussed, wiping Hersche's forehead and making him comfortable on the upper deck, next to Benjamin.

Hersch? Oh yes, of course we brought Hersch with us. Benjamin insisted. The Thomashevskys and the Adlers had children with them or who could they train for the future? Personally I wouldn't part with any child of mine that easily but – well, Annie and Lev had a lot of others and plenty on their minds. 'His talent is his destiny,' they'd nodded sadly.

Drushki, weak and pale herself, but too proud to complain, kept reading over and over again the booklets Lev had let her bring, hardly able to endure the time until she could bring freedom single-handed to the poor slaves of Americhky. Her English dictionary book was mine now, since Annie and Lev had told her how the Bund would insist on Yiddish worldwide. I worked hard at the words with Pinchas as Drushki was too ill to argue. It suited her, being poorly. She was much pleasanter for it.

So this was the Port of London.

Pushing through to the front of the rails around the battered ship, we Rubenovskas seemed to me to look as conspicuously valuable as pearls in a jar of garden peas. Around us sea-weary East Europeans ejected from their homes and with no sure welcome anywhere joined silently in the deliverance prayers of gratitude that sang from pious mouths like Pinchas's everywhere.

Whatever lay ahead the Baltic Sea was between us and our enemies.

In the dropping of the wind as the harbour surrounded and protected us, the water hung limply now as if held up by under-mud. And the weather was warm – very warm, just like Wisherodik in the spring. Mama said Avrom always saw the worst in everything and he had always written of the rain and the cold in London.

Even those laid low and sickly the whole journey began to smile and move about, warmed by the welcoming English sun and the pleasure of being nearer to the time when they would stand upon blessed ground that does not move.

'The Goldene Medina!' an old man cried out, tears running down channels already dug by years of previous sorrows. 'Oy! The Goldene Medina!'

A hundred voices told the old fellow he was only in London yet but still he cried out his wonder at having arrived at last at Americhky the Golden. Many others clustered around him, convinced that the boat had taken, maybe, a wrong turning and missed England altogether.

That it was only London, and that the trip to Liverpool was yet to be made tomorrow, the day after or next week was bad enough in the explaining. But that the tedious crossing of the Atlantic also lay ahead was too much for the old man to listen to. So he shut his ears and ran from rail to rail searching the distance for the 'shtarke shiksah mit de lempel.'

Through the laughter at the rails the Port of London came closer. Though the buildings were blackened and patchy, to me they looked important, official and safe. Though it was worrying that the King of England was a little bit related to

Tsar Nicholas, Cousin Avrom always wrote that if you worked hard enough in England and made enough money you could live how and where you pleased. Was Poland ever like that?

I leaned my head down to watch the colours in the water and to dream. Before the journey to Liverpool perhaps Avrom would show us King Edward's Palace, then the Yiddish theatre in Thacker Close Tata talked about, and maybe see that big shul that hadn't been burnt down in over a hundred years – imagine. And then Americhky. Mama said Cousin Avrom might want to go with us. She said he had been handsome like Benjamin when young and nearly as good an actor though he never could hold a tune.

'Why so slowly we're going?' Hersch said, smiling again and no longer green in the face, fresh in his clean knickerbockers.

'That hooting you can hear,' said Benjamin, from whom Hersch had been so inseparable throughout their mutual sickness that I had been almost jealous, 'is from the tiny tugboats. They have to be like the eyes for this big ship as she's too clumsy to get into such a small space by herself. Can you hear them? "A bissel left, a bissel right, enough already", they're saying.'

What a father he'd make.

Was I expecting yet? Was Leah? Did you feel it grow from the very first day? Surely you must. Cousin Tillie used to be sick all the time and Mama said that was a good sign. But how can you tell between baby-sickness and sea-sickness? We're all too young. We shouldn't be going to Americhky. Alone we shouldn't. Mama.

'Nothing, Leah. I'm just crying from excitement.'

'Can you see Cousin Avrom yet? What does he look like?' Hersch said.

I saw him last when I was six, seven, when Benjamin was nine, ten. Just before Bubba died, he left. Avrom had a joke habit of brushing down his thick moustache and eyebrows to make us laugh when we were little but would he be doing this on a dockside? I could remember nothing else about him.

There was much pointing of fingers and shouting now as the

tip of a large crowd started between the blackened building with a flag flying and a round glass thing without a flag. Like raisins in a lockshen pudding in a bad week they came at first – only a few. With bright eager eyes, they searched the decks as the decks searched them, broken halves of family trying to lock together again and seal the cracks. How long before we . . . ? Thicker came the raisin faces now, all eyes lifted to the rails, everyone welcoming anyone in the warmth of arrival. Sometimes a name would be cried out, recognition, weeping, but mostly there were sighs of safety and hope. As the faces became clearer, many had waved themselves silent but still the children cheered and tirelessly swung their arms above their heads and sang, Hersch amongst them, taking off his cap and letting the wind bend it about in salute.

Nearer and nearer. Years change people. Many had shaved off their traditional beards for English moustaches. Some were fatter then or thinner, some in English-style clothing, many were coughing into their handkerchiefs. And Avrom? How would we know him? A typical Rubenovska, Mama had declared, forgetting each of us would visualize a different face from that description.

Anchored. Through the cheering and the praying, through the pushing and the lurching, the moaning started – not the small boat business again.

Bundles were being unwrapped, boxes distributed amongst the able-bodied, children put to the breast in urgent necessity even amongst the turmoil, leather straps were tightened around bags as a small queue of rowing boats dipped and clung to the side of the ship to take us all ashore. As ladders swung down the side, the sea air filled with Yiddish curses. Elderly people everywhere shrugged their inability to climb down ladders, and their spirited intention to stay right where they were, t'ank you, and go back to lovely old Poyln rather than drown on the way to Americhky. But they had their baggage dragged from them, and were handed from step to step, their cursing ignored until, safely seated in the ferry-boat, they screamed threats to the next terrified down-climber to hurry, please hurry.

Pinchas helped Leah who helped Hersch who helped Benjamin who helped me. Drushki managed on her own.

Rubenovskas. We stood in London, England, for the first time with none of the chilling wind we were dressed for; nor any of the rain. It was hot, stiflingly still and sticky as the time moved nearer to midday.

We stood uncertainly like all the other families, acknowledging by our stiffness the fear of the uniforms around us everywhere. Customs officers, they whispered one to another and then to us. Ah, not soldiers, then. Hard to relax when in Poland behind every raised hand, raised baton, raised flaming torch glinted these same shiny buttons and polished boots of a uniform.

You could see what lay behind the repacking of every family's bundles on every foot of dock space; we were anxious to conceal our precious candlesticks, the last of the family shmay-drays, the letters and photogravures, though everyone was sure, that whatever we did, however we pleaded, these, valued or worthless, would, simply because they were the property of Jews, be seized or destroyed.

Yet though the officers of the Customs were often cold and unsmiling, and although the baggage was searched with undignified thoroughness, once chalk-marked, belongings were respectfully handed back as interpreters stood by to ease the difficulties, stay the questions, overcome the suspicion. At least that's what happened to us and those around us. Eyes were examined for disease; heads checked for lice whether we liked it or not; the sickly put into temporary quarantine, not without resistance; the hysterical calmed or not calmed.

Those who were to go no further than London crowded towards the immigrant entrance, yearning towards their folk across the barriers that like the Red Sea only a miracle could render passable. But what's a miracle for a Jew? A common-place; so they pushed and shoved to be first.

The Rubenovskas were pushing in the other direction with the other half. Where Pinchas said we should go, we went. The letters said 'In Transit', whatever that meant.

Here a bottleneck was forming of such a muddle that even

the most downtrodden, intimidated, patient soul must protest. More officers appeared, a further desk or two was opened. Passivity spread again under this fairness, then chaos rose in a new wave until yet another table was dragged out under the pressure.

Hersch slumped against the bundles. Benjamin urged him forward when necessary, cursing the samovar now we had to carry it. We'd stopped looking for Avrom. Pinchas had been told by an interpreter that Avrom's address was a five-minute walk from the dock so we would go there soon and surprise him. Could the poor man be expected to meet every boat? Mama must have seen our arrival a little rosier; just us on a boat and only Avrom there to meet us. Besides, the picture Drushki had in her side-pocket was of a smudged Avrom in his best clothes on the occasion of his wedding so long ago and though we would search and search there was no one with the Rubenovska cheekbones standing around the quay in a top hat.

The problem of Avrom's absence dissolved like shmaltz on a hot stove when we reached the head of the queue and met real trouble.

Hadn't I written my play about this? How many warnings had we had? What were Annie and Lev doing to let this happen to us?

And Pinchas. Pinchas had been the judge, the hochum, the scholar who had so proudly spelt out and explained the letters to us, NEW YORK, UNITED STATES OF AMERICA, printed clearly. The officer couldn't see? We craned forward; there, we could make out the words for ourselves.

'Nisht goot,' the hot, perspiring officer said again in what sounded like the only two Yiddish words he knew. 'Nisht goot,' he said, waiting for the interpreter at the next desk to be free to explain to us. 'Do – you – speak – English?'

Pinchas stood forward. 'A bissel,' he said modestly. 'London, England,' he pointed. 'Then, New York, United States of America.' He smiled back at us. All sorted out. The poor fellow was tired and had been there jostled for hours by us all. A natural enough mistake.

'Nisht goot for New York,' the officer sighed, pointing to some tiny words. 'Not valid for New York. Nisht goot.'

Pinchas stared then grabbed the tickets, pushing his fingers against the tiny little words. 'Not valid for,' he pronounced slowly. '"Not valid for" is nisht good?'

Pinchas stared on at the ticket, his fingers running under the new little words, tears falling down his face. Leah came to stand very close to him. No one spoke. No one moved. I pushed to the front. One thing I knew: Mama says money opens every door. The keys to the Goldene Medina could also be bought. I used my English for the first time.

'Pliss. New York. Ha much?'

The officer looked down at me, counted us. 'Roughly? Let's see. Five? And a child? Kind? In zloties –'

He added up a final figure and pushed it over to me. With tears running down my face, I handed it to Benjamin. An epitaph for the Rubenovska headstone.

Seeing our despair, Drushki thrust away the piece of paper and starting cursing the ticket-seller and his genitals to amens from all of us but saintly, infuriating Pinchas.

I could see for myself the look of gratitude on the officer's face when he saw that the interpreter was free and on his way over with a file of papers.

'Look,' said the interpreter, drawing us away so that the arguing, impatient family behind could step forward. 'Look,' he said, kind but with a job to do, 'walk over there, near the archway. Those people, that's what they're here for, to help with these problems. Tickets, tickets, it's all we hear. Listen, it's not so bad here in England, believe me. See how happy Montefiore is here? Did he take his family to Americhky?'

Holding Drushki back from his throat, we shuffled after him, demanding answers as we went.

'Listen, half the passengers behind you will be, you'll excuse the expression, in the same boat. But there are people who can help.' He nodded again towards the line of desks ahead.

'These people, who are they?' Benjamin said.

'You've heard, maybe, of the Shelter? That's who they are.'

The Shelter. We stiffened and stopped. Who hadn't heard of

the Shelter? A wonderful thing, a splendid institution, a credit to Jews everywhere. The Temporary Shelter for Jews; who hadn't been told mouth to mouth the address in Leman Street? The Jews blessed every person connected with its development aloud to the heavens – and prayed in their souls they need never have any truck with such a handout. Giving charity is easy. Indeed it is the duty of every Jew. Taking it is another story.

'The Shelter,' Benjamin said firmly, 'we don't need. We are actors,' he added by way of explanation and with no intention of further dealings.

'. . . But we thank you for your kindness,' I tagged on, avoiding his furious eyes.

'All the same,' the interpreter shrugged, 'on the docks you can't stay. Arrangements you'll have to make.'

'What's happening?' Hersch demanded, the rest of us hanging on to possible answers. 'How do we get to Liverpool? Where's Avrom? What today are we doing?'

Benjamin seemed to have taken charge. He swept the interpreter to one side and stepped through the crowds as if he were wearing his finest cloak and this were only a temporary setback before his final triumphant curtain.

My man had style; more I couldn't ask for.

More queueing. Many in front of us had thought themselves only 'In Transit' too. Many had learned the words 'not valid for' and wails and laments rose and fell. Rumour and counter-rumour echoed back to us. The most consistent of the rumours was that any immigrant found to be of poor health or positively ill would be sent back on the next boat. Never have frail, poorly passengers perked up so quick. Pale cheeks were pinched into rosiness, coughs were stifled, limps were modified, backs straightened everywhere.

As we stood, weight first on one hip, then on the other – how Mama would have shouted at us and warned us of the 'revmatizm' we would suffer in our old age – seamen unexpectedly handed out bread and salt herring, shrugging off suspicious insult and proffered money with equal blankness. We took some but Benjamin gave his to Hersch, disdaining such unearned titbits. Men and women clutched at us, at everyone, clamouring for 'charity' showing dirty crumpled 'licences' in their hands for such collection. Pockets opened willingly enough until a further rumour came back from the front that these were merely clever beggars and that not a coin would ever reach either widow or orphan. Ahead of us only tears and sobs came from groups of children and adults whose Statue of Liberty's torch had been doused if not for ever then at least for now.

'May a black pox descend on the bowels of the family of the ticket-seller,' Benjamin said, when it was our turn at the table under the banner of the Temporary Shelter.

(He couldn't first have said hallo or shalom?)

'We have been outrageously cheated and robbed. We wish to know how to obtain our rightful passage to New York. We wish to know this quick,' he added. Benjamin took the tickets from Pinchas's hand where they lay crumpled into damp, useless bunches. 'The swine who sold these worthless tickets to us was of medium build, greying hair and beard and with –' he looked at us for confirmation – 'very large brown eyes?'

We nodded, remembering the swine.

The man whose lapel badge of authorization claimed that he was Israel ben Melech known as Igor Lottenstein looked up.

'The blackguard looks just like me?' he said, his large brown eyes smiling wearily at us over his grey beard. 'Not that it's anything to joke about,' he added, sharp to the change in Benjamin's face. 'A tragedy it is. Perhaps they may catch him if you tell us where he goes, what he does; perhaps not. But they rise as quickly as they're cut down,' he frowned.

'Like the Jews,' said Pinchas, speaking for the first time since what he obviously considered his disgrace and fall from favour.

'You're right, angel,' Leah said adoringly.

'Ssh,' said Drushki. 'Let the man speak.'

'I'd like to find the best possible way to help you,' he said, warming me up with his close attention as he addressed me straight in the eyes.

You think being crazy in love with Benjamin would stop me

seeing Mr Igor Lottenstein's interest in me. Leah may be the beauty in our family – she'd be the beauty in most families – but the Rubenovskas are uniformly olived-skinned and dark-haired and my throwback red hair and milky skin automatically attracts some men.

Aside from writing plays if there's one thing I'm good at it's reading people's minds and I knew the answer to my Benjamin's question was that the money we had paid was lost and nothing could be done and the fellow hated to say so. I watched him bridge his nose with a thumb and forefinger to pinch at the inside corners of his eyes.

'Every day you're here?' I said, achingly sorry for this tired, kind-looking man.

'Wednesdays,' he said smiling. 'Every Wednesday except the Holy Days for six years. Just temporary they said it would be. That's how these things are. You take them on and you're handcuffed and no one can find the key.' He stopped, looking a little shocked at himself for speaking out. 'Nice of you to ask about me. People think we're just a file and a pencil. Look, I'm glad to be able to do this job. Now . . .'

No matter how he shuffled the papers and looked at lists and added up our assets, London was where we were staying for longer than just to greet Avrom and see the Castle of Buckingham.

'Of course we shall help you with temporary accommodation for two weeks, providing you search for work daily and take whatever job you can get and . . .' misunderstanding the look between me and Benjamin, '. . . a two week limit may seem very harsh to you, but . . .' he waved behind us to the crying, restless valueless-ticket-holders still to come.

'Yes, yes, yes,' Benjamin said impatiently. 'My dear sir, we thank you but our cousin lives here in London and will provide for us until we have accumulated enough to take us on to our destination. Our new situation is shocking but we are in no need. We have . . . connections.'

'We are,' Leah confessed, 'in fact, the Rubenovskas.'

We stood back and beamed.

'The Rubenovskas. Indeed,' said Igor. 'Indeed.'

'So, my dear sir, if you would be kind enough to direct us to – this address, which is where my cousin is believed to await us and if you could tell me where are the Yiddish theatres, especially this one – can you read this? T'acker Close?'

'Thacker. Thacker Close. The Behrens is it? A coincidence. I know the Behrens well because . . . but I don't go myself to the plays. When you've learnt maybe some English, Up West you can go and see – oh the theatres there, they're wonderful. Still, first things first. A bed and a job you need first. So, where does your cousin live?' Igor Lottenstein put out his hand.

My Benjamin held back the paper with the address on it. 'Excuse me, but Rubenovska? It means nothing?'

Igor hesitated then shook his head.

'The Rubenovskas. The theatrical family,' Benjamin said louder, as if Igor were merely deaf. 'We are known from – here to here,' he said, covering such a wide area with his gesture it could have been from East Prussia to the Ukraine.

'Our own theatre we're opening in the Goldene Medina. So at the Yiddish theatres in London we'll act for a while until we have the tickets and then . . . Now this address. It's far?'

Igor Lottenstein frowned. 'You're sure this is right? Only – well, this you can take with you,' he said taking a battered map out of a box and shaking it out of its folds.

'You', he said, marking it, 'are here.'

We saw our first motor car two minutes after we'd started walking. Was it safe with all that smoke around it? Hersch, who had been complaining of hunger and tiredness for so long, wanted to wait until another one came along. But we walked on quickly, eager to say shalom to Avrom and lay down somewhere soft.

Yet in the letter Pinchas took from Benjamin's shocked hand it was quite clearly number fifty-eight. There was a closed up warehouse taking up most of that side of the road and on the other, into another warehouse, an open one, sides of meat were being carried on the blood-soaked shoulders of some hard-capped porters.

Between the dockside chandlers, public houses, boathouses, lock-up stores and abattoirs of this street we wandered up and down; there were, however, just a few houses.

Children played and cried out in shabby yards, then stopped to stare at us, Pinchas in particular, shrieking with laughter as they bent their thin bodies and rubbed their hands wearing pretend beards from the ample mud that lay everywhere. My Benjamin approached them and they ran ahead of him screaming in terror to the exposed passage of a hallway as if they'd played that Jew-game a million times before but never had anyone come after them to beat them up.

Benjamin, with all of us trailing behind, was met at the door by a solid chunky man with his collar off and his collar stud open. There was a look in his eye somewhere between faint suspicion and murder.

In his grandest manner Benjamin enquired after Avrom and why number fifty-eight had disappeared. The man frowned.

'Look, I don't talk Jewish but sure I can tell you those kids weren't doin' no harm. Sure they're just playin'; you know what they're like. So bugger off.'

Pinchas was called in to translate but, not knowing the words kids and bugger, was at a linguistic disadvantage. Into a closing door Pinchas inserted a loud, 'Excuse, pliss.'

As the door relented a little, the hanging bottom half scraping on the step, a thin sliver of wood sliced off to lie with others.

'We look for our Cousin Avrom – Abraham Preiska. Abraham Preiska? You know? Fifty-eight? This road?'

'There's no Yids lives here,' he said. 'Sure aren't you always looking for your relations? For meself, the less I see of mine the better.' He shook his head as the children inside the house began to scream and shriek again.

'Yids and kids,' he laughed, closing the door on us. 'Kids and Yids.'

So Mr Lottenstein had been right saying that this dockland

area was not the usual place for Jewish families. Most of them had moved nearer to the synagogues and kosher butchers in Stepney and Bethnal Green.

Maybe Uncle Preiska's doubts about Avrom's long silences and lack of news meant he had married, God forbid, a gentile wife.

So we stood, defeated, right in the middle of the road, trying to face ourselves in the same way as the hard-to-follow old London map with only the main streets marked. The Golden Grapes stood behind us and the Unicorn in front.

'Relying on Avrom has been a disaster,' Benjamin pronounced grandly. 'We must rely only on ourselves.'

'That man, Ivor? Igor?, said to come back if there were any problems,' Hersch said sighing and sitting on his bundle, his arms round Leah's legs. My money-belt had only Polish money in it; it had seemed so precious until we arrived here where it was as worthless as our damned tickets. Nothing to eat since – hours ago. How long since Annie's food; the gefilte fish, the mandelbrot, the rye bread and the olives? Better not to think about it. I looked guiltily at Hersch. He was in our care and look at him: red-eyed, exhausted and starved.

I bent closer over the map with Benjamin and Drushki.

'Brick Lane!' I pointed. 'Mr Lottenstein said something about the theatres being around Brick Lane. Definitely.' Benjamin looked at me. 'I think it was, wasn't it?'

They looked doubtful. But Leah, at a wink from me, agreed that she remembered it too and we exchanged a quick smile. Anything was better than standing here. Benjamin gave way to the pressure and with his fingers, measured from where we were to the docks and then over to Brick Lane.

'Why didn't Cousin Avrom . . . ?' Hersch complained, moving to his tired feet. 'Where's the trees? You said,' he accused Benjamin, 'that we'd sleep in a goosefeather bed tonight and eat chicken, and English apples straight from the trees.'

'Yes, I did, didn't I,' Benjamin said vaguely, promises

meaning very little to him either way.

'Cousin Avrom never thought anyone would come to London to uncover his lies, that's what this is all about,' Drushki said angrily, putting her hair that Leah had brushed so prettily around her wide face back into its unflattering, habitual, black band. 'The Preiska part of the family; what can you expect?'

The streams of dockers heading for one pub or another were thickening. Mostly they took as much notice of the Rubenovskas as of a hole in the road to be stepped round but a nudge here and a sudden splash or two of laughter seemed to be hosed at us and I began to wish we definitely had a safe bed for the night ahead. Benjamin said that the first theatre we came to would give us a place to lie our heads but . . .

Would Mama have let five and a half strolling players into our front parlour? Never.

The Unicorn seemed the more popular public house. The door was propped open to let in the sweet warm air of the last-of-the-summer-nights. A piano started to play and the whole lot of us straightened to listen critically. Unfamiliar tunes but easy peasant lilts; nothing Hersch couldn't handle and that voice joining in was just terrible. So we nodded to each other in unspoken instant optimism. If the worst came to the dreadful, we could, better than starve, retreat from our standards a reluctant mile or two and cobble together an act to drag around these English alcoholic drinking houses.

'Like Bubba, that's how she started,' I smiled at Benjamin.

'Never,' he scowled, as if the very same thoughts hadn't been going through his head. 'Come – if this Brick Lane is right, if this map is drawn correctly, we've perhaps, I'm not sure, an hour's walking to walk.'

At once our feet felt swollen, our bags looked heavier. Such a shlep and maybe for nothing.

'It's easier if you sing as you go,' Pinchas said softly, remembering.

'Sing? You sing if you want to,' Drushki said, lifting her

bundle and holding on to her side. 'That far I'm not walking. For one night the Shelter can't hurt us. Somewhere we've got to sleep and eat. On the street we could be murdered.'

We scoffed but were indecisive until two men were hurled yelling out of the Unicorn to fight it out on the pavement. We picked up and hurried off; only I saw the same two fellows, arms around each other, going right back into the Unicorn in comradely love.

So we walked back to the dock gates, back to Igor Lottenstein. I pictured him still calmly at his desk – if he hadn't gone altogether – symbolizing orderliness, safety, belonging. He had been so gentle. Truly we needed any shelter we could find. Benjamin was all bluster but had finally agreed with Drushki, so things must have looked bleak.

And Mr Lottenstein? Not gone, as I'd feared, but not at his desk either. He stood at the side of an empty throbbing horseless carriage surrounded by clouds of smoke and a pointing staring crowd.

The London politsey could barely write fast enough to record all the recriminations a hundred eager witnesses swore, pointing at poor Mr Lottenstein.

The motor car seemed to be his, we agreed in amazement. Sticking out from underneath it was a large woman wrapped in a blanket, groaning in pain and holding her head, whilst those bending over her rose periodically to scream at Mr Lottenstein.

'Come on, come on,' Drushki swore. 'It'll be night-time before we can talk to the man.'

'He must be ungershtocked with gelt', said Benjamin admiringly, 'to possess such a motor car. Look, Herschele – look at the lamps and the chrome so shiny and the little buttons in the leather on the seats.'

'But he's hurt someone with it,' Leah reminded us.

'It's a fuss about nothing,' Drushki said. 'It seems to me there's not much wrong with the woman. Look, she's laughing when she thinks no one's noticing. It'll be all right.'

Something in the scene jarred, worried me. Mobs

screaming were nothing new in the streets of Wisherodik. In fact riots were what we had come all this way to avoid. But then – a lovely thought. Of course. This disturbance was not against the Jews. I could be neutral and uninvolved. A pleasure.

The politsey had finished talking to the excited crowd and turned to Igor Lottenstein with a clean page turned in his little book.

'Now, Mr Cohen,' he said.

'Pinchas? Why does he call him Mr Cohen?' Perhaps I had misunderstood.

'Because, Zelda, he sees that Mr Lottenstein is a Jew and is being as rude as he dares.'

'Even here?'

'Even here.'

Then I remembered the taunts of the children and another illusion smashed like Bubba's glass. Still – no horses, no clubs, no fury. And this English Jew had been allowed to make and keep enough money to buy such a showy luxury as a motor car. England might not be a bad place.

Hersch's obsession with the motor car had thankfully delayed Benjamin's usual impatience. 'It's hard to make it move, Cousin Ben-Ben?' he said, finding a space to stare from the running board.

'Easier than a horse. It has no will of it's own. If someone showed me, in an instant I could drive. It's the first thing I shall buy in Americhky,' my Benjamin, the one who was penniless in London with no place to sleep, declared. 'If Pinchas painted Rubenovska on the sides – here and here – how much better than any poster.'

There was laughing and screaming behind us and we turned to watch. The woman under the car was holding up a banner and a photographer retreated under a cloth as she lay still for him. The moment the explosion had finished, she and her group strolled away unfurling the banner between them and chanting as they marched.

The policeman pointed to the motor car, shook his finger at Mr Lottenstein and walked away slowly.

Mr Lottenstein looked after him and said politely in Yiddish, 'A conflagration in your intestines.'

Only the Rubenovskas were there to laugh and the policeman turned, uneasily aware that some subtle insult had been made but couldn't be proved, that the sting of the 'Mr Cohen' had been spat back.

Mr Lottenstein frowned at us all, yet how could he be expected to remember us from all the others? It was me, he recognized, of course. My hair, I mean. He smiled. 'The actors? Yes? Trouble?' he asked Benjamin who leaned back against the motor car whose engine had stilled itself.

He heard our story gulped out in patches, each of us playing a different part, but it seemed to me he'd heard it all before.

'So,' he said, taking out his file from the motor car, 'another family for the Shelter tonight.' He took back the map he had given us before and marked a cross at the Shelter and another at Thacker Close where that theatre was supposed to be, and reminded us that we had only a fortnight to find both accommodation and work.

'I've a business myself, however,' he said suddenly to Benjamin but looking directly at me. 'Perhaps I could find something for the three young ladies. Only if there's difficulty with your theatricals, that is,' he added hastily, knowing an arrogant refusal when he saw one coming.

'Ah, it will be reassuring to know there's a last resort,' my Benjamin bowed, sure he was being gracious. I exchanged a wince of apology with Mr Lottenstein that made his face shine. He handed his card to each of us. 'If I can ever be of help to you – we all', he said, gazing at me, 'need somebody.'

He swung a handled stick at the front of the motor car until it jumped and rattled and he rushed into the two-seater saddle putting a pair of eye-protectors on.

'Good luck,' he shouted into the smoke that drove us back. 'Don't go to the Goldene Medina without saying goodbye. Or perhaps I'll come and see you at the theatre.'

'We'll send you some seats,' Leah waved, coughing.

Watching him go, we lifted our bundles and trudged in the direction of the Shelter, as people shook their fists at him and

73

shouted. Only we and the London children stopped running to look enviously as he jerked and banged elegantly into the fading evening light of the English summer, fainter and fainter until he was gone.

ACT II

SCENE II
Thursday 8 September 1904

Rubenovska, Benjamin. Rubenovska, Zelda. Rubenovska, Drushki. Rubenovska, Pinchas. Rubenovska, Leah. Rubenovska, Herschel.'

We sshd Hersch's protests; here in England we were all Rubenovskas. It's good for business, it's nice and simple, listen, don't argue, the man's waiting.

The clerk at the Shelter sighed. Shame on him. Was it so long ago that he'd been a greener here? He looked more straight-off-the-boats than we did.

'The boy? How old?'

The pride in Hersch as he pronounced the magic word 'ten' painted pictures of summer birthday parties laughing by Annie and Lev's stream and made me, if not him, homesick for their love.

'T, t; you want I should put him down, ten for school, thirteen for work?'

The only thing we were in London for was to earn money to get to Americhky. Every Rubenovska must pull a little weight, sacrifice. As a rehearsal pianist Hersch could earn a lot by day, perform at night. We nodded our decision firmly one to another. No question about it.

'School,' Benjamin said.

'Ten,' wrote the clerk.

(The other way of looking at it is that as we pictured Hersch in our various ways – actor, rabbi, doctor, pianist, anarchist – it followed that he needed the sharp weapon of education to slice himself the prime cuts of life.)

'All right, so – Jewish Free School's full, it always is, Christian Street School . . .'

'It must be Jewish,' said Pinchas. 'The boy's orthodox.'

'Don't worry. Even the schools that aren't Jewish close early on winter Fridays for Shabbos and all the festivals. If they didn't, who would be there to learn anyway? Don't worry. Listen, you don't want to be too fussy, you should excuse me. If I can find him a place anywhere he'll be lucky. Fickland Street – full, Brick Lane – full, Deal Street – full; full; full. To go every morning and queue up until a place comes you don't want, no? Well, look, you want me to try to get him a place at Lantern Street?'

He looked up and I thought he seemed pleased to see our faces one to another clouded with suspicion at the way he'd spoken.

'For learning it's good,' he said. 'A lot of scholarships they get.'

'But there's something wrong with it?'

'It's tough. But they all are. It's – a good school.'

'So what's the problem? It's expensive maybe?'

'No, no. Free. They're all free.'

'How comes?'

'People. They give money. School's free here. But . . .'

He was going too slowly for us. Drushki couldn't bear it.

'With "free" how can there be any "but"?'

'Wait, let the man speak.'

'To tell you the truth,' he said slowly, 'I just remembered I think Lantern Street School is also full.'

Leah and I turned down our mouths in disappointment. Now what? But the others were muttering, smiling, consulting.

'Our Hersch would very much like it if he can go to Lantern Street School,' my Binyomin said unexpectedly politely. 'Is there some way . . . ?'

'Luckily . . .'

We relaxed. This script we knew.

'. . . if the boy's the right type, I could get the teachers there to squeeze . . .'

A rustling of paper money, a nodding of heads, a thrusting into pockets and Hersch became the 'right type' of boy to enter the learned gates of Lantern Street School.

'Give me your map,' said the clerk, marking it. 'Take him there and give them this – and this letter. Here and here, I'll mark them in red, there are workshops and factories. You might get work there, right near the school. Anyway you know the rules. You have to try. And take my tip, even if it says 'no vacancies' outside a workshop – that means workers they don't need – go in just the same. Just that moment there may be a broygus, a fight, someone walks out, someone drops dead over their machine – it happens and nah, a job.'

'Thank you, but we have,' Benjamin said again, checking his pocketwatch, putting the papers for Hersch and the map in the pockets of his best cloak whose creases had fallen out easily under the steam-kettle I had borrowed, 'connections.'

Hersch wouldn't have cared what school it was, just so he didn't have to attend it in secret as he had near Kovno. So surprised we weren't when he didn't look back as a teacher put himself in charge of Hersch, stopping only to advise us we should meet the boy at four this first day.

'Not a word of American he knows,' Benjamin said doubtfully, walking reluctantly away with us.

'When he comes out he will,' Pinchas said. 'He'll be the first of us all to speak English properly.'

'And in Americhky English they understand?'

'Of course.'

'I wonder if Cousin Avrom speaks English. We must never give up looking for him,' Leah said, slipping her arm through mine.

I nodded guiltily, but really I was dreaming of writing English plays and though Mama would have died to see me, I kicked an English stone along with my foot from me to Leah and we hummed an old song cheerfully together through the East End street in the bubbling excitements of newness. Never mind the problems, London is an extra even Bubba didn't guess we could have.

Maybe in the houses there were people, but it seemed to us as Benjamin called out the turns to us that surely everyone must be out here on the streets.

Rolled-up newspaper cricket balls were being hit by bent-stick bats from lamp-post wickets through the bowed legs of smelly tramps scratching under their caps as they walked. Italians sang hokey-pokey slogans and tiny barefoot children who had earned or stolen a coin or two lined up in squabbling rows for the cold, slushy red and white treats. We stared and stared. Unattended babies, they were. Ragged, thin, weasely scraps, eyes everywhere, smiles nowhere. It should never, we prayed, come to a child of ours.

Elderly women with a tooth or two squatted on the pavements with a few unwanted unwantables for sale on cloths by their sides – a proud kind of begging, spat on by others with only a wheedling tongue to open the seething pockets of the East End.

'How can you tell who's Jewish?' Leah whispered as we walked.

A good question.

The meshugah frum, not orthodox like Pinchas but ultra ultra, were easy to pick out in their sombre eighteenth-century costume and sidecurls as distinctive here as anywhere. But for the rest? Maybe this one? Definitely not that one, at least I don't think so. For twenty years, immigrants had been flooding in. Many had conquered the language and the manners and, Pinchas said, had to be guarded against as they exploited the waves of us greeners, stepping open-mouthed into the strangeness. Easy game, easy pickings. Then, too, streetsellers, clinging to their baskets of plums, of ribbons, of lace, of matches, had picked up the Yiddish phrases necessary for trade and used them loudly. No help there.

Only two days until Rosh Hashanah and nowhere to make the honeycake, and nobody but ourselves to celebrate the New Year with. I could easily have felt very sorry for myself – if it hadn't all been so exciting.

Leah and me, we were light-headed from the wonders of the

mantle and dress shops. In the bootmakers and the hat shops, in the china and glass, never had we seen such things. We had furnished a thousand homes from new-style pleated sarsenet silk lamps and Chinese lacquered tables, sofas and velveteen cushions, scrolled looking-glasses and thick, soft double beds with a little nudging and blushing, despite Benjamin's impatience with us at every halt.

We were mindlessly, covetously, thrillingly half way up the – what's that big long – yes, Bethnal Green Road, before Benjamin started frowning that we'd come too far and turned himself upside down to get the direction of the theatres again. For the theatre, maybe, we were on the wrong road but for Leah and me – at home in Wisherodik all our clothes were a question of choosing some cloth from the travelling waggon and making with the needles and buttons.

Then no sooner had he stopped us from enjoying ourselves, than he was arguing with Drushki in the grubbier little roads that ran between as she stood pointing, staring angrily into small grey windows of workshops where women sat merged together, faint, sore, in frantic tongue-minding silence, soaping seams, sewing, machining, buttonholing.

'Look at them,' she pulled away from him. 'Sweating! Those steam-irons, they make their lungs bad, Benjamin. Working illegal hours; slaves. Look at them. Coughing. Thin, like lockshen. It's worse than Lev knows. They'd have been nearly better to stay where they were.'

We shrugged, impatient for her to walk on, knowing it was senseless to argue with her. Had she forgotten pogroms? So soon?

A couple of lefts and a right and Pinchas was peering longingly into little synagogues and study-houses sighing and singing catches of choruses.

'To pray with a minyan again . . .' he said sighing, none of us listening as Benjamin hustled us on 'only two roads down and left,' his excitement catching.

Down these tiny alleys and threads of streets were the shops where they mended the grand boots, tables and coats we had passed in the main roads when years had gone by and they were falling to pieces. Through a market – fruit and vegetables, rolls of cloth, bulkas and bread, handbags, scarves. Not unlike the markets near home, in fact. Easier to see who was who here: Jewish housewives, no matter how few wore sheitls over their hair these days, or how much like their English neighbours they dressed, were unmistakable when buying poultry.

Hinna. Boilers, roasters, stalls piled high with chickens. Yet to be a Jewish housewife is to be sure that the only hen fit to feed the family is hidden deep down in the pile or perhaps – for the really shrewd mother – the one she seeks is 'out the back', where the poulterer has hidden it. She puts up with and returns with spirit the insults and curses of the stallholders, who should know better by now, than to try and control this larder Diana. The mama shoves and discards, parting wing and feather, pinching pulkas, kneading brusts, peering distastefully into entrail after entrail like a diviner on piecework. And, once she's chosen, the poulterer flatters his customer on her sechel with a hand in the air, whilst with the other hand, the one Mama told us to watch, he pulls the chicken on the weighing-pan down a little nearer to gravity. We chuckle and nudge each other feeling very at home.

Grudgingly, they take our zloties for some honey; it feels nearer to Yomtov to stick a finger into the jar and taste, so we all do and soon there won't be enough for a cake and anyway who's got flour or a stove?

It became simpler near Flower and Dean Street to find Yiddish-speaking people to ask the way but somehow we went round and round seeing Fashion Street three times.

'Oy,' I said, leaning against a wall. Benjamin, sure now of the way, took my arm and smiled into my face that golden way he has so you forget your feet hurt. Up Brick Lane, left then right into a tiny, narrow alley. It couldn't be the place. But it took pity on us as we walked and widened to the bulge of a miniature square courtyard with an exit alley directly opposite. Thacker Close looked on the map, and in reality, like a cooking pot with two slender handles. And in the pot bubbled the life of the restaurants, the steady hum of machinery from the workshops, the statue of a broad man shielding his eyes as he faced appropriately into the sun, and there in letters for anyone passing to read, over double doors, were the words 'Behren's Yiddish Theatre'.

No cowshed; no secret. Oh Mama; look, Tata. The dust from the lane outside the disguised theatre in Wisherodik rose to my throat.

At the front of this theatre, a canopy built out to protect the queues from the weathers with side panels for the advertising, and posters everywhere.

'Dreadful.' Leah examined them happily. 'Look, Pinchas, what you can do for them. Old-fashioned, too much to read.'

'You're right. Almost the whole plot they tell you. I could . . .'

'And the same old plays.'

'A grandfather they're using for juvenile lead,' Benjamin pointed at the circles of the faces of the actors. 'New life we'll bring them before we rush on to Americhky.'

Despite its locked-up deadness we tried the doors, knocked at the leaded lights, walked round and round the building, held our breath to listen, gossiped and bustled, impatient to set up shop, to Rubenovskaize London. Knock, knock. What a welcome when the door would open.

But you know the saying that not every horse relishes the same oats? Where was Drushki, whilst we knocked and banged? Over at the other side of the alley staring at another poster in Yiddish.

'Look!' she beckoned us across with a lit-up expression on her face that reminded me that when she was smiling, her face didn't look so awful. 'Rudolf Rocker!'

We raised our eyebrows, drew down our lips, shook our heads and whispered together. She had a good memory, that Drushki. Us? None of us could remember an actor by that name.

'Arbeter Fraint! The Workers' Friend! Lev gave me some articles by him. Look! Just two days ago – if we'd been here two days ago, "Tuesday 6 September 1904 In Person". I could have heard him. Maybe even talked to him. They say he's a genius. He's nothing to look at but they say he's a wonderful speaker.'

'So am I,' said Benjamin in that voice that had made me weak with love for him since my baby-teeth had started dropping out. 'He'll help us make a living, this Richter?'

'Rocker.'

'He's too fat and square for my taste. He'd look terrible on a stage. He doesn't even look Jewish.'

'That's the point: he isn't. He's German. He learnt Yiddish only to help our poor downtrodden brothers and sisters, he . . .'

We shushed her embarrassing solo street meeting and she snarled back at us. Drushki is a good soul, caring for the oppressed, the hungry and the meek. When she reaches her allotted span (may it be hundert tsvantsik) the Lord will delight in her and the voice of the people will rise to bless her in time to come. But whilst she's here on earth, Drushki will never write a pamphlet on fun.

'Why aren't they here rehearsing?' Benjamin said, pulling the doors just one final exasperated time, leaving Drushki gazing again at the poster on the other side of the alley. 'Can you imagine having a theatre like this and not being in it every minute? When we have our own place in New York, in the mornings we work on new plays, the tidyings-up of the play that's on in the afternoon, performances at night and – my dream – training youngsters at lunchtimes. Here in England they've gone slack. Think how we longed for this in der Heym.'

'No fun, you don't want them to have?' Leah said, mimicking Mama wonderfully, at the cost of a fleeting pang of loss and worry between her and me. 'When you're free, acting must be a job like any other. Who wants to work all day and all night?'

Benjamin was too mortified to answer and even I laughed at him. 'If you try to work us like dogs, Drushki will put up a banner and close you down.'

It was hard to pick out someone who might tell us what had happened to the Behrens. A young orthodox boy hurried past us fingering his sidecurls anxiously. His family would regard us as idol-worshippers and we let him pass. Two girls in smart home-made dresses, frilled bodices under their waisted jackets, their hats touching together chattering confidences close to each other's ear, approached. As Leah stepped forward they walked even faster, gasping a little, hands to their bosoms, round the corner quickly in fright.

The close was alive with posters: 'No Jobs', 'No Hands Wanted', 'Part Of A Room To Let', 'Closed – Bereavement – Cutter Required', 'Fellers, Finishers'. That last one was torn and scrawled on but never taken down, just in case. Earnest men in sombre clothing, caps firmly on, came and went, in one dark doorway, out another. Thursday morning, the week nearly over, New Year treats to be cooked, work to be found, livings to be scraped. How could you stop fearful men like this to chat about theatrical matters, for Heaven's sake?

'Even if I missed Rudolf Rocker on Tuesday,' Drushki said triumphantly, turning from a stark red and white poster, 'I've found out the cafe where the Workers' Union meets: the Sugar Bowl.' She pointed back the way we had come. 'That place we came past after the big shop with the furniture? – the Sugar Bowl every lunchtime. On my own I can't go: we'll all go.'

Whilst Benjamin and she argued, I put my arm through Leah's and made 'crazy she is' faces as we walked around the close looking for someone to talk to. The others soon joined us. Even Drushki could understand we needed to find the Behrens.

'Excuse me,' Benjamin stopped at the door of a small front room turned oil shop, three doors from the corner. 'The actors? Soon they will be at the theatre? Natalie Behren? Maurice Behren? You know?'

The old man continued exactly what he was doing, searching for something in a lidless cigar-box to repair an oil lamp in front of him. Around his feet were heaps and jumbles of lamps broken, dented, in pieces, dead. A boy shifted a thin grey hand-rolled cigarette to the side of his mouth with his tongue, a tiny hammer never stopping in an attempt to beat out the damage in a copper casing. His cap covering all but his chin, he jerked his head over his shoulder.

''Offman.'

'He doesn't understand Yiddish,' Pinchas said softly. 'I'll try.'

''Offman,' the cap and the cigarette jerked again. We walked nervously away and clustered outside. Soon someone would be along to ask, surely.

Still carrying the little hammer and using it as a baton, the boy came out behind us and pointed across the square to a shop half-hidden by boxes of old books outside with more spilling from the inside.

''Offman, 'Offman.'

Forced, then, by our stupidity to spend all at once what was apparently a ration of words, he reluctantly counted out a few more.

'At the side. Upstairs a restaurant. At noon they come. Bleddy show-offs.'

He turned his back and the sound of the steady little hammer followed us across the road.

'It's early yet,' Drushki said. 'To the Sugar Bowl we'll go first and come back?'

Nobody answered.

'Hoffman's Restaurant' was painted in yellow letters on the glass door with an uneven scroll flourished below. The letters of the word 'Closed' (schliessen, Pinchas told us) swung backwards and forwards on a small dirty card hanging from a brown cord as Benjamin pushed open the door. It released a life-enhancing, staling smell of old cooking-oil and elderly meat. Half the wooden tables were still bare, chairs piled on top of them, the boards still faintly damp with the familiar paraffin and mildew combination of a woodwormy building.

'Closed is closed,' an unfriendly waiter raised his hands, eyebrows, shoulders – but not a smile. 'A half after eleven, open,' and the flash of red striped cloth followed his disappearing back.

Benjamin put up his two strong arms for two flimsy chairs and set them down.

'Sit yourself,' he said firmly to Leah and me, reaching for

two more, Pinchas getting his own hesitantly. 'Sit, sit,' Benjamin waved to him. 'A long wait, but we'll wait.' He unfastened his cloak to let it fall neatly back over the seat and pulled straight the watch-chain Uncle Preiska had given him.

He smiled at me. How thrilling he was. I reached out an impulsive hand to him but – of course. He was already in rehearsal and he kissed it grandly with the objectivity of a star to its public. Well, it's not that I mind, but you know what I mean: you feel sort of lonely.

The waiter swung back through the door. 'Oy oy oy oy oy,' he said through his teeth as he swung a tablecloth on our table, decorated it with cheap salt and pepper pots and a stand of toothpicks, making it quite clear we were in the way and unwelcome but otherwise doing nothing to move us.

Leah and I unbuttoned our jackets and in the silence Leah and Pinchas whispered together sitting very close, making me feel angry with jealousy. Every time Drushki's mouth opened out fell 'Rocker' or 'the Sugar Bowl' and there was just nothing for me to do or say. I sighed a bit but nobody took notice so – a playwright is never without a piece of paper and a pencil, and when you're writing you never feel lonely: there isn't time. Tata would be amazed how my second journal box is filling up. And not on those big sheets all the same size with the top cut off. Anything, now: backs of bills, the end of an exercise book little Katya gave me, a packet of shipping labels we didn't need.

Leah keeps staring at the door, fidgeting. And Benjamin's also staring at the door – harder now it's nearer the time for opening. And me? I'm staring at my Binyomin, wet-eyed with boredom and worry. At the Shelter we're parted; how long before the six of us are settled? How long before Mama and Tata can come and . . . that's what I miss. I can't imagine making a palace behind a door like Mama made, where you could pull your family round you like a shawl, where the meal-table was full of laughter and loving as the cradle that rocked you, where tempers blazed only enough to warm you, sulking only enough to cool you off. Me? I could make a home like that? What if we had made a baby already? It happens.

How long would we stay here before moving to Americhky? Was it worth getting comfortable? Could Leah and I buy curtaining and sarsenet silk lamps and then leave them behind as we journeyed on? Lucky Benjamin, with his eyes and mind on one thing at a time, and me with a thousand problems and no solutions. Enough writing. Drushki's left her English dictionary book on the table and it's time I studied. This way the time will pass. Nobody wants to talk to me, who cares? Good morning. Good day. Good what? Night? The 'gh' they don't pronounce? So why put it in?

Half after eleven, a clean, striped glasscloth over the arm of his crumpled, sweaty jacket, a waiter, expressing the ancient contempt of the Jewish restaurant waiter for the Jewish restaurant customer, was forced to acknowledge our determination and reluctantly came to our table, lifting his head very slightly.

'Was willst?'

The lemon teas came quickly, undrinkably hot, uniformly black, the lemon slices thick and ungracious. He took our Polish money without comment but very clearly the word 'greeners' came back to our ears before he returned with our English change.

Unasked, unsmiling he sat at our table with the handful of coins. 'This money,' he said. 'Farshtayt?'

'Of course we understand,' Benjamin lied instantly, not having appeared to change his glance from the door.

'Well again I'll tell you,' the waiter said, unimpressed. 'Twelve of these make one of these. And twenty of these make one of these. And don't take these or these,' he said, digging them out of his pockets. 'Gornisht, they're worth. See? Remember. And this is a half of that, and that's a quarter or half of a half and that's three of those and that's six of those or two of those threes. Easy. You'll soon know. And, if you order maybe something in a cafe and want to give a tip, you'd give one of those and one of those, maybe. Oh, thank you very much. You need any more help, ask me.'

We sipped through our first glass until nearly twelve, had used the badly-kept toilets downstairs out the back and ordered a second glass for everyone before the restaurant began to fill.

Hungrily we had watched the shelves fill first; flaky Austrian apple strudels, squares of moist coffee kuchen, poppy-seed rolls, hot potato latkas and cold gefilte fish. The waiters interfered with each other's arrangements and tables, argued loudly amongst themselves and raised their hands in boredom at every early customer's request, implying that, frankly, it was more trouble than it was worth.

I held it all in my mind and wrote on a new piece of paper; *A Fly in My Soup*. Cast: a man, a woman, two waiters.

Moving fast from right to left my hand wrote the easy funny dialogue. Perhaps if I told the sketch to Drushki, with a dictionary book the two of us could work it out in English. Ah, but how long before I could make jokes in this foreign language?

Just as I was going to ask her, Drushki stood up, clumsily tying her hair back again in another black band. 'Some of that English money I need,' Drushki said. 'I have to go. That Sugar Bowl has a pull like a magnet, you understand?' she appealed to Benjamin who didn't move.

'Tomorrow it'll also be there, Drushki,' I said. 'Today . . .'

'Dead we could be tomorrow,' she said, taking a handful of change from where it lay on the table and making towards the door.

In the flurry as we nullified her dreadful words with the customary spitting three times to stave off the evil eye, Pinchas stood quickly, sighing and exchanging his skull-cap for his hat. As Leah half rose to go with them, Pinchas spoke softly into her ear. Leah nodded and settled herself.

'Back at the Shelter about two?' Pinchas said turning at the door, 'Or here?'

I nodded.

People were beginning to arrive. Hunger-making smells wafted and teased. Benjamin turned to look at us. 'Take off your hat, Zelda. No, perhaps not, leave it on. And pinch your cheeks, Leah. No, later we'll eat. How can we look attractive with bulging cheeks?'

How different actors are from human beings.

It was a dragging, wearisome twenty minutes before Benjamin's foot tapped mine lightly under the table to signal the rising of the curtain on this cafe cabaret.

Actors.

Two came, three more. Another two. Minor characters, of course, arriving early to warm up the Hoffman audience. They preened. They rapped for speedier service. They demanded in tones above their station until superceded by two, three, four more ambitious stars laughing together, one singing softly.

But wait. The long table in the corner by the kitchen, growing chairs like porcupine quills, swollen with noise, was heavy with laughter, but directly opposite, by the greasy skylight another table was filling up with actors, but quietly. And passing between the two tables? Looks, they were giving each other. You know? Looks?

We noticed. We smiled at each other. Wasn't our own Mama the world champion of the 'look'?

Grander actors began to arrive. Unmistakable, they came singly, pausing at the door, arranging themselves for glory, taking in the temperature of the mood of the restaurant, stopping to taste a compliment here, flavouring with a pleasantry there. As Mama says, if you can learn to kiss the public foot it maybe won't be used to kick you.

We had decided between us that the table-by-the-kitchen-group had been the cause of whatever arguments were in the air. This was easily detected by their cheerful, carefree laughing ways. And if you're thinking that isn't logical you should ask yourself who goes off whistling after a street attack – the victim?

The skylight-group, on the other hand, held themselves with dignity. A clean-faced man listened attentively to the stout dark woman in the silk blouse but all the time they watched the door. Like Benjamin. Whilst Leah and I turned our heads everywhere and no time to cram in all we had to say, he sat there at one with his chair as if it were privileged to bear his weight.

Hoffman's buzzed. People rose to greet and flatter one

group or another, we noted, but never both. So here was a deep-down argument with a long memory.

The Hoffman waiters, however, joked with them all. What difference? So long as they all came here, even to glower at one another, business was good. Everybody likes to mix with actors. Except me.

After the arrival of a handsome couple in their middle thirties, who even moved Benjamin's eyes to follow them to the skylight table, that group seemed slightly to close in upon themselves. Gracious, splendid, they acknowledged a raised hand here, a slight bow there.

'Even so,' I said following Benjamin's eyes to the woman, 'they haven't anyone like Leah over there.' And nobody anywhere has anyone like my Binyomin, I didn't need to add.

Benjamin closed his book. 'The same conclusions we come to,' he said, magnanimous in the rising tide a promise of action brings. Still, it was praise of a sort and I reddened from it.

'Come.'

Leah held me down with a strong angry hand, turning pink without pinching her smooth cheeks this time. 'Nowhere I go that I'm not wanted,' she flounced, the old Leah with a fixed mind of her own came racing out from where it had lain hidden since Pinchas first came back from his Siberian holiday. 'We do not beg. If they want us, let them come to us.'

We smiled at each other over her head.

'You're being difficult for nothing, Leah,' Benjamin said. 'Must they guess who we are? When I nod, you'll both walk over. Watch me.'

Where else would I look?

He rose to give his first English performance, approached the skylight table and tapped the head of the group on the shoulder.

We saw nodding, hand-shaking, Benjamin was brought a chair, we held our breath but still could not hear anything though we strained and stared. Leah noticed at the same moment as me a sudden stiffening at the table – we nudged one another. So the name Rubenovska had travelled. Everywhere, hands fidgeting at lace collars, smoothing hair, sweeping up eyelashes. Yes, I know. Benjamin's had that effect on me forever.

Yet, look again, they seem to be staring past him. All of us, Benjamin as well, turned to the door.

A Great Man stood squarely in the doorway until he was sure he had the maximum concentration of attention. Then he stepped a little back, allowing a lady to reach the top stair and step inside the held-back door of the restaurant. She paused slightly, bringing the skirt she wore after her as if she were its shepherdess. Her awareness that her beauty made every male bristle with hunger, every female suspicious with envy, just coloured the tips of her excellent cheekbones with enough colour to seem ingenuous.

'Natalie!' they called, at table after table as she spent her smile recklessly, relentlessly. 'Natalie! Natalie!'

Looking quickly at Leah, I seemed to see her anew as a pleasant young Polish Girl in a cheap dress – and I hate to think what I looked like. But as Natalie and the Great Man sank into their thrones at the large, unruly table by the kitchen where the underlings had risen in respect, Leah winked at me and in the flash of an eye and a raise of the chin became 'Natalie' for a second. 'Make-up and corsets,' Leah said scornfully. 'She must be fifteen years older than me.'

'But . . .'

'But, nothing. I like the look of the others anyway. Without the Behrens we can manage.'

Benjamin, on the other hand, had turned from the still stiff, still silent group frozen in position under the skylight and, walking towards the other table, spoke in his crimson voice somewhat between a storm at sea and dew on a marigold.

'Ich hais Binyomin Rubenovska.'

My golden-skinned greener with the stall-killing voice and the wonderful cloak – please G-d may there be no room in that spoiled little bodice, deep within Natalie's cream lace ruffles, no room for a pang.

A terrible thing, is a pang. Think: Cleopatra, Salome, Josephine, your cousin. One pang and a family dynasty can end up – gone.

The Great Man stood his silver-topped cane between his feet like a landlord in any number of plays, his eyes narrowed against the smoke of his short cigar.

'Rubenovska? Of?'

'Wisherodik, sir. Not far from Vilna, Mr Behren. Like you, our family . . .'

'We come originally from Russia, nearer to Odessa right down south from your – Wisherodik. By your accent I would have known, of course. Pleased I am to know you. You'll come maybe to see many of our performances.' And dismissing Benjamin, he sat down and flicked his fingers at our suddenly animated waiter.

'Mr Behren, I see that you are hungry but – my family are the Rubenovskas, sir. For three generations they ran an underground theatre in Wisherodik. You will have heard of our great Zaider Yaacov Rubenovska? Bubba Rubenovska? Rosa, Dovid . . .'

'Underground.' Maurice Behren frowned. 'Yes, yes, so many of these small groups in Poland. Very good, very creditable. You will come maybe to see many of our performances.'

Benjamin stood still, too proud to move away and simply sit down while Maurice Behren turned to the table and began to eat.

Personally, I was furious with poor dead Bubba. London, it seemed, was not Wisherodik. And what about Americhky the Golden? Even further away? Rubenovska meant nothing.

The chair next to mine scraped, moved and was still. Benjamin was back.

'Come,' Benjamin said quietly, for the second time. This time he meant go, and Leah and I reached for our jackets.

Some rustling behind us and a voice as deep as Mama's spoke. Natalie Behren wished to make our acquaintance and was requesting permission to sit at our table.

Whilst the whole restaurant stilled at this baffling rarity, Benjamin bowed deeply and pulled out a chair. Leah inclined her head prettily and spoke flatteringly of knowing Natalie anywhere due to her likeness to the photogravure outside the theatre when we had already discussed that it must have been taken twenty years ago. There wasn't a lot for me to say, my mind full of pang.

'You're living where?' Natalie asked my Benjamin as she stroked her jaw – either to show off her fine nails, or to keep it from sagging, maybe.

'We arrived only yesterday' – the way she showed surprise would have set Mama off into fury about overacting – 'to find that our cousin who has a fine big house in London is temporarily . . .'

'You're at the Shelter.'

Tact, beautiful people like her don't bother with. I know – haven't I got a beautiful person for a husband?

Hot with the disgrace, Benjamin nodded.

'Mrs Behren, we are there only . . .'

'Call me Natalie,' she said standing. 'Come. Bring . . . She waved at Leah and me meaning that he was to bring his packages with him just so long as they didn't have speaking parts.

'Sit yourself,' Natalie said, inviting Benjamin to sit next to her by means of getting the young man already there in the chair she was offering to move so sulkily that I wondered if it were more than the seat she was demoting him from.

Double pang.

Leah and me were allowed a place in the other less important bend of the elliptical shape we now made round the table.

Chicken blintzes, worsht sandwiches and pickled cucumber were ordered, yet more lemon tea arrived and hands everywhere reached for the piled-high rye bread with the carraway seeds. Wrong again, Mama, English food is just like our own.

Even though I sat forward and spoke to no one, I couldn't hear what Benjamin was saying to Natalie, but from her laughter and her wiggling and her crinkles ready to turn into wrinkles any day, I could work out for myself that cursing her he wasn't.

I whispered to Leah, she shook her head and it took three more whispers before she rose to her feet and I followed her to the top of the table. With all the Natalieness of the real thing, Leah motioned two actors to change places with us and before their mouths could close properly, we were removing our jackets once more over the back of the chairs next to the Great Man.

'The ginger girl is my wife,' Benjamin pointed out reluctantly to Natalie, 'my wife the playwright; her sister, Leah, a fine actress who can sing like an angel, my brother-in-law, who will be here shortly, is a great artist and my own sister will – would, er – might be an asset in the – backstage. I myself have always played the lead in every . . .'

Couldn't my Binyomin see for himself how less interested Maurice was in us all than in one of the many flies on the wall?

Natalie smiled. 'A whole company of your own, you have.'

'Well exactly. But to begin with, with you we'd be honoured to be – associated.'

'So.' The silver-topped cane hit the floor for emphasis. 'I will be frank with you, Rubenovska. You are a threat to us. Already in London there are – factions.' He scowled across the room to the skylight-group but they had turned in upon themselves and missed the quality of the scowl.

'You'll forgive me, Mr Behren, but London is a groys place. And in it room for many companies, no?'

Benjamin took out that piece of paper we had spread flat many times on our journey and he read out the names of ten stars and actor-managers Mama and Tata had raked up for us from letters and old newspapers. At each name Behren banged his stick and snorted.

'I took them in,' he shouted. 'And now? Dead. Gone to Americhky. Another in New York, then another. So good I train them, without me they can manage. Loyalkeit? Who has loyalkeit these days? But it's not so easy. Without Behren's management and Behren's money – without Natalie Behren – the public, they love my Natalie, love her, idolize her.'

'Understandably,' shmoosed our three voices, guess which two insincerely.

'One big, happy company, we used to be.' Another wasted scowl. 'But him – the madman over there' – pointing at the skylight-group – 'has to start a company of his own – may he end on his knees.'

Wasn't it easy to tell we weren't wanted? That the man was saying don't bother me?

'A year? Two years ago? Him,' he said, pointing again, 'he crawls back to me after his back room "theatre" – he's calls it a theatre – is closed down by the fire-regulations. Give him a job? Starve, better. The ingrates. New York, New York – everything's Americhky all of a sudden. All right the Kesslers are making money hand over fist. And the Adlers. But as fast as most of them open, all around they're closing. Only Behren's has the strength of quality. Quality. I insist on it. Anyway – how comes to Americhky your family didn't also send you to get rich quick?'

Before the word 'tickets' could leave Leah's honest lips, my Benjamin made eyes at her then turned to Maurice with ten lit candles in his eyes. 'My family, the Rubenovskas, hearing of your great work – of quality – for the Yiddish Theatre here in London, Mr Behren . . .'

You'd think the bigger they are, the more suspicious they'd be of outrageous sycophancy, but not at all. They love it, love it.

Mr Hoffman himself – yes, he and no seraphim – delivered the ordered lunch for the Great Mr Behren at this moment, not forgetting a complimentary this and that to ingratiate himself. The busikeit and the clattering didn't stop Benjamin's wonderful flowing rhetoric and by the time the food platters were down to soggy parsley garnish and torn, empty, greasy doileys, friendships, enmities, employment and accommodation had all been discussed and arranged.

The skylight assembly had left raw places in his 'quality' theatre and with Natalie's underwater shoving, Maurice found himself shrugging into an agreement that if they proved half as good as Benjamin swore they were – maybe, perhaps. Small salaries for now, small parts for now, two spare attic rooms for now, box-room under the stage for now, skivvying for now. Benjamin agreed without a glance at us, which was just as well or we'd have been back walking the streets, looking for the skylight company to bed down with.

And in my head, one of the attic rooms with flowers, a rug, curtains made of some material I'd spotted in the market on the way here. And one day, a nineteen shilling and sixpence lamp with double pleated sarsenet and coronet draped of the highest quality, many other colours available.

The very first time Behren begged me for a new play, I'd write my best but refuse to let them play it unless Leah had the lead and Natalie played the Bubba.

'It will be an honour one day to play opposite the great Natalie Behren,' my Binyomin concluded his meal with a graciously hidden belch behind his knuckles and a bit of complimentary wind to match. Unaware, as ever, of the grinding of teeth and the hissing of breath from all the other hopeful leading men at the table, he took a thin, black, celebratory cheroot from Behren without showing any aware-ness of his 'place' in the Behren hierarchy as Maurice continued to smoke his own very superior thick cigar.

'One thing,' Behren added, 'one unshakeable rule – in our company we are all equal. We have no leading actors. Fervently I believe in democracy,' he said, nodding at the young actor who helped him on with his cape, and walking to the door, waiting for someone to open it for him.

Leah and I stared. With the manager and his wife auto-matically starring in every production? With Behren Behren Behren all over the front of the theatre? Not only Benjamin failed to query this glaring lie; the little actors were nodding at us in a self-satisfied way and believing themselves equal, poor shlemiels. Good thing Drushki wasn't listening.

Pinchas didn't mind and Drushki wasn't openly angry when we went on talking so earnestly and left the restaurant nearer to three o'clock than two. We hurried after the Behrens, my arm through Drushki's but she wasn't, of course, very interested in her brother's triumph, or in box-rooms under the stage or in fake equality, even.

Drushki was on a committee.

In England thirty hours, and because she'd stood up and

spoken up (shouted out, Pinchas called it) passionately, decisively during the debate in the room behind the Sugar Bowl, she'd been noticed and asked to stay when the meeting broke up.

'All this way from Poland they've heard of our Lev,' she told them excitedly.

'That's more than they have of us,' Leah sighed, holding on to Pinchas's arm ahead of us, trying to tell him everything in one breath.

'You're nervous,' Maurice Behren smiled vaguely at Leah, misinterpreting her sigh and clicking his fingers for one of his equals to wrestle with the stiff padlocks of the Behrens' theatre doors.

My Leah? Us? On stages since birth? Nervous? Of course.

Inside the sudden dark interior, directly opposite the doors, stood the glass-fronted office with dark wood-panelled sides. The way into the theatre was left or right of it and up two staircases set at either side.

'A balcony,' I breathed. How we'd planned for one on the boat.

'A dress circle,' corrected Behren. 'Before performances we use the stage door at the back, of course.' Fancy, a stage door. 'But in the daytime, secondhand clothes they sell there.'

The doors into the stalls had been unlocked and we could see into our first English theatre.

Gilt? Plush? Tassels? Drapes? Tiny angels holding lamps? Raked seats? Ashtrays? We gave silly gasps and foolish cries. We had fallen in with the Rothschilds.

It was a lot later that we noticed the dreadful flooring, the cramped set of the seats, the peeling plaster, the mended tears in the curtains, the frightfulness backstage.

One marvellous thing we noticed; this was no cowshed.

While Leah and Benjamin stood deep breathing as Mama always insisted before performances, and then squabbling over what piece to do (the choice being between one that showed my Benjamin to his best advantage and the other that did the same for my Leah), Drushki had emerged from her committee chrysalis and was fighting Pinchas on every front.

No, she wouldn't help with the wardrobe, no; she would not sleep in any box-room. She would be no slave; she would fight for the workers – no point in joining in.

I sat next to where Drushki had gone to sulk and took out my lucky pencil. When would Tata be living with us again to buy me another?

In a Strange Land, I'd call it. Act One – the Docks of London. It was important to me to remember how alone we had felt in those dreadful moments without the tickets and no trace of Cousin Avrom before we had forgotten about it altogether; to record Igor Lottenstein's kindness.

A small, neat woman touched Drushki's arm. 'Please? Backstage? I'll show you.' Even as Drushki's mouth opened to a 'no' the woman walked confidently off down to the front and amazingly shooting only one sulky pout at me, Drushki followed her.

Benjamin, up on the stage already, beckoned Pinchas, crouched to whisper, then put down his strong arm to lift light Pinchas to the stage. Straining, they pulled a piano from the wings. Pinchas brought on the stool and immediately began to play.

Maurice walked down the side aisle. 'A moment,' he commanded. But Pinchas had had his orders from Benjamin and went on playing ploddingly through one of the two tunes he could pick out if he had to – best not to stop him in the middle – setting the scene for *The Blind Singer* by Abraham Schutz.

My Binyomin, not blindfolded, no dark glasses and with absolutely no groping with his hands outstretched walked onto the stage deliberately to one far side of the centre and you just knew that he had never seen grass or trees or a red-head's hair.

Tears came to my eyes in pity. Into the shocked silence, just to be sure we knew who was shef, Maurice Behren lowered himself into the second row and muttered that he could begin.

'Ssh,' Natalie hissed peevishly. 'Ssh.'

'. . . Alone? Never!' wept Leah, clinging beautifully round unseeing Benjamin's knees, five minutes later. 'For Europe tours a little while you must wait. I am . . . with child!' she whispered.

Child.

Gevalt! Hersch!

In the faint sniffings and clearing of throats from Behrens' company, I put my hand to my mouth, picked up my jacket and ran out of the theatre, flinching as I heard the door bang behind me.

How long had we left Hersch on his own with nowhere to go, no one to care? No home and no family. May Annie and Lev never hear of this, I prayed as I ran. Out of the alley, right here, no there, that way, past the market. Running, pushing, blind as the singer now to rolls of curtaining and pyramids of apples. Left now.

'Pliss, Lantern School Street,' I rehearsed as I ran. 'Pliss, Lantern Street School,' and kindly fingers pointed till I arrived panting and red; better now, seeing that children still hung from the sewage pipes and chase-screamed in the playground.

'Hersch. Hersch!'

Not all on his own as I'd feared. In fact he was surrounded. The seven or eight boys darted away screaming as I came towards him.

'Nice,' I smiled, relieved at his safety. 'Friends you've already made.'

'Yes,' he said, sniffing, sniffing again.

Problems. His eyes were as red as my hair. I'd do what Annie would do. But what would she do? I'd ignore it. That's safest.

'So, school you like? English already you can speak?'

'Pliss, can I be excused,' Hersch said suddenly laughing. After he had explained it to me we chanted it all up the next two streets until he'd made it into a song and looked much better already. Kids. Kinder. In every school they are cruel. Time to dare a question or two.

'Teacher says I'm clever. English is hard, so to special lessons I have to go to in another room with lots of others. Sums I liked. Playtime I didn't like,' he ended bravely, waiting.

'Some good, some bad,' I said vaguely, half back in the theatre again, anxious to hear what happened to my Binyomin, to all of us. 'Soon everything you'll like. So much news there is, Herschele. We went to a big, big restaurant . . .'

INTERLUDE

4 October 1904

Before we even moved our bags and bits into Behren's our address I sent to Mama. How long letters take. I think I made it sound as if things were all right despite the tickets, despite no Avrom. Pinchas has printed a beautiful bunch of cards with AVROM RUBENOVSKA in enormous lettering and put them in the newspaper shops. They stand out from all the hundreds of others like a worsht in a cheese shop. One day he'll come to Behren's and ask for us and he'll maybe be rich and send us on quick to the Goldene Medina – if he isn't already there. Leah's cutting our curtains tonight to put over the skylight. Me, I quite like to look out at the stars, though they're all in the wrong places, I'm sure. Mama, Tata, Annie and Lev; they're not asleep but watching the other side of the night sky and thinking about us? Mama, Mama, if you were only here so I could tell you how it was when Leah every day is certain a baby they've made straight away and me, I cried myself asleep when I saw the brownish blood on my cream wash-cloth. Silly. Plenty of time. But anyway, when did I ever tell Mama every little thing like Leah did? To myself I like to keep myself.

20 October 1904

This morning when I woke up, again it was raining. That's the worst of London. The doctor said Drushki couldn't expect to be well if she stands around in rainy parks shouting all day but he softened up when he saw how really ill she is. When he said he'd call in again tonight, we looked at each other and whispered pneumonia but pray we're wrong. When I got up to dress I pulled our iberbett of goosedown over my Benjamin and just gazed at him. He clings to the edge of the bed and his dark heavy hair grows just right to frame his golden forehead.

He'd his hands up to his mouth like a squirrel with an almond. No wonder Natalie Behren – may her appetite cease – can't take her wrinkled eyes off him. Up on our mantleshelf, Bubba's lucky piece of glass winks at me between the little clock and the music-box she gave me.

I woke Hersch up and told him to ssh so Drushki could sleep till the doctor came. Then we both said the Sh'ema and said our own prayer for Drushki. Then we took a deep breath and looked and thanked G-d and perhaps because we used Shabbos wine in his water, the little bird with the funny feet is still alive. Thursday is Nature Study and Hersch wants to put it in a box and take it to school and by the time we find a box and put holes in it – well it's only what Annie would do. He's clever, Hersch, and he's teaching me English by talking it to me and putting me right without laughing. From a couple of the boys he still gets trouble so I told him bring them home and tea they'll have with us and it'll all be all right. But he says if they don't want to be friendly, he doesn't want to be friendly with them. Would Annie agree with me or with him? Benjamin says he's right, I say he's wrong. So I watch him go with his precious box and he waves nice from the end of the road and I hope I'll know what's right when I'm a mother.

Then for breakfast I make fried potato cakes with fried eggs on top which is Benjamin's favourite but the smell wakes Druskhi and I'm half pleased – at least she's alive even if now she's complaining. It'll be a while before Pinchas eats as he lays tefillin first and Leah? Oh dear. It's the smell of the frying, I suppose. Every morning she gets sick, the lucky devil. I'll later make some weak tea for her.

It's funny, at home I did nothing, suddenly since we've been here it's me who's keeping house – all through the holy days, first the honeycakes, then the over-eating before and after the Yom Kippur fast. Then the dressing of the lattice with the fruits and eating in the open despite England's endless rain. All very nice but hard on the money I'm supposed to make last and on the time I have to spare. Why didn't G-d spread out the feast days a little?

27 October 1904

Thursday again. Nature Study. That bird must get tired, in and out of the little box. Hersch swings it from his finger on its string like its a conker. Since the boys at school found out he can play whatever they ask on the school piano a hero he's becoming. Mama's right. When I have children, PG, an instrument they'll have to learn. Igor Lottenstein came to the theatre today, just as Natalie was explaining to Maurice how she really loved the new play I'd written but felt the audience isn't ready for such cleverness. (Not a big enough part for her, she means.) Mr Lottenstein was really pleased to see me and shook me by the hand. Every Thursday he collects rents, he told me, and Mr Behren pays every last Thursday in the month. Shocked, I was. So the theatre belongs to Mr Lottenstein and not to Maurice and Natalie at all.

I couldn't wait to tell my Binyomin but he said what difference does it make and even though I explained that it meant we could maybe have one of our own sooner, if we didn't have to buy it, he shrugged and said he'd wait for ever but the Rubenovskas would own it just like the cowshed. Yes, Benjamin, but it isn't a cowshed we want, I said to myself. And speaking of cowsheds, how comes no letter from der Heym? Now I'm Mama to them all, advice I could do with. All the time I'm writing writing plays and the Behrens, they won't use them, though Leah says they're wonderful. So just to feel useful I bake and I scrub and I clean. For what?

The doctor says Drushki's going to pull through. She's had two good nurses, he said.

3 November 1904

Drushki's over the crisis, thank G-d. And maybe no more bills. Another thing to keep from Mama now it's over.

It's Thursday again and despite the prayers the bird was dead this morning. 'Too dead to take to school?' Hersch said, staring. So I wiped his face and said when I go for a walk with Leah we'll keep an eye out for another poorly bird as that's all we're short of.

4 *November 1904*

In the streets are children with sacks dressed up like a man who tried to blow up the London government hundreds of years ago. Money we're supposed to give them. Crazy! I told Herschele – not a farthing he's to give. Turns out he's been collecting. Collecting. Begging. Benjamin wouldn't beat him for it. He should.

28 *November 1904*

After Pinchas said what he said about Charlie Marken, Drushki walked out. I told Pinchas it was none of his business and just to be pleased Drushki was well enough again to be so difficult but he said quietly, nicely, that morality is everyone's business and then he said if Drushki couldn't change then he felt she should simply leave. And she did. Rashi has a lot to answer for, I said to Benjamin. Crying, I was, to see a family broken up.

The same night, after promising to play my short piece about the tailor who made a fool of the tax-inspector, all of a sudden Natalie said Maurice was 'too tired' (from counting his money, maybe) to be tax-inspector to Benjamin's tailor and they'd substitute her one-acter where she is the angel and Benjamin's the nearly dead body. Nothing I'm earning for the family, I sobbed to Benjamin later. She won't buy anything from me no matter how good. Better I should get a job. And just like that, Benjamin says it's a good idea and goes to sleep. I'm running the family, saving every penny I can and gratitude I get? Mama, I'm beginning to understand.

ACT II

SCENE III
Monday 5 December 1904

'How comes the other end of the street it always is?' I complained to Pinchas, looking around his large umbrella as it dripped great droplets on to the hem of my best navy blue gaberdine skirt.

A shop loudly selling meerschaums, tobacco jars and gold-tipped cigarettes, 'My Darling' brand (a speciality), proclaimed amongst its generous gilded paint the only numeral we had seen so far in the whole street. One hundred and three was still a long way from the number nineteen we were looking for. The wind blew the rain under the umbrella in a mean, thin spray, grey with anger, turning the cuff of my bloused jacket to a damp cardboard bracelet.

Seventy-five, fifty-nine. The bottom corner of my shawl returned soaked to lie soggily near my tookas. Thirty-three a printer, twenty-one a Jewish workmen's club, no number at the next one, but ah – 'I. Lottenstein' in thick sculptured black letters. With pillars, yet.

We raised wet eyebrows at each other. The steps up had been scrubbed, the brass bell-plate polished, the foot scraper shone. Shame to dirty it up with our mud and drips. 'I. Lottenstein' repeated the mat furring and unfurring beneath our wet boots. A man with a Vauxhall motor car and his own name on a mat must surely be the richest man in London.

I was sure it was true that Mr Lottenstein was busy but half way through the ten minutes we stood there, I started to get angry. All right the woman was also busy – looking for some lost document or maybe trying to memorize those six bundles she'd untied on the desk a dozen times – but at least she could have told him we were there.

Kneeling now on the floor and going through more thick bundles of paper under a far table she seemed to have forgotten us anyway. As the pool around the point of our umbrella widened under Pinchas's boot I made a face at him.

'Excuse pliss,' he stepped forward, bending to speak to her under the table. 'Mr Lottenstein now is ready?'

The woman glanced up quickly, said a soft sentence very slowly, then sighed and repeated it in Yiddish.

'You hadn't understood, I'm sorry. Later he'll be in. I don't know when. You're relations, perhaps? No? If it's important you'll wait; if it's not important you won't wait.'

As basting hands, we'd earned so little the blisters on our fingers had cost more to bandage than we'd made. Then we'd tried two days at the cattle-market, Pinchas and me, packing unspeakable offal, retching and damp with slime. And the third day there, laid off for 'tardiness' though in line with everyone else. A woman put off the same time as us ran screaming, her hands to her mouth. Ashamed, it made me. Starving we weren't. Petty smallness to be saving up to rent a theatre. But first, since we'd had to burn the bug-infested beds the Behrens had 'rented' to us, a bed so high and plump a ladder you'd need for it I'd seen in Gardiner's and with my own money I'd buy it for Benjamin and me; such babies we could make on a bed like that.

After the cattle-market, I folded sheets at a laundry until they got someone cheaper and Pinchas hired himself out to a bimah or two. When it became the off-season for sweet-voiced chazanim, he had a grand idea. But the lump still shone faintly from his forehead as a reminder that the shop-front sign-writers of Spitalfields and Whitechapel were as brilliantly organized against outsiders as in Drushki's wildest dreams of workers' unions.

So – no work anywhere.

It was important.

We'd wait for Mr Lottenstein to arrive.

The woman rushed to take her employer's umbrella, rubber overshoes and thick navy overcoat. Under all this he seemed groomed and dry. I pictured myself; as if I'd just arrived at the docks all over again, that blue skirt, no longer crisply starched, clinging uncomfortably around my ankles and thin boots, which were already slippery inside with wet London rain, my hair – oh my hair. And just look at Pinchas. Mama would be furious at how we'd 'let ourselves go', as she would have put it.

But Mr Lottenstein was kindness itself.

'Mrs Isaacs, you'll bring lemon tea for these people to my room. I'll take them to the fire or they'll catch a chill. Then if you could go to the bank, please. Ask for my deed boxes and get the porter to bring them here. The papers I asked you for may perhaps be in those. Your husband's better? I'm sorry. My own doctor will come to see him this week, would you like that? Then I'll arrange it. You'll excuse me. Rubenovska, my dear sir, madam . . .'

Steam rising from my skirt, Pinchas's thin raincoat and the glasses of tea made our interview clustered around the little fire like Yom Kippur confessions in a Turkish bath.

As the level of the tea dropped to the top, then to the bottom of the silver handle of the cup, Igor Lottenstein's sympathetic patience with our problems (even though it wasn't Wednesday, his day on duty) squeezed the juice from our worries as we had from the lemon slice we had squashed so ruthlessly against the glass. We had, I saw for myself, exasperating but not-very-sad circumstances. We needed the Behrens and they only wanted us for slaves. The Rubenovskas were all of one opinion: they must be up-stage or they were nowhere. A creditable stubbornness it wasn't, but we are what we are.

'So,' he said, poking at the fire with an unnecessary poker, soot-blackened up to its waist. 'For now, two jobs you want. Then you want me to rent you your own theatre so that your plays you can put on in your own way. Then you'll take the money to run to America and the Behrens, who have paid me every month on the dot all these years get broygus with me for helping you and when you're gone I've got not one but two empty theatres. That's the proposition you're putting me?' Mr

Lottenstein looked at me very carefully; I saw him glance at my hair, smile into my eyes. 'How could a good businessman like me say no to such a thing?'

'You're saying you can't help us, sir,' the humourless Pinchas frowned, missing the joke.

'You know how to use one of these?' Mr Lottenstein said to me, pointing behind him.

'It's hard to work?' I asked, wildly attracted by the black typewriting machine with the golden scrolling, the letters on it jumbled up and not in sensible alphabetical order like in Drushki's learning book.

'So, night school I'll send you to learn it,' he shrugged briefly. 'Easy. For English also night school you can go to,' he added in a rush of helpfulness.

He listened carefully as we bragged about Leah and Benjamin and Hersch and how well they fitted in with the Behrens – easy enough not to mention Leah's pregnancy and Drushki's defection and the rats and bugs in the attics. No need to worry him with the smaller anxieties: that from no one had we had the slightest news from home, nor did we hear of Avrom and our first savings had been devastated, if willingly, by the fees for the doctor who saved Drushki from the pneumonia crisis. For plots give me a sad story every time but in real life good fortune suits me better.

Looking at Pinchas and seeing how frail and pale he looked, how weak and indecisive, a few good words I put in for him about his gift for art and his Siberian-spun stamina until Pinchas stopped me, frowning. 'My family I want to protect,' he said, with that cutting away of triviality that makes me feel so foolish. 'Any job you have I'll do.'

Speaking now in English he was telling Mr Lottenstein about me. They kept turning to look at me, nodding, smiling, shaking their heads. She this, she that. I could understand none of it so looked somewhere between modest and magnificent to cover it all.

'Speak Yiddish,' I frowned at Pinchas.

'Your brother-in-law says so clever with words you are, English you'll soon learn. Mrs Isaacs,' he said waving his hand to the woman outside, the thumps from the bundles still easily heard from inside his warm easy room, 'will be leaving, and . . .'

'Just because some papers she lost?' I said, hot at the injustice, ready to march with Drushki, hand out leaflets, deface the lettering on his mat.

'Illness in the family.' He laughed out loud – at me, I think. 'But before she goes, everything she's trying to leave tidy. So, a personal assistant I need, an experienced typewriter who is fluent in English as well as Yiddish, good at figures. That's what it says in my advertisement in the *Jewish Chronicle*. A Yiddish playwright it doesn't ask for but how did I know that's what I'd get?'

Very high, the wage seemed to us when he said it. He laughed again when I said so and told me I had more than English to learn yet. In exchange for a large amount of money, it seemed to me he was getting a skinny rent-collector too weak to push the barrows of furniture that were often to be moved from one set of rooms to another, and a typewriter unable to read, write or speak English. Also, if the telephone instrument on the desk should ring I would hide until it stopped. That Igor Lottenstein really knew how to get value from every English penny.

Pinchas frowned. 'Mr Lottenstein, one other thing: you know that I am orthodox? That in the winter early I must leave on Shabbos, all the holy days I go to shul, the week before Passover . . . ?'

'All right, all right. Go, the pair of you, before I change my mind. If I closed down now, a richer man I'd be.'

Nice man, Igor Lottenstein. He'd be our Tata until our own came over the water to be with us.

INTERLUDE

12 January 1905

At last a letter from home and though we shrieked with
pleasure when it came, good news it doesn't have. Tata has
that coughing again and they aren't getting full houses
anymore. That's since my Binyomin left, I said, and Leah got
jealous – I thought she was too pregnant for that – and she
pointed to where Mama says people are leaving Wisherodik,
that's why. Every day Tsar Nicholas wakes up with an idea for
a new edict. One day there's going to be a new fashion for
loving the Jews – then watch us fall to pieces.

20 February 1905

With me, if I write things down they don't worry me so much.
But the rest of them have to talk, talk, talk, as if talking makes
it better. A family conference we're having tonight after the
performance. Me, I'm taking with me a list of the things we
have to discuss and make them go through it orderly, fair – or
March it'll be when we finish. My English homework for night
school I've done. Verbs in a different place, they have. (Easy,
that isn't.) For tonight, the list.

One: Cousin Avrom – I could maybe go on the way to work
tomorrow to this man on the list at the Shelter. Why not?
Thirty – forty others we've seen. It's my turn; Pinchas is
always running. He'd like to bring all these lost men home
with him like puppies. A good man. But impractical.

Two: how to send money to Mama. Only once out of all the
times has she had our letter unopened and the money still
inside. Happy Birthday, Nicholas.

Three: what to do about Drushki – no, at the end we'll put
that so that Benjamin can walk out in a huff without holding
up the rest of the decisions.

Next: my new play. Mr Lottenstein wishes to take us to see Henry Irving's farewell at Drury Lane. Surely we ought to see the opposition if we're to open our own theatre? Wish Benjamin would come and learn English – even Hersch is beginning to get impatient with him. There must be some day class Benjamin could go to. I'll write English lessons on this list. Make that Four.

Soon Leah will be too fat to work. Pray Benjamin won't make me come back on the stage. I love being with Mr Lottenstein. I shouldn't say this, but he thinks everything I do is wonderful: a nice change it makes. So, next item. Five: Benjamin must start to play leading roles. Here – a new piece of paper. At the top of the list we'll put that. One.

28 April 1905

Passover wasn't right without Mama spilling the first cup of wine all over the tablecloth before the four questions were even asked. (Even now I can hear Tata's voice saying 'T, t, t, one question, four answers!' and us forgetting the very same thing the next year.)

We had the Seder on the stage. Very nice but for me, Seder is where you've no room to move because too many you've invited to be comfortable and your egg in salt water you have to eat in sittings because enough bowls there aren't. Which reminds me: Natalie, of course, is Sephardi and all the time a business she's making about the differences between Sephardi and Ashkenazi sedorim and anyone can tell which she thinks is superior. Rice and beans, they're allowed. Well with me that's all right as long as I don't have to see them. Then eggs in salt water they don't have – such a face she makes when we're eating. Them, they boil the eggs, what did she say? Ten hours? Ten days? But with a face acting like she cares she says, 'Brown, they go. Dark lovely brown.' Amazed I'm not.

But I understand better now why Benjamin's so fond of her. For her Benjamin can do no wrong and it's pleasing for him. Like me and Mr Lottenstein. Me adoring Benjamin isn't enough. In fact it irritates him. But Natalie he needs; I don't even mind any more. And as she's so good with him, perhaps

I'll get round her to talk to Benjamin about his sister. Ridiculous it's getting. I can only see Drushki in secret now. A couple of hours every Thursday Mr Lottenstein lets me off and I meet Leah at the market and together we go. And you know what? Sitting with the two of them, great pudding-basins sticking out of their frocks, *so* jealous I am, into the Thames River I could throw myself. Even without a husband, Drushki fell for a baby. All the time I'm thinking if I went to a doctor, how could he help me? Would he sit by our bed and shout advice? Perhaps when we can buy that new bed it'll be lucky for us.

3 May 1905

It's ten pounds only to go steerage to Americhky now. They were shouting in the streets the end of last year when it happened and people were talking about packing up the next day. But when they'd thought about it a bit there wasn't after all such a rush. Me, I can't see where it makes much difference. Ten pounds is still ten pounds and there's going to be, PG, seven of us when the two babies are born. And first Mama and Tata must be here: one thing the family conference agreed on, we're never going to Americhky without them. So that's ninety pounds. And food for the whole crossing. Steerage is English for starving. And then we need just a little extra so a theatre we can buy when we land. Worry, worry, worry.

27 May 1905

Families need Mamas to hold them together. Standards have lowered. Look at us. Look at me writing up here in the attic on Shabbos. I don't even feel that guilty about writing today when it's not permitted and Benjamin – he's talking about Saturday night performances through the summer before the three stars are out. Certainly we need the money but it's not right. Pinchas went mad. After the baby's born he swears Leah'll never go back on any stage – let alone one where Shabbos is made a mockery of. The baby's only a couple of weeks overdue but poor Leah looks twenty months gone. Natalie's face must be sore from the thick young-girl's make-up she's been forced to wear these last months in Leah's place. Please, please let Pinchas change his mind or it'll be me up there in a wig and a torn dress in Act II. Still – perhaps then Maurice and Natalie would be forced to do one of my new plays. Mr Lottenstein lets me work on the typewriter any time we're slack and he's given me my own key to just one drawer to keep my plays. He's so proud that I can write them – he often asks to see something and I give him, maybe, some scene I think is really good but it's disappointing because never does he give a word of anything but praise. I'm not used to it. Maybe, after all, they are no good. But even if Benjamin doesn't say much, when I get him to read a part for me to hear how it sounds, I can't get over how wonderful are the words. Or is it just his voice? Could it be? Leah. I can hear Leah screaming. Thank G-d. She sounds like she's dying. Mama always said that's a good sign.

29 May 1905
A boy! Jacob. As pale and dark-haired as Pinchas. But with rounded bonny limbs you wanted to bite lumps out of. None of us is getting much sleep.

22 June 1905
Tata's coughing is much better now the summer's come, Mama says. Next year in London, she says and it's as unlikely as 'Next Year in Jerusalem.'

14 August 1905
Drushki had her baby, Sarah, safely a few days ago – on the eleventh it was. Perfect. Hair like fluff. Cry? I can't stop. Why not Benjamin and me? Drushki doesn't say much but even she must have some feelings – she loves that baby and will hardly put her down. Doesn't she ache for Charles Marken to be with her? Even Pinchas has forgiven her. Over Benjamin surely she must be breaking her heart – not coming to see her like this is cruel and foolish. As I said to Benjamin – well I didn't say it, I was pleading and crying at the time – she's your sister and what's done is done. (Every day I sound more and more like Mama.) So Leah and I, we buy fruit and every day we go to see

her. Right there in her hospital bed, speeches she's still giving. The poor, the downtrodden, the exploited, she shouts as we ssh her. Descriptions of herself she's giving, poor thing.

It's damp and it's disgusting, the rooms she lives in, over the printing press with Charles Marken. He believes, too, that women are the absolute equal of any man. Which is why, maybe, till the last week he let her shlep heavy packets of paper? Why not once has he been to see her whilst she's lying-in with his own child? Why Pinchas will have to go to shul for Drushki tomorrow if the baby is to be named and blessed as it should? Why making a baby is good and making a marriage is bad?

21 *August 1905*
When the Tsar slits open my letters to Mama and Tata all he can take is the money. The censoring I've already done. Who else writes to them? Only me – they rely on it. 'Tell them this,' they say when they see my writing-case out. 'Say that,' and 'Did you remember to mention . . . ?' Not once do they ask to read what I've written or scribble so much as a note on the end. So they can't blame me if I write what I think it's good for them to hear. No point worrying them with our worries when they're hundreds of miles away, performing plays amongst the pogroms all around, keeping house, giving singing lessons far away in Wisherodik. Less and less do we talk about Wisherodik, about Vilna, with any devotion. Things are bad there and looking back you can see it always was. It's family we miss. If only Mama and Tata and all our cousins were . . .

So I write them the funny things and the tiny triumphs – the way Benjamin had the Behrens' theatre standing to cheer him in the mean tiny part Maurice Behren allowed him to take in *The Honour of the Family*. And a mention in the *Daily Eastern News* he got – I bought another copy and sent it to them. Someone will translate it for them – Mama will talk about her 'Prince' Binyomin – she only ought to know what her 'Prince' is doing to her own Princess. Does Mama know that I'm not writing out in the rain? That it's tears that dimple so many of the pages of my letters?

8 November 1905
It was a masterpiece, my description of the wedding dress
Drushki didn't wear for the wedding that she and Charles
Marken never had. Well, it seemed sensible to get them
married in my letters or how could I write long pieces about
lovely baby Sarah with Leah's boy, Jacob – the way they smile
and kick and hold your fingers so tightly. 'A bit quick with
Drushki's baby,' Mama wrote back sniffily, her words saying
clearly that it was, however, no wonder, as in any country
Drushki was not much of a bargain. Thursday mornings, Leah
and I still go to see her. We buy our fowls and hers too and take
them there to kosher them and it gives us an excuse to stay with
her a few hours and sometimes while I'm talking Leah will
clean up a little – or the other way round. They live like pigs.
But in exchange, books Drushki lends me, ideas she gives me.
She isn't all bad, whatever Benjamin says. Charm she hasn't
got – but her brother's overdose of it is fine on the stage,
though for me, at home, a little less would do.

24 December 1905
Oy, am I tired. Leah and I couldn't get through the market
today for Gentiles. It's their Christmas and big chickens
they're shlepping home and geese, even, and birds I don't
know what they're called but kosher you can't get them. On
Sundays, normally, it's only Jews you'll find in the market. But
the goyim, on their Shabbos money they're allowed to spend –
their Shabbos anything they can do. (Most of the murders they
do on Sundays, it said in the *East London Advertiser* last
week.) These days we usually get a top-quarter of fowl to boil
for soup for Cousin Avrom and the meat we then bake in short
gravy with carrots and in the cold weather tzimmes we make.
Oh yes, we found Mama's Avrom – dead he isn't. Arthur
Ruben, he'd become. We found him on an old list from the files
at the Shelter. And when we all went, there he was – a skeleton
version of my Benjamin, aged about two hundred, lifting up
his bent head, a light in his dull eyes, staring at us when Pinchas
demonstrated again what had happened on his first hopeful
visit.

'Cousin Avrom,' he said softly, 'Rubenovska?' and the light brightened inside his pupils. 'We're all Rubenovskas: we're Rosa and Dovid's children, from Wisherodik. We've come to take you home.'

Avrom's hands tightened and clasped and made shapes. His fingers crossed and recrossed, his mouth opened then went still, his eyes dulling.

'Good, good,' the rather mad-looking doctor said vaguely, his attention taken by rising noises in the terrifying dormitory behind where this grey silent cousin of ours sat, looking down at the reddish flagstones of the dirty conservatory. 'Not loony, this one,' the doctor said, nodding at our Avrom, but distracted by screams, standing quickly at some crashing. 'Just gone away. Harmless. Improve? Never. If you'll sign here – Bolton, the Jacket!' he screamed himself, running back through the dormitory.

Throughout the horror and the violence, Cousin Avrom sat on through our tears and despair and our powerlessness, safely unaware. Pinchas argued rudely, we pleaded insultingly, when the doctor came back. But sign or no sign he stayed here. If only we'd found him sooner, Pinchas nagged, holding Avrom's hand and whispering Rubenovska at him to see his eyes light, again. But it would, the doctor shrugged, have made no difference. He had been well-dressed and well-fed when they'd brought him in half-dead from a snatching somewhere in the back streets of the Nichol. No wallet, of course.

'There are ways in which we could make him more comfortable, more, er –' the doctor sighed. 'But . . .'

A great deal of money changed hands. Americhky the Golden shifted a few months or years further off and who knew whether the money would be used for Avrom at all. But we paid up with good heart, trying to remember Tata saying that there's no sweetness in nothing. Visits home he can maybe have sometimes but to live with a family, no, no, no. If we signed, 'arrangements' could be made; if we signed, a proper funeral he could have; if we signed, luxuries we could bring him personally; if we signed, visitors he would be allowed. On the other hand, hospitals had their rights, so if, Heaven forbid, we didn't sign – well.

We signed.

Outside in the darkness dirty children with crowns made of paper and coloured ribbon danced round by the Salvation Army band who played those Christmas songs that make you hum along with them they're so good. Christmas in Wisher-odik just meant boarding up the windows again for the Jews-killed-Christ bottles and stones. Here? We call 'Happy Christmas' to our Christian neighbours and they don't know any better – or come to that any worse – than happily to call back, 'And the same to you.' You feel to join in such gaiety would be nice. All right, all right, Pinchas. It takes more than a piece of holly and a couple of choruses to turn even a theatrical Jew into a goy.

26 April 1906

So long since I've written in this book. When my Tata died in February I just cried and cried and fondled and fondled those wooden boxes he made me so long ago. Nothing I wanted to write except how much I loved him. We send as much money as we can and Mama is coming. She's really coming – as soon as she's 'settled' everything, whatever that means. Annie and Lev say their organization is even bigger than before and so long as Mama can get to them, papers and travel are much better arranged than when we came. I tell Leah Mama'll be different without Tata – quieter, sadder. She used to annoy me with her bossy ways; now I'd like to hear them again. Is that growing up – letting your own mother be herself? I don't know. I always felt closer to Tata with that way we both had of keeping the big things to ourselves. For instance . . . Perhaps if I can finally force myself to write it down it won't hurt so much? (Pity I don't believe that. It'd be a wonderful thing.) Hating Natalie I've stopped. Benjamin didn't have to be tempted. Or even if he was, he didn't have to do anything about it, did he? After all, is he short of someone to love him? That day I couldn't stop crying at my typewriter. Every minute a handkerchief I'm using. A bad cold Igor didn't believe and in the end I told Igor everything. All of it. I was ashamed after, but I suppose he's my only Tata now. He was so angry that I could sit crying, yet pleading for Benjamin. Me. Ten minutes before, the Tsar I even preferred. How do you get over it? When do you forget it? How could he, how could he, thunders in and out between my jagged anger and the flashing of despair. Her fault? His fault? My fault? Who cares. He's Natalie-Sephardi-Behren's lover.

I saw them.

ACT III

SCENE I
May 1906

'You're still awake, Zee-Zee?'

Neither me nor my candle lighting this journal were expecting ever to recover from the shock of the opening and shutting of the door and the uttering of my childhood name; but we did the world a favour and stayed lit.

So early tonight, my Benjamin? A good sign this could be? If he'd taken the trouble to come in any night straight from his final curtain he could have found me here just like this, doing what I was doing. Awake and often sobbing, trying to put into words the hatred and resentment you feel for an unfaithful husband just makes you more clinging and unattractive to him anyway.

What's this? A strange new courtesy from Benjamin; he's pulling over the stool near to mine as if – how amazingly unusual – he will wait for me to finish anything that isn't actually for him. I shall go on writing just to be difficult but the words will have to be rubbed out; they lie limp as wet unstuffed cabbage leaves, the brisk fury steamed out of them at Benjamin's entrance. How come? He walks in with a cheap 'Zee-Zee' and all of a sudden I'm trembling? Five minutes ago, if he came sobbing, shuffling on his knees, his clothing all torn in guilty despair, enough it wouldn't have been.

And what does a nice Jewish girl from Wisherodik, who's only been in love once, know from married men and mistresses? To hate Natalie is also a waste of time. Better to despise Benjamin for being tempted by someone so obvious and so pathetic.

Which makes it more unbearable than ever that I lowered myself to ape her, trying to dress like her, talk like her, as the Zeldaness of me didn't seem to be what Benjamin was looking for.

But I saw them.

Only once, right there on the stage and with only me for their unscheduled sickened audience but their performance runs in my head every time Benjamin's voice softens and lowers as I heard it then, as I hear it now.

'You're not tired, Zee-Zee?'

I'd worked up just enough anger to be able to scream, 'How could you? How could you?' at him, but before my mouth even opened, whilst I was still writing, hoping to make him feel uncomfortable as I ignored him, he stroked down and down again the finger on which I wore my wedding ring as it lies holding this journal steady.

Steady?

It's just skin touching skin, I signalled to my head. Nothing to get excited about. There is a lot to discuss and there are new rules to be made. A bit of nagging would also be nice.

'Zee-Zee,' he says, running his fingers now down the side of my neck. 'I'll never love anyone but you, Zee-Zee.'

Such dialogue. Where was the confession? The apology? His wonderfully-shaped breast would look even better for being beaten a little. Looking up now I can see – oh Benjamin, no tears. Not one? After the half-Volga I'd wasted?

Chewing on my neck is not enough to cure the pain or smooth over the feelings of foolishness, helplessness – nor is biting on my ear with such tenderness I would be able to recall the feeling for weeks ahead. Locked in the prison-cell of my natural resentment are a great many biting, cutting, woundings words needing to be spoken.

He's looking at me.

I put down my pencil. For war there's always another time. I turn round in my chair to make a brief statement in a grown-up forgiving way.

'May your organ fall off if you do it again,' I whisper, holding out my arms.

*

Since my Benjamin gave up Natalie and fell in love with me, how goodly are my tents. Should I be rude and write here in my journal all my feelings? Tata would have said a journal, it's private, write what you like. But will my eynikl — see the confidence I'm getting that I can believe in grandchildren? — blush his pimples to read how Bubba Zelda burned with love for Zaider Binyomin? Ach, I'll write it and maybe my memory will last long enough to remember to tear it out and throw it away when I'm old. But not now. Another time.

There was a family argument about Tata, because of tonight. It's only half over, the year since Tata passed away and, strictly speaking, parties you shouldn't have. But when was Tata ever 'strictly speaking' about such things? And Pinchas, I nearly reminded him, is no Rubenovska except by marriage and such a big say he doesn't always have to have.

So a party we're having and it's up here after the show and as I look up at the big cloth covering all the food Leah and Drushki and I made hours ago I get such a big smile my face hurts. It's good to be hostess in charge of the tea and the kichals and all the time pulling straight the new quilt and apologizing that it's cramped and receiving with modesty all the praise I'm entitled to.

I missed Leah a lot when they moved into their own rooms — have I written about that? I just checked. Not a word. That's a story. Another time. But, you have to be honest, sometimes husbands and wives, it's nice not to have to whisper. You know? And of course their room is now our parlour and we can have proper meals sitting down and not so much of the Awful Natalie at Awful Hoffman's.

Leah and Pinchas, they're happy enough over the Zigman's fishshop though the smell from their clothes sometimes — all the time — I don't know how they bear it. And Leah is always coming here with Baby Jacob. Whatever Pinchas does he'll never scrape the theatre out of my Leah. But he's getting meshugah frum now, the sort of orthodox where all the time he's telling you what to do and t, t-ing at what you don't do. So he wants Leah to give up this dreadful, indecent, immodest, disgusting play-acting without which the Rubenovskas wouldn't be the Rubenovskas. (Wasn't Moses a showman?) Their Jacob's lovely. He's walking now and it's like he can never stop smiling. Drushki's Sarah is dumpy and serious and though you try to love her – I don't know – you don't get that chuckle and joy inside you get from Jacob. Jealousy, I suppose. My babies are a long time coming. This I don't want to write about tonight with such a lovely evening ahead.

Igor's coming. Well, it's two years today that we stood like glumps at the dockside with our tear-stained 'not-valids' crumpled in our fists. Can you think of a better reason for a simcha? We survived, didn't we? Through bad times and awful times? At least this is what I said when I gave my idea for tonight. Does everyone have to know it's for my marriage I'm giving a party? And I don't know where we'd all be without Igor. He's been – isn't that dreadful that I was going to say like a Tata to us, like anyone could replace our Tata? I suppose I mean he's the only Tata we have and all the time something kind he's doing. Pinchas wouldn't approve if he knew how much of his rent has been filleted away from the real cost by Igor.

I feel nervous of Igor coming up here. Seeing him every day either at his office or here at the theatre is one thing – up in our dreadful rooms is another. I mean they're lovely when Benjamin and I are in them alone but – you know. Strangers.

There's been a skin of embarrassment between Igor and me that was never there before – since I told him about Natalie, that time. He was as happy as me to know it was over but warned me what would happen. And it did.

Broygus, Natalie is.

Planning something, Natalie is.

Nice it won't be.

Already she's nearly starving us – if it wasn't for Igor (how many times a week do we all say that?), we'd be begging on the streets now. Natalie and her equality. The new rules are small part, small wage and you can guess the size of parts Benjamin and Leah get nowadays.

Pinchas, the big-shot, was just part-timing for Igor as he was anxious to teach Hebrew, to sing at weddings, to recite for the unread at gravesides. At such jobs a fortune you're not going to make and Mama's anxious to begin the journey to Annie and Lev and pray G-d she got our letter telling her to have nothing to do with the moneylenders that she wrote to us about.

And my letters? More and more secretive they're becoming. 'Tell me everything, Zeldele,' Mama writes. 'Even the bad news I want to hear. How I miss you and long to share it all.'

Some letter I could send her. Full of worry. Full of fear. But Benjamin's in love with me – that I could tell her if I hadn't been lying about it all along.

Despite all our troubles, we're two years here in London, pogroms we don't have, we're healthy, (p,p,p) and the family's happy enough.

To tell you the truth that's silly. I'm so in love with Benjamin being back in love with me that lately I can't even notice who's sad, who's angry and why. Does it mean that people are only sympathetic and understanding when they're dying of misery themselves? How dreadful if that's true.

Two years since we came here looking for the Goldene Medina and how long since anyone last mentioned Americhky? Perhaps we'll travel on one day when Mama gets here, perhaps we won't. Perhaps when our children come, Benjamin and I will have decided what we want to do. Maybe. Ach, too many maybes.

Lovely. The family together in my parlour. And quite right. Any excuse will do for a party. I felt like an adult, when the buzzing of the talking got louder and louder, everyone waiting for someone else to take up the gavel and thump with it. Why not me? In a minute, perhaps, when I'd straightened the curtains again and passed round the kichals. And Benjamin and Drushki were fighting. Nice. So they felt at home enough to argue, bless them.

'Hersch,' I said, winking at him and watching his boredom melt. 'Excuse me, Pinchas, but Leah wants Hersch to rock

Baby Jacob a minute while she's helping me. You don't mind?'

That Pinchas. A year until Hersch's barmitzvah and already Pinchas had begun to drum it into Hersch's clever head. Sedra, Sedra, Sedra, he's a young boy yet, with that twelve-year-old body that looks like flesh and hair will never grow on it. Still he's too quick for a laugh and lark to be too badly influenced by Pinchas, I hope.

Everything seemed to me just right when Igor arrived. You know how some days you look how you'd like every day to look but it doesn't always work out? I tried not to bustle about too much because it annoys Benjamin, but soon Igor was settled in the big wing-chair with Leah's loose covers smooth under his best black broadcloth and the bowl of freshly roasted, salted almonds just where his hand could reach it. Friendly and easy.

Three bites into his kichal and a sip of his lemon tea and Drushki has to open her mouth.

'So what's what, Zelda. All night we don't want to be.'

Not a party, any more. It's a meeting. Drushki would like us all to sit in rows and smoke a lot; Benjamin would like footlights, but this is a family and a family does what a family does. It sprawls on the floor and cracks monkeynuts in its teeth and throws back its head in laughter and burps a little after a glass of lemonade.

So I'm surprised to find that it's me breaking into the glorious Rubenovska racket, holding up a hand and saying, 'Perhaps if we all spoke one at a time . . .'

This unnatural idea scandalized a sort of silence.

'. . . about what worries us. I mean – Mr Lottenstein,' I turned to him apologetically, 'when we lived in Wisherodik we all used to go to my Tata and –'

'Go on, go on,' he said, waving his cigar as if the fifteen sentences I'd planned had already been spoken.

'We're all agreed, aren't we,' I said, feeling like the assistant cheder teacher of class gimel that I had been at the age of sixteen, 'that to stay with the Behrens any more isn't possible?'

Good Lord. I only said what groups of us had been whispering in corners ever since my Benjamin had come back to me and Natalie showed how much she had it in for us in every way she could. You would have thought I'd suggested voluntary mutilation for us all so that we could take part in the penny gaffs down the road.

After a few seconds' shocked pause at my rude trench-opener everyone wanted to jump into the hole I'd made. We all shouted at once, said things twice over or more, failed to listen to anyone's point of view, were unfair, imprecise, random, rude, impractical and just plain silly. Oy, how I love my family.

Through four almonds that he threw from the salty heel of his hand into his mouth Igor mumbled, 'Will you leave them in the lurch if you just walk out? Haven't you promised them some sort of notice?'

Leah, released from all her recent quietness by the doses of family freedom we were all drunk from, stood up, put her shawl round her head and her hand to her forehead.

'A broken promise is like a broken vase – you can't put it together again, Shaindl!'

We clung together laughing, howling, knowing we were free at last to discuss, next time we were koshering chickens together at our weekly session, Natalie and the Great Affair; how it felt to be the Wronged Woman; how, perhaps, To Make a Baby.

I looked at Igor. He was frowningly unsure why everyone everywhere was acting more bits of *Mirele Efros* and clowning around as though nothing was serious. If we left the theatre right now, this minute, all we'd be was a little bit homeless, hungry and unemployed. What's to be serious?

'Something you wanted to say?' I smiled at him, sad that he didn't have a family of his own to despair of.

'Ssh,' I called to my family. 'Ssh a moment.'

'I have,' Igor said, looking everywhere but at us, 'should you find it useful, if it might be the answer to your problems, if it'll keep you together, but of course you are under no obligation and anyway, maybe it's impossible . . .'

Not a sound. Not even from Drushki.

'. . . I came tonight, Zelda was kind enough, well she told me nothing of your problems but, for myself, well I could see, and I have . . .'

Leah took Baby Jacob from Hersch's arms and tried to rock and rock him out of his hiccups. I winked at Benjamin.

Igor said, 'You know Leman Street? The Shelter?' and stopped again.

Know it? In our memory surely we could still taste and smell it. So a reply he didn't expect.

'Past Hooper Street there's a turning. You know? And on the corner a public house – the Sheep and Shearer. Yes? Well, naboch, the publican died. Shame. Young he was – TB. So it's empty.'

'You're very kind, my good sir,' Benjamin smiled, getting to his feet, weary of Igor's amateur performance, anxious to audition for us himself, 'but drinking we know nothing about. Acting we know.'

What can you do with my Benjamin? He didn't actually say that Igor Lottenstein was a waste of time or that the Rubenovskas would starve rather than stop acting but everything was insulting, just in the way he stood there, Bar Kokhba in his prime. If I wanted to spend for ever loving Benjamin – yes, yes, – much of the time would pass covering up for his rudeness. But before I could smooth or speak, Drushki had spilt tea everywhere, cloths were run for, skirts needed to be sponged and I was on the damp boards kneeling when light began to drift through Igor's purpose as he shyly went on speaking.

'Strip the Sheep and Shearer out, if you like,' he said. 'Make it a real theatre: it's big enough. Live over it, be the Rubenovskas again.'

I saw mouths beginning to open everywhere, full of the wrong words. Benjamin frowned ready to assure him that we always had been Rubenovskas and didn't need him to hand us any permission, Drushki narrowed her eyes to work out the absolute maximum percentage she'd let Igor rook us for, Pinchas to make conditions that on even the most minor of religious festivals the theatre that hadn't opened yet would be closed. Nobody was saying 'thank you'.

So, smelling of wet dishcloths, I just reached up to Igor and kissed him.

INTERLUDE

23 September 1906

My darling Mama,

Perhaps this will be the last Rosh Hashanah that we eat our apple and honey without you. Soon, soon make the journey to Annie and Lev before you need your winter boots and Bubba's fur. Where did Lev collect so much money for you? It's wonderful; it's also true that a mother can keep seven children but seven children can't keep a mother, isn't it? There is much good news, Mama and – oh even as I write this I know I'll never send it. It's the fifth time I've tried to write lately. But tears come to my eyes every time I read what you said last time. Soon enough you'll find out how I've been lying to you and when you say, 'Tell me all the news, my dear, even the bad things or it'll be a shock to me when I come, please G-d, to live with you again', I realize how wrong I've been.

But what else could I have done?

You want the bad news? Strikes? You want to hear about the strikes? All right. Strikes. The tailors' or the bakers'? The tailors' strike was as violent as the bakers' but more frightening because Drushki was out there fighting with them. Actually hand-to-hand, Mama; bottles and bricks, Mama. And me looking after her Sarah, hushing her when she cried and saying her Mama would be back and all the time wondering if Drushki might never be back and I'd maybe adopt Sarah and put her into some decent clothes for once. No, Charlie Marken didn't go out into the streets with her, screaming and pulling hair. Of course not. Up in that hot room he stayed with his machines printing. Printing leaflets, leaflets, like anyone reads them or acts on them if they do read. A little thing I forgot to mention: they aren't married, Mama. Which makes Sarah a mumser, bless her.

Another piece of news you wanted. Our Cousin Avrom – we found him. Loony, Mama. Put away. 'Gone away,' the man said. How? Beaten up in a back street. But it wasn't because he was Jewish, that's the good thing. It was only for his money. We see him, we take him things; but he's lost, Mama. Sorry.

Then Pinchas. He's becoming crazy and the latest thing – all right, he said it kindly, but you know how stubborn he is – that when Leah falls for a second child it's all over with the acting and she's to call herself Mrs Rottman and they'll have a room somewhere and he'll bring in a great fortune davening Mincha and Maariv and being the cantor at weddings and barmitz-vahs. Can you imagine? Leah's a Rubenovska to her glove-buttons and nearly as talented as my Benjamin.

Benjamin. Now there's another piece of news I shan't tell you, Mama, now it's over. Natalie's only got two pulls to her curtain – up or down and believe me, is she down since Benjamin behaved like a mensch and ignored her. I could almost feel sorry for her except she's so hard. The other day Hersch came home from school stinking of paraffin with his head shaved. (Not such bad news, Mama, don't worry, nits is common here, nits the whole of London has.) But Natalie screams when she sees him and says he can't come inside 'her' theatre – Sephardis don't get nits? – and Benjamin, for once says the right thing: 'No Hersch, no Benjamin', and Natalie screeches, 'For my part we'd be better off without all of you,' and we all wink at each other because we know about the Sheep and Shearer but Maurice and Natalie don't and . . . Now, that, Mama, I can tell you about in your real letter because that really is good news. Every minute we're there when we can and –

My Darling Mama,

ACT III

SCENE II
October 1906

Problems. The Sheep and Shearer floors were rotten, the walls uneven, little steps up and little steps down, corners and arches, and that wall, the one over there, between that half and that half, what could you do with it?

Nights Benjamin and Leah worked their heart out on the stage for the wages we desperately clung to. Days and nights the rest of us were builders, strippers, painters, barrow-pushers. Benjamin knew how it ought to look when it was finished; Pinchas did consent to draw Benjamin's ideas so we could all see the same vision but still tried to persuade us that for good Jews, theatre isn't quite proper.

Problems, yes, but since the days when we had been all together at home with Mama taking care of us, there hadn't been so much laughter and closeness.

I suppose if you're not looking for brickdust in the hair and distemper in the fingernails you don't see it. But with such bad giggly whispering conspirators as us, how we hoped to fool the suspicious and furious Behrens, Heaven only knows.

Natalie should have thrown us out the day Benjamin stopped shmoosing around her. (Easy to be clever like that – did I throw him out myself? No: I sat there waiting for the mumser to come back. Women. What chance do we have? Didn't I know the pain she was suffering? She'd be worried if she knew how much sympathy I felt for her. Me sorry for Natalie? Well, I am.) Too late now. Leah and Benjamin were working over every tiny part they were grudgingly allowed;

expanding, ad-libbing audience-catching extras, show-stoppers, their exit applause out of proportion to the importance of their part. Not good acting behaviour, of course; but the crowds for them outside the back exit at night made it hard for the Behrens to complain. Well, not so much hard as bad for their business.

So the Behrens dug their own grave, letting us live and work with them whilst we Rubenovskad the Sheep and Shearer, flirted with their audiences and planned their downfall.

Daytime, there was no one better to mix the Portland cement, the lime and the water into the mortar for the bricks than Leah. She said it was a lot like getting batter ready for blintzes and sang as she shovelled. At night they had to put up with my infinitely more sloppy mix, the work slowing down not only from our tiredness. Daytime, my Benjamin had wonderful ideas – imaginative, thoughtful, idealistic. At night we took the tools that Igor loaned us and without even knowing what they were called we used them to huck and to chip and to smash our way ignorantly towards Benjamin's visions.

This wall that we all kept wishing wasn't there – well it wasn't going to disappear. So I took the thing with the flat bit and the hammer with the iron on the end I could barely lift and I banged the first with the second. For hours. If you take out one brick, I thought to myself, the others would just fall down, and surely the way we had put bricks up, to take them down would be just as easy. Scenery, Pinchas the weed could paint, ideas Benjamin the great actor could have, buckets Drushki could hump as easily here as from the well in Wisherodik, walls were mine to remove. I didn't hear either their sighing or their annoyance. I'd wheeled my last barrow until that darned first brick came out. The more it stuck and chipped away and stayed obstinately lodged, the greater my anger grew for all the injustice I considered I'd suffered. Torn away from Wisherodik, thump, thump, Tata dead, whack, whack, Mama in danger, huck, huck, Benjamin seduced, wham, wham, wham – a hole – Pinchas made a prayer, a shercheeornoo.

How much time had that taken? Times how many bricks in

the wall? We all played about peeking through from one side to another – look, no matter how long, it had to come down. Perhaps if we all – we all left the sensible essential jobs. But after the first brick (or maybe it's the way I did it) it wasn't all that bad, except for the mess and the pain in the arms and not knowing how to finish at both ends where the bricks stood in their in-and-out pattern.

Benjamin's clever face frowned sternly as he gazed at the wonderful clear auditorium we had made. 'You've thought – it's maybe a supporting wall?' Sweaty, panting, grey with dust, shoulders hunched with wear, I shrugged them just a little, carefully so as not to irritate any muscles still in working order.

'Supporting what?'

Taking Hersch, Pinchas, and Igor's Chesterman-steel-wind-up-tape they pounded about measuring here and above, tutting and arguing whilst we waited down in the rubble with exhausted patience to the slow boiling of the tin kettle on the spirit stove.

Footsteps. Voices.

'Luckily . . .' Benjamin said.

It was like Paradise. We were so happy that night that even after our noisy careless return to the Behrens' attic to make noisy careless love I couldn't sleep and stayed up till the candle went out writing the bones of *Enough is Enough*, not realizing until Benjamin held it out in his puzzled hands to me in the morning that I'd written the whole play in English.

'My G-d, Mrs Behren,' Benjamin shouted, hitting his forehead in a gesture so theatrical he would never have used it on the stage. 'How long must I go on playing second fiddle to your one-string violin?'

Into the silence, breath taken and never let out again, bodies stiff in their anxiety not to be noticed, Benjamin came so far down to the edge of the stage that his boots hung over the edge.

Jumping down, he snatched up his new cloak without glancing at me although my arm had been lying on top of it; he spoke as if privately to me though at gallery-reaching volume.

'With such people, Zelda, we shouldn't mix. With such

people I cannot act.'

'Indeed you cannot, Mr Rubenovska,' Natalie shouted from the back of the stage. 'You have much to learn,' she screamed. 'Perhaps, were you to take some advice from Maurice and me, in time to come you'd be maybe as successful as –'

'Vos? Any actor that would listen to your ideas on acting,' Benjamin spat, putting his gloves on as if every finger of them had insulted him personally, 'would be no actor.'

'In that case, Mr Rubenovska, the Behrens' school of acting should suit you very well, being not much of an actor yourself.'

'Thou offspring of a maternal parent and a large horse,' Benjamin said pleasantly. 'I go. With me go my family and – your hopes. Who will you look to to draw the crowds, to bring the applause?'

Curtain.

But the silence didn't last. Maurice and Natalie stood screaming from the stage and all of us, Leah, Benjamin, Drushki, even Hersch and me, released all our sewn-up politenesses in some harsh truth-telling, secure in the warm knowledge that at the former Sheep and Shearer we had, tonight, somewhere to go. Rooms had been hastily furnished from Igor's secondhand stores, stairs had been swept, larders had been stocked, belongings had been smuggled out from the attics the Behrens thought were our only refuge. Thinking us imprisoned by the lowness and meanness of our wages, the Behrens felt free to insult us, misuse us – as I put it in my play *Enough is Enough*, even a shrivelled-up raisin swells if you soak it in brandy.

'Even a shrivelled-up raisin swells if you soak it in brandy,' I shouted proudly at Natalie as she screamed that we were killing the chicken that laid our only eggs.

'I don't get it,' Leah whispered. 'About the raisins, Zelda. What do you mean?'

'All right, I'll rewrite it,' I snapped.

'Let them go back where we took them from – the streets!' Natalie raged.

'A good idea,' Benjamin bowed. 'Come. To the streets, kinder.'

A nice feeling, being free.

Also, not a nice feeling.

Out in the darkness, Spitalfields, Whitechapel, Mile End scuttled and hustled. Bundles of cut-make-and-trim seemed always high on the carts on the move to and from the outworkers. Skinny, starved kids pushed those barrows and though the tailors paid them as little as they could, the pennies they earned like this still kept family after family in food and out of the street.

We passed plenty of doorways with crumpled unofficial guests in snoring exhaustion, most of the empty market crates make the only home an orphan could wish for.

From upstairs windows as we walked came smells and laughs and shouts. When I was little in Wisherodik I used to worry what went on in all the other homes. Ours was strange and different because we were the Rubenovskas and I ached to be like normal girls of my age, ached to live in a home where the Mama sat to do embroidery after she'd dug the potatoes and the Papa studied Gemorrah after lifting sacks of dung for the farmer. You know? Normal?

But here in London, what was normal? How could I ever find out? The Behrens lived and breathed theatre like the Rubenovskas and when we met the Adlers and the Thomashevskys in America, they too wouldn't know the time of day unless it was curtain-up.

'I'm hungry, Ben-Ben,' Hersch said in the last year of his high voice. 'When the gevalt started I was just going to eat a . . .'

'To my home we're going,' Leah said, taking his arm. 'Before I feed Baby Jacob something nice I'll make you. All of you.'

'No,' Benjamin said, walking too fast in that way of his as if the world must run to catch up or miss him. 'Tonight we eat like kings. And Hoffman's is not the only restaurant in London. Somewhere near to –' he paused, 'our theatre, is a restaurant which we will make our own. People will flock there to see us. First, the theatre we must agree on a name for and . . .'

Benjamin talked on like an emperor with a new kingdom to play with. I sighed and thought about the bed I'd seen in the window at Gardiner's, the furnishers. When we'd earned enough to buy that bed, babies would want to get born there.

'I'll still first have to feed the baby, Benjamin,' Leah said, 'and I'd like Pinchas to come with us but we can only come if the Zigmans will take the baby into their room. And then there's Drushki – you'll want to pick up Charlie, won't you?'

'No,' Drushki said, changing the sleeping Sarah to the other arm. 'Sarah can stay with Baby Jacob tonight? It's too cold to take them out tonight. In the new theatre I'll also sleep.'

So. Enough of Charlie Marken she'd also had. Charlie with black from his leaflets in the thin deep creases of his palms and the same blackness in his conscience and the place where the morals go.

Nice idea to use another restaurant, my Binyomin, but as we passed Hoffman's, where the soup-of-the-day announced itself clearly as barley, it seemed to me that the nearest soup is the finest.

Hersch jabbered as we walked, full of dreams with him in the centre as a song-writer, Leah tut-tutting the ideas half-heartedly in Pinchas's absence, my playing putting words to the snatches he sang.

We walked towards the smell of Zigman's. Six o'clock one of the busiest times of their day. Heaving uselessly at her too-long apron straps Sadie Zigman still had time to crease her wrinkles at us and wave an oily hand. 'Ahzoy? A simcha you're making tonight, Leah? Fish you'd like maybe? The two babies? Every half-hour I'll see them. Go. Go out, enjoy yourselves. You're young yet. Look, you want that tail of haddock, yingele, you can have it but don't touch it with the fingers, yes?'

Up the stairs. Oy, that Mama, may she come soon, should see Leah live like this. Yet why not? She was happy, wasn't she? She was a mother, wasn't she? The smell of the fish oil? What was that to a pious man like Pinchas?

Kissing the mezuzza on the door-post, Leah shoved four times before the door opened and Baby Jacob tottered unsteadily to her, stomach out, one foot making longer strides than the other, joy everywhere on his lovely face.

Love, this place had. Somewhere in the Talmud it probably said that not even to whitewash the walls let alone put up a bright picture or two was not only a mitzvah but made you a better Jew. And Drushki the socialist agreed in her possessions-are-the-devil idealism. For religion, against religion, what difference? Fanatics are fanatische.

'Why so late?' Pinchas asked, redder in the face than usual. 'An hour he's been whining. Up and down I've been walking, every minute something he's touching. That range – a fireguard we have to have. And . . .'

Such problems I should also, please G-d, have.

As Leah warmed some milk and cracked the egg Mrs Zigman had given her for Jacob, we settled our baggage around us and all shouted over one another the wonderful news of our departure from the slavery of the Behrens.

Pinchas had plenty of pessimism to share with us about the wisdom of rushing out on a quarrel – 'as Nachman said', he frowned, 'as the Lubliner Rebbe was fond of explaining', he pompoused.

'But Pinchas, didn't Rambam also say that a good war is better than a bad peace?' (My, that sounded real. How could he quarrel with that?)

With Jacob and Sarah reasonably pacified and settled to sleep, we left them to Sadie Zigman's care and walked.

At the bottom of Leman Street on the left hand side at the corner of Hooper Street, the Sheep and Shearer lettering had been crudely painted over until we'd finished arguing about what to call our very first English theatre.

Our very first – oy, what a mess. It had seemed better yesterday when we left it. A couple of panes of glass had been broken – that you've got to expect. A top-class neighbourhood it wasn't. After we'd scrubbed the outside yesterday, Drushki and me, it had shone with wetness. Now, dry again, even in the dark it looked dreadful.

'That's nothing a little paint can't cure,' Benjamin shrugged, knowing that Great Actors don't use little paintbrushes.

We opened the amazingly wide door, which lacked only a handle, into the entrance lobby, which could do with a spot of lino. The desk that Igor said was dying of woodworm looked all right from the front and the short leg was propped by the round strong lid of a biscuit tin, the rest of which stood ready to be filled with profit.

'Pictures,' Benjamin said, looking round in his demanding way as though he had been expecting pictures to drop like manna. 'Lots of pictures of us' – you could tell he meant 'me' – 'in costume. It's what they do at the Britannia, I believe. It's fashionable. We'll go to a studio – no, better, we'll have a studio come here.'

Nobody, but nobody, even queries whether this was possible, or even how much. We all listen to Benjamin and we run around obeying and pleasing him and he never has sleepless nights like the rest of us worrying, having second, third thoughts. He says 'pictures'. You wait. Before you know it the lobby will be papered with them. Shame we painted the walls.

'Come see,' I said, tugging Benjamin up the stairs, anxious to reveal our best surprise.

'A moment,' he said. 'First things first,' and swung open the doors to the stage and the stalls.

An irritating man, Benjamin.

Except that the seats Igor had helped us bid for from the old Albert Palace still had to be trundled here six at a time, it was amazing how ready the place was. The dusty blue curtains were hung, if unhemmed, the walls were whitewashed neatly, the lights worked – sometimes – and what wouldn't Mama and especially Tata, olev hashalom, have given for such luxury?

'Goot, goot,' Benjamin said vaguely.

We shlepped, shovelled, dug, plastered, painted and planed and my husband 'goot,' he says.

'But I wonder –', Benjamin pondered.

You've maybe noticed when someone says, 'But I wonder' it's either impossible or costs a lot of money.

'The Pavilion it isn't, of course . . .'

The Pavilion? Two and a half thousand they cram in there every night and turn away the rest. The place is crusted with gold – they say it's real gold – chandeliers as big as the Crystal Palace hang for no reason at all and the stage must be sixty, seventy foot across. The Pavilion this wasn't; just an old public house two and a half thousand times better than a cowshed.

'. . . so we have to be – different.'

'Different, how? We don't let them pay for the seats?' Drushki sounded so hard and looked so sulky it made me feel just a bit less impatient with Benjamin who was being, it hurts me to say this, a pain in the backside. It would kill him to say something encouraging?

'A family business.'

New? We all moaned at him. The Adlers and the Thomashevskys, we whined. All the back streets and the main roads were full of bakers' sons and marching gran' pas. The whole of the East End was families.

'We make a story and we get the East End papers and the *Jewish Chronicle* to tell – always they're looking for a story. You'll write it in English, Zeldele. The family built the very theatre with their own hands, you'll say, our fingernails broken and bleeding, you'll say' – he held out his clear, clean, golden-skinned palms, which had moved quite a bit to explain how things should be but had never shoved at an obstinate brick or gripped at an angry wrench – 'and having made of a simple public house, a comfortable, homely playhouse – in English that'll sound good, yes, Zeldele? – the family will only act in their own family-written plays using only their own actors from the family and . . .'

'It's good,' sighed Leah, rubbing her leg where last week she had showed me a varicose vein like the inside tube of my fountain pen. 'Mama'll love it.'

'My Leah will have to be at home when – the Lord blesses us again.' Pinchas pinked but spoke with great firmness. 'This I have said many times.'

'Stupid,' Benjamin said angrily. 'Such nonsense you talk, Pinchas. Surely we should use what talents we have been given by the Almighty? No – when our froyen begin to grow big with our babies, we will make a place in the play for a woman carrying a child.'

'Or maybe, a fat woman,' Drushki added.

'Or when two of us have quarrelled I'll write for two black eyes and a crutch.' We doubled over, laughing.

Jokes you can't make when Benjamin's being serious. This I still haven't learned. And despite the worries his ideas are bound to bring, for myself I can see how good and clever it is to use our disadvantage as a bridge to walk our audience over with nice warm feet.

'What about Mr Lottenstein?' Hersch said, frowning. 'Family he isn't.'

Educate the kinder a little and what do you get? Questions.

'An uncle, we'll make him,' Benjamin says without taking a breath even to think it over. 'An uncle – Uncle Igor. Zeldele, you'll tell him in the morning?'

As I led Benjamin up with his eyes closed to see, at last, my surprise I heard the screams of laughter as Leah imitated me telling Igor that all that money he'd spent had bought him the honour of being our dear uncle.

'Hmm,' Benjamin said, when I let him open his eyes. We had unscrewed panels of thin soft wood just from one end of a storage area upstairs to find it gave direct access to the downstairs seating – a gallery; a balcony, in fact. I'd measured the one chair we had and measured the space we would have when we took off all the other panels screwed to the carved struts and on the three sides there could be ninety, ninety-two extra seats for each performance.

'Maybe.' He banged on the floor. Steady enough. He shook at the bars. Sturdy and strong. Did he think we hadn't done all that?

'Permission, we'll need.'

This also we knew. Hadn't I gone with Drushki to see the fire brigade man and the licensing officer? Two unspeakably awkward, awful men they'd been too. When they come here to 'inspect and approve' as it says on the letter, let Benjamin take them round and fight with them.

'Unscrew the other panels.' He indicated the hours of

planing and smoothing and varnishing with wise clean fingers and all of a sudden my poultry knife I'd have liked to hack off those pointing fingers.

Blind, love isn't.

'There's still much to be done. I'll go down. Hersch – make for me a list while I remember,' he shouted as he walked down the balcony steps. 'Soon here we can perform. Here we will learn,' he said in irritatingly restrained calmness. 'Leah, you'll go with Zelda, arrange who sleeps where tonight? On any floor better, sweeter than the Behrens' featherbed.'

I stayed where I was, thinking. On the first night, or maybe the second when we were speaking again to each other, I'd go and get Cousin Avrom from that shambles he lived in and he'd maybe light up again. Every time I thought about him, I saw Mama screaming at us for how little we'd done. Chicken we took him every week but he was still there – maybe if one day we had a proper home. A house away from the theatre . . . Smiling babies with fat thighs and patiently wound ringlets darkened my vision like a bandage. When would the babies come?

From up here you could look at the family and pretend they were strangers. Drushki didn't look well. How come I didn't see that before? Dumpy people don't look bad as quickly, maybe, but yellow she looked, like a bad pomegranate. The look she had I had somewhere seen before – ah yes, on me in the Natalie days. Hatztsorus. So for awful Charlie Marken she was hungry, poor Drushki. Later I'd talk to her, try to help. And my Leah. Even in that ridiculous headscarf Pinchas made her wear to cover her shining hair nothing hid her fine bones and that like-it-was-made-for-her nose. Hersch – babble, babble, never quiet unless he was singing or humming or banging the piano or tripping over things that weren't even there – like any twelve-year-old klutz. A lovely kid. Would Annie and Lev be sorry the way we spoiled him? Who wouldn't spoil such a boy?

We ran about a bit putting bundles into the rooms we had chosen, temporary this and temporary that, maybe the others didn't mind but a little regret I felt for the comfort we had made in the Behrens' attic and the curtains we had left behind to cover that skylight view of the stars. The paper on the walls of this other skylight room only a publican would choose to live with. Still – I knew I'd get fond of it. That bed from Gardiner's would be our first purchase and it would, I knew, be a lucky bed, G-d willing, touch wood, cross fingers, as they say here in Whitechapel.

Only kosher restaurants Pinchas would go to, so when Benjamin had locked the door and put the key inside his second-best cloak, I took his arm up Gowers Walk into Commercial Road where there were plenty of places to choose from. And as we walked we argued names. Only tomorrow Pinchas had time to paint the front and the posters. Money he had to have before we opened and he had barmitzvahs to teach, a wedding this week and maybe, if we were lucky, a levoyah or two. Without him and me 'earning' – for nothing, Igor was paying me these days – the materials we needed to open couldn't be wheedled out of anyone even with a promise to pay over six months. Everywhere in London, it seemed, theatres were being rebuilt, refurnished, ripped out. Good thing. Pinchas would go to the public libraries to read some building magazines to find the news of theatre refits and then hurried round with a barrow for any props or furnishings our necessity could invent.

Names, names. Serious at first: 'Rubenovska Revels.' 'Rubenovska Palats.' 'Rubenovska Yiddish Teater.' But then silly names we were finding. 'Royal Yiddishe Palace.' 'Alexandra's Yiddish Business.' 'Binyomin-the-Boss's Place.'

And glorious Binyomin-the-Boss his passionate eyes smiling, was holding me and laughing, trying to trip me up by kicking my ankles together like that night in Wisherodik. Who cares how far the restaurant – I'm too much in love to be hungry.

'We've been walking for hours and hours Ben-Ben,' Hersch sighed inaccurately. 'Where we going to eat?'

'Here.'

Frankenberg's. It didn't look very clean.

'This will be "our" restaurant,' Benjamin explained. 'People will, once the theatre opens, come here to mix with us and we will do them a favour and mix with them.'

Frankenberg's.

Plenty we knew about the Frankenberg's.

Old man Frankenberg, Morry and Lily Frankenberg and their two sons were a boil on the face, a pox on the buttocks, horse-muck in the horseradish, bed-bugs in the soup of life – how did we know? The Hoffmans told us every day, that's how.

The two families had boiled, fried and grovelled to their own regulars for decades and screamed awful curses, shuddering with disgust at each others' chopped liver. Who knows what small thing began this so long ago – could they even remember?

At Hoffman's, which looked cleaner but was much smaller, the seats not full of the tookases of actors, were filled fully by the cabinet-makers of Curtain Road. Here, down in Stepney, Frankenberg's was full of cap-makers and milliners, the dusty windows of which we'd just trudged past. The sample-makers, queens of the trade, were a sight in their something-special-hats made from bits of nothing in their own free time. I saw Leah fidgeting with her headscarf, eyes greedily searching from one to the other for ideas.

Frankenberg's – if it was true what they used to make the soup go further, what were we here for?

No less self-importantly than the actors at Hoffman's the hatters stared at us, unfriendly, whispering, shrugging as we were squeezed and pushed into the tiny table, the worst table in the place, near enough to be hit each time by the ever-swinging kitchen door, near enough to smell the oil and the waste-bins but not near enough to be noticed.

For all Benjamin's gesturing and clicking of fingers and calling, the waiters came when everyone else was suited. They came in their own good time and with the bored shrug of the put-upon.

Passing trade! Regulars were bad enough.

'What do you want?'

The reluctant waiter stood, his fat hand at his fat hip like a fat dancer waiting for the music, looking everywhere but at us, suggesting nothing.

'What's good tonight?' Benjamin said, his charm dazzling – to me, anyway.

A fat shrug.

'Soup everyone?' Benjamin counted round – not me; not likely.

'Chopped liver.' Even if I was starving, just in case – not for me.

'Saubraten?'

'Not tonight – enough we didn't make.'

'Tzimmes?'

'None left.'

'Goulash?'

'Neyn.'

'Ben-Ben, at Hoffman's the soup they bring right away– '

If Hersch wasn't sorry he'd spoken he ought to have been, even though he spoke for us all.

The waiter had disappeared. Maybe to get the soup, maybe to give us time to think better of staying.

When Benjamin had finished the begrubbing of Hersch, he shifted us all an inch along from the wall so that both arms he'd be able to use at once. 'Nice here,' he lied loudly. 'I feel at home.'

After they'd drunk their soup, swallowed their liver and I'd finished half a plate of caraway rye-bread and three dill-pickle cucumbers, they brought us some gristle and bone, tepid vegetables and a grudging bissel this and that, (though the lockshen pudding was marvellous).

'Oy, what a meal!' Benjamin said, wiping his mouth and winking at all of us. 'Kelner!' The fat one didn't move, just lifted his head a few chins to listen. 'More glasses of tea and tomorrow the same table we'd like,' he called.

An eyebrow raised in the bank of Frankenberg's behind the long sandwich counter at the front.

The tea when it came this time was hotter and the lemon slices seemed first-hand – nearly. Lily Frankenberg brought it to us and stood waiting.

'Setz?' I asked.

'Azoy.' Hersch's chair was removed and he sat at the edge of the table listening, sensible, aware how important this meeting was.

'So?'

Maybe the Jew just hasn't got the time for long conversations – there is, after all, a living to be made, a family to be loved. Lily knew what she meant by 'so' and so did we.

So our life-story Benjamin tells her.

'Vunderlekh,' Lily smiled coldly. 'It's where, this little theatre of yours? It's called?'

'We have transformed the Sheep and Shearer public house into a delightfully cosy theatre,' Benjamin said, his smile as cold but wrapped up warmer. 'The corner of Hooper Street. You'll see the boards go up tomorrow. 'My wife's brother-in-law is a great artist, he . . .'

'It's called?'

'The Family Theatre,' Pinchas said, as if the name had never been in dispute.

We swallowed, we considered, we frowned, we smiled. It was just right. Both ways it meant something; it had taste, it had something, it had everything.

'Vos?' whispered Benjamin.

'Mishpokhe,' I whispered back. 'Family, mishpokhe.'

'In English you're going to write it?'

'In England English we'll use. Soon even plays in English we can do.' Me, I had to open my big mouth.

They were all shouting fors, againsts, efshers, maybes, maybe-nots. Lily was sitting amongst us puzzled. I touched Leah's arm and catching eyes here and there we returned to selling ourselves to the Frankenbergs. After all, somewhere we had to start. Posters we needed to put up somewhere. Free publicity we had to get from someone.

'. . . and you shall be our honoured guests,' Benjamin smiled, getting up as Lily retreated back behind the counter. 'Free first night tickets for all of you,' he smiled.

The place was emptying. Just us left and early yet.

'When we open, packed you'll be after the show,' Leah

reminded Lily quickly. 'An advertisement you'd like to put in our programme?'

She shrugged cautiously. 'We'll see.'

'We'll open with *Motke Goniff*,' Benjamin said firmly, folding his arms as if they were boneless and he were already on the stage in the part where he's a clown in the circus.

'No, no,' said Leah, whose part in *Motke* was insipid. '*The Blacksmith's Daughter*.'

'*Motke* is stronger, funnier.'

'*Blacksmith* is deeper, yet lighter.'

'*Blacksmith* not everyone knows. The songs not everyone can join in.'

'And *Motke*? Every word everyone knows. That's good? Behren's *Motke* they have all seen.'

'Zelda? Drushki? Hersch?'

Suddenly we counted.

Drushki held out her hands. 'I'll be the whiskery grandmother in one or the bearded lady in the other, so what matter?'

To hear Drushki make a joke was like seeing lockshen swim.

'Blacksmith,' Hersch said definitely. Well, he'd be playing the songs wouldn't he?

I tutted like my mother. 'No. I think we should start with a special Family Evening. Each of us, we'll do something special ourselves and then perform our own play. A Rubenovska family performance without a word of anyone else's work. A big long evening they get for their money. Then in the papers they can shout for us that the Family Theatre is, well, a family theatre.'

Into the deadness I had made, Lily nudged Morry who brought a wet and smelly dishcloth to smear our table. Clearly giving an unhidden yawn, she made it plain that to wave goodbye with the same cloth would also be a pleasure.

'You know, Zelda, you're right.' Benjamin said, placing his arms back on the table, the cloth ribbing the greasemarks.

'You'll forgive us . . .' Lily said, blowing out the gas-lights above her head and not looking sorry at all. 'Myself I don't get tired, but my husband – some early nights he must get before you, mit mazl, fill us up until the middle of the night. Gei gezinterheit.'

'Till tomorrow,' Benjamin said, taking off his hat in the English way.

Hersch ran ahead of him, shrieking with laughter, taking off his cap and bowing 'biz morgen, biz morgen,' into the darkness.

After ten. The small shops beginning to shut, already. One of Hersch's friends from the buildings, lucky to get a night job after school and after Hebrew classes, yawned as he weighed out, winking, a bag of broken biscuits a little on the heavy side for Hersch – good thing Pinchas didn't notice. Some black bread, sugar, a pinch of tea, a lemon don't forget and we were on our way home.

With a full stomach, your family round you, a place of your own to sleep in and my Benjamin to sleep with, who notices a little screaming and hair-pulling outside the public houses? Who worries about the bright glint of knives, blankness in the faces of starved children searching a crate to crawl into? Who is, any more, after two years in London, startled by beggars with parts of their body missing you shouldn't know of?

Me, I did. I noticed.

But what could I do? Sweep up the filth of London with my lonely broom? Give every child a place to lay its head? Stop this terrible drinking here in London? A start we were making – one public house we'd closed.

Pinchas waved the copy of the *Forward* Lily had picked off the floor and straightened for him.

'In here they say that in Americhky now, the latest thing, they don't print all about the characters in the programmes. Just the name they give you.'

We ignored him. How would the audience know the landlord had a secret sorrow and a weak heart if the programme didn't tell them so? They'd think the actor had a bissel indigestion.

'And another thing: they don't make with the cheering and the curtains after every scene. At the end only they do it.'

'And still in Americhky they make a living?' Tch, Tch. So

many worries, changes we didn't need to make.

'All the photographs now are of the stars in motor cars.'

'All right, Pinchas, so we'll borrow Igor's. You'll arrange it, Zeldele? At the wheel I can sit and look better than Boris Thomashevsky.'

More worries. Igor. I was cheating him. Hardly any work I did for him these days and still money he gave me. For his paperwork I must find time. But how? I was a builder, a painter, a felling-hand, a personal assistant to a man of business and the best play I'd ever written I'd promised to the family for the opening and not a word written yet.

Outside the Sheep and Shearer – how long before we stopped calling and thinking of this lovely place of our own as that – we stood in a neat family row and gazed at the blank brown front.

The Family Theatre. That's what Pinchas would write large in gold, with curlicues, tomorrow. Gold? Gold paint? From where?

Charlie Marken's workshop was full of paints, wasn't it? So a stone jar or two of Ardenbrite Liquid Metallics he wouldn't miss. And quite right too; nothing else he'd given poor Drushki, except a baby, of course. Look at her. Pale and limp as if Charlie had shaken her temper till its neck broke. She was more lumpy than dumpy now and the roundness of her jaw sagged here and there with a yellowness replacing her ill-natured red. I scooped up a few crumbs from the sweet swollen kuchen of feelings that were always wrapped ready for me to give to her brother and hugged her with them. She didn't pull away, shrug me off, tch-tch me either. She shivered and smiled up almost like thanking me. A red flag waved in my head; someone else we must find for her. She was pining for awful Charlie. Now we had a theatre of our own we must find a big strong chap for her. A cabinet maker who could build the scenery, fix us a table, rebuild a chair, make us a mantleshelf when we needed one. A walk-on, a scene-shifter. A mensch.

'The posters you'll also do tomorrow, Pinchas?' Benjamin scowled, but taking my hand and smoothing the palm of it with such tenderness that I was forced to shrug to keep my head from flying off.

'Of course,' Pinchas agreed neatly. 'You want?'

'*Motke Goniff* – starring Benjamin Rubenovska,' said Benjamin.

'*Blacksmith's Daughter* – starring Leah Rubenovska,' said Leah.

'– Starring Leah Rottman,' said Pinchas.

'Music by Hersch Rubenovska,' said Hersch.

'An Original New Play by Zelda Rubenovska.' I added my oar too late.

'In the morning, in the morning,' Benjamin said impatiently, but stroking me again so that I didn't care if morning never came.

'In the morning, Hersch, a day off school you'll take and start with a barrow bringing in the seats.'

Tomorrow this, tomorrow that – Benjamin issued the orders like a general who would be on the top of the hill with his men but he'd already told me where he would be: choosing a photographer and being measured at a tailor. 'Like kings and queens we must look, only better than their King Edward,' he had said. 'On the stage or on the street they must idolize us.'

'Early, before we eat, everything else we'll decide,' he said, unlocking the big front doors to that smell of shaved wood, drying whitewash and drains.

'Come, Zee-Zee.'

Bundles. Boxes. Building bits. The bottom half of an old bed. Bubba's lucky piece of glass centrally in its new place on its new mantelshelf.

Alone with my Binyomin.

A blessing.

INTERLUDE

Friday 2 November 1906
So Mama formed the village Friendly Society herself as a copy of Annie and Lev's idea in Yemolsk, and when they came to her and said the money to make the journey to join the family had been put aside for her, no wonder she cried. In her letter she says she had packed before they'd finished speaking; Leah and I know better. First she mended the tears in the back drapes, then she changed every bit of dialogue in the play that was running and then she packed. Isn't it vunderlekh?

Monday 5 November 1906
It's like Shakespeare. You know? They say when one person's on stage talking to themselves it's the truth they're speaking? Like that with me – in this journal, I mean. Mama's coming, that's all we can talk about but am I the only one who's worried that when she comes here, all of a sudden, children we're going to be again? Soon enough we'll see. No good putting a bucket ready until there's a leak in the roof.

How Annie and Lev must worry about Herschele.

Friday 9 November 1906
One thing Mama may be able to do – keep control of Benjamin. We can't. Sleeping is something he doesn't think we need bother about until the theatre is open. In two directions at once he sends us, to do two jobs together is not enough; eating, except by him, should be done in the hand and on the move. It's so nearly ready and more and more exciting that I don't really mind. The whole place is blue and white and Pinchas has used the blue material we picked up in the market for everything. Benjamin thinks it's vulgar so the people will probably love it. Also Pinchas got some gold paint that would

stick to the curtains and they look – well with a noise you can describe them best. You know? Hmmnah? Considering Pinchas's fears about the theatre leading to sin and impurity, for love of Leah he was keeping decently quiet about it and only occasionally muttering to himself.

Oy – now what are they doing? 'Benjamin. They don't fall to the ground fighting. Quarrelled, I wrote. You want I should write the quarrel out? Of course, darling, if you really feel a fall or two would be better . . .' To end this good marriage all I have to do is mention Jacob Gordin, again. Gordin's rule is that no word is ever changed once it's been written. He gets up in his seat, they say, and yells at the actors if they play around with the words. Me, how I'd love to do that. But, blast my Benjamin's elbows, now I see it, the silent fighting *is* better than any words. All right, all right, my scribbling I'm stopping, in a moment I'm on. With such a few of us, an actress I have to be also. Best part I ever had, though. Nothing I say. Not one single word.

Tuesday 13 November 1906

To get an asbestos safety curtain that cheap, something had to be wrong with it, of course, and it still sticks a gap from the ground whatever they do with their slides and grooves and I'm sick of hearing about it. Inspector this, Inspector that – I don't see what good they are. Every day in the English papers is fires – fires burning down this theatre, fires in that public house show, fires at the music-halls. They said electric lights would stop the fires. Did they stop? At least here in England, fires start by accident, not by Cossacks. Shall I tell the Inspector that?

Wednesday 14 November 1906

This is, without doubt, my best work. – *Only One Day*. So much there is in it. Too much, maybe. It's like three plays. In fact if Mama was here to play around with it, to knead it a bit, six she'd make of it. I wrote Benjamin a part for a perfect and loving husband. Some fun a playwright has to have and who knows better than me how he brings his role home with him;

except when he's angry or tired or worried or hungry or concentrating on something else, loving he is to me. What more could a wife ask? Last Friday when we popped some fish in for Cousin Avrom, Leah and I asked at the hospital if he could come for the first night. No, they said, without looking up. Well, we'll see, they frowned when we said free tickets there would be for someone who could stay with him. How long since he's been out? A part I could maybe write him where he just sits through the play? Family, after all. Maybe now about Avrom I should write to Mama – warn her a little. Shame she isn't here for the first night – still, bosses enough we've already got for that. Igor's been more than a father to us – money he gives us, time he gives us. In his speech Benjamin must thank Igor over and over – but I don't dare to mention it. That first-night speech is another thing we don't talk about. So many things I can't say to Benjamin now, when I do open my mouth I feel like a mother bird feeding her chick only with safe morsels.

Thursday 15 November 1906

A long letter I must write to Annie and Lev – but for long letters how can I make time? Today even Igor frowned a little when I asked, again, to leave so early. Today, Thursday at least, he expects me to finish up the books for the week to carry him over until Monday. Silly, it's getting. And not fair, either. Twice I've said, 'Look, someone you'll get full-time', but Igor always says, 'When you're here you work hard.' And I keep quiet and stay on because where would I write my plays if not in his quiet office with a nice solid desk, my wonderful typewriter that I can nearly use properly, and the peace of mind I never have anywhere around Benjamin.

Yes, to Annie I must write, I was saying. Hersch, at school a lot of trouble he's getting into. Of course. When is he there? Would we keep our own child away like that? (The answer to that is probably yes.) A lovely boy, Hersch – responsible, grown-up sometimes, and so funny and the songs they shake off him like the crunchy brown leaves of this week's trees. But at school they're not interested in the theatre, in songs.

'A scholarship boy must study, study, study,' that Mr Cranborne said to us when we were sent for. 'Truancy we won't stand for. Not at a grammer-school. There are hundreds of other boys who, given this golden opportunity, would . . .'

Why didn't Benjamin say something instead of sitting there nodding like the father in *The Halfwit*. As if Hersch had chosen to stay away, not been forced to by our desperate need. And the part Hersch had worked up for the show was so rich. Kuchen without streusel without him. Besides, as a willing shlepper he had no equal. I wanted to say to the teacher that this was also an education for the boy but how could I? The man was only trying to whip our skimmed-milk boys wrenched from the pogroms into fine English cream. So I frowned and said we had 'family problems' that would soon PG be better and then I felt terrible because he was suddenly so kind, remembering that Hersch had no parents, only us, and there he was sympathizing with our 'problems' when, in a way, we don't have any. Maybe to Annie I won't write about it. Troubles enough she already has. Trying to be fair to Igor I stayed later than I'd planned so when I walked in on the latest 'running order' battle and Benjamin shouted at me because I was late when all the numbers I'd been adding still stuck to my fingers and the inside of my ears, I called them 'a bunch of show-offs altogether' and went to our room to have a good cry. But there was no comfort in our room. Still not much different from the day we walked in, and no bed from Gardiner's yet. Here comes my Benjamin – look at his face – there's no good arguing. I'll just apologize, go downstairs and get to work.

ACT III

SCENE III

Opening Night, Tuesday 8 January 1907

Family. A wonderful thing, a family.

Drushki didn't feel well and out selling tickets she scarcely bothered to hide it; Hersch all the time running to the toilet – nerves, I think; Leah's Jacob had had an oil burn two days ago when Sadie Zigman took her eyes from him for a moment and Leah could think of nothing else; Pinchas wasn't back from shul, Benjamin had had second thoughts about – to tell you the truth he'd had fourth and fifteenth thoughts about everything and we'd all stopped listening. Hersch's friends, useful though they were for fetching and carrying, selling the programmes, selling the drinks, taking the tickets, were, to be honest, more tsorus than pleasure. It wasn't that they didn't work, it was – you know? – they weren't used to theatres. No, I've got to get used to these intruders, these outsiders. Family Theatre or no, soon we'll get bigger and we'll employ other actors, too, like other places do and one day we'll have maybe two theatres or three and make it more of a business than make such a business of it.

Avrom. Why didn't we think to send him some clothes? How did he look? Mama must never see him like this. In the middle of the front row, Pinchas has put him. Tomorrow, whatever money we made, clothes for him we must buy. A haircut, a shave. So ashamed I feel that I didn't think of it. The man who brought him doesn't look much better. Good wages I suppose they don't get. And to be in a front row for nothing the man can't believe. Every minute he's turning round, smiling.

Poor Avrom just sits. Igor's seat the other side of him is still empty. The Zigmans sit in the front row over to the left in their best clothes.

Shrieks, there are, from the ladies as they arrive. Those flowers we bought for nothing in the closing market last night were a masterstroke. Not just a new theatre, a new play, a new family but free flowers? Quick, put up the price of drinks; profit is also no disgrace.

Out here I'm smiling, I'm being a Rubenovska, I've done what Benjamin told me to do but without me they can also manage and where I really want to be is where the panic is.

So I go round the back, after I've seen the sight we all hoped for – people are arguing because all the seats in the theatre aren't front row centre.

Here, backstage, if you shut your eyes you could be back at the Behrens'. You could be in Wisherodik, except that Mama isn't here blazing; you could be in any theatre that Benjamin's in – they all feel the same. He wants to bellow – it's his way – and because there's an audience, a great big, fat, growing audience, he can't shout, so he pouts and gestures and throws his hands to his forehead and he finds us disappointing, inept, dumb, inefficient. Unbearable man – until we'll be back in our own room, at least. Such a fuss he makes that it sounds noisy although it's all done in whispers.

'Ssh,' he says the minute he sees me instead of throwing me a loving glance, a kiss, or even one of the cheap roses we bought. 'Ssh!'

I've never been backstage before? And why do I have to shush for him to do what he's doing? All right, for mime, make-up has to be just right but tip-toeing past his mirror needs 'ssh?' I lean closer – I thought so: that's Natalie's mirror he's using; the first money we get – I get – that doesn't already belong to our stomachs, one of those big triple glasses I'll get him before Natalie's mirror gets 'dropped' and a chair mirror to see the back of his wigs and a big light to see by but none of this before the bed from Gardiner's. I looked at it again this week with Leah when we walked down to Cousin Avrom with his piece of chicken. It's still lovely. You can feel the bounce in it through the glass.

'We'll be full tonight,' I whispered, kissing his ear.

He pushed me away as if I'd tried to cut his head off.

'Tonight the Rubenovskas are new. New they'll always come to see. But they'll maybe never come back. It's tomorrow you should be worrying about.'

'All right, I'll worry.'

Cancel the bed. Who needs it?

A ripping tear and a shriek. And another ssh from Benjamin.

'What'll I do, Zeldele?' Leah stood, tears in her eyes, net had parted from net right round the waistline where it would show. Pinning wouldn't do – this was a neat-tiny-stitches job. And me, I'm crying too, because all the time we were with the Behrens it never was like this. Every little thing matters now, everyone pulling the same way, our own gescheft. Quick, I threaded two needles and Pinchas and I sewed her back into her costume, working from opposite ends and meeting again at the front in triumph. So tiny and tight the little stitches, even Pinchas's, that soon with the fine-pointed scissors we'd again have to cut it off.

You've family, maybe, in the theatre? Then you'll know what it was like before the show began. Not just a new baby but a first baby in a fine frilly basket. An atmosphere it had like swimming with crocodiles, not knowing if it was their dinner time or not.

Benjamin says anything's unlucky if he means he doesn't want it done, but even we all think looking through a chink in the curtain is unlucky but who could stop themselves doing something so exciting? Just a little peep – what harm can it do? Oy! Give a look! Oranges, they're eating; black bread crusts they're throwing on the new floorboards; outside it's raining tonight and mud children are grinding into the cracks. But still, it's our very own theatre. The Rubenovska Family. If Mama were only here to see it. If Mama *were* here, there'd be nothing but complaints and rows and angry silences. Still, I missed the way she had of mixing our individual prunes and carrots into a luscious sticky family tzimmes.

'Ssh!'

It's Igor Benjamin's sshing this time. Igor, who paid for most of the Family Theatre. The building's his in the first place. He's that most important thing in anyone's life – the landlord – and for Benjamin, Igor must crouch and whisper and tip-toe like the rest of us.

'How are you doing?' said Igor very softly, kissing me and looking nervously at my awful husband.

'Wonderful – nervous.'

'Naturally, but what you and your family have done – a miracle. More proud of you I couldn't be if I was your – father.'

Well it wasn't the first time I'd dreamed of Mama coming here and falling for Igor, but why should I even wish such a life on dear, mild, kind Igor?

'Help you don't need?' Igor was fidgeting with nervousness and I saw his head turn from confusion to confusion.

'You're very kind, Igor, but . . .'

'Zelda,' Benjamin whispered angrily at me like a sewing-machine snagged on velvet, 'get these people back to their seats. A clear mind I must have.'

'These people', that Benjamin was talking about being only Igor, I blushed red like borsht, but Igor shook his head at me, raised his hat in the English manner jokingly and whispered 'Mit mazl' as he left. Another mistake – good luck you don't wish actors so we all spat for the evil eye and ignored him; good as Igor is and clever too, an outsider he'll always be.

Everything you can't think of. Nobody had thought to practise turning off the audience lights. On, off, no, yes, that one and the one maybe next to it? Not that, no, no, no, oy, try those three, or efsher the ones under . . . G-d be praised it was dark, and everyone cheered good-naturedly. It was a bonus we hadn't intended but the warmth reached us and even Benjamin threw off the thick socks of his ill-temper that had been pulled over his face all evening.

From a few people, theatre-wise enough to know good art when they saw it, the moment Hersch had drawn the curtains back on the painted backcloth, Pinchas got his first scenery applause. It could have been any of the little villages the audience were from that Pinchas had created, but most of all it was an eyeball's worth of Wisherodik hanging there, with chickens running at the front that I could put names to. A gift like Pinchas's could get washed away like mud on the boot-scraper outside a Yeshiva study-house door.

A big round Gouda of light shone in the right place on the stage tonight. Inside it sat a peasant, whistling, whittling at a stick, waiting for his horse to be shod. The fellow's clothes hadn't been washed for a long line of Shabboses, even from the balcony he seemed to smell bad; from shtetl to shtetl he'd been pushed by his own laziness and wildness, but everywhere he was loved for the fun about him. This time, maybe, too far he had gone. A Cossack's horse he had borrowed. Noch, a horse with markings that everyone knew. Borrow or no borrow, horse-stealing from the Russian Army isn't encouraged. In fact, as a punishment something worse than death they wish they could think of. So Hersch, playing the angry Cossack (in boots that would one day, please G-d, fit him), has all the power of the Tsar behind him to face this one saucy, beggardly Jew. But don't worry. It's Benjamin who's the peasant, so of course he gets away with it in the end.

They just wouldn't stop.

Calling, stamping, standing, cheering. Throwing some of the roses we gave them back on to the stage.

Quick, while they're in the mood. Put Pinchas and Drushki on now, not later. No one argued.

A family.

My idea, this one. From watching the humourless effort of my cousin's twins with cartwheel rims a hundred years ago when we lived at home. (Would we see them again? Already the boys' barmitzvah we'd missed.)

Our own two natural born twin-klutzes, Pinchas and Drushki, walked outside the curtain and with blank faces and half a dozen oiled, birch Indian Clubs, juggled, visibly bored and apparently quite unsuccessfully. Every drop, every mistake, every narrowly missed head-smashing, from the audience came screams of delight. Children and zeidas were crying with laughter. Avrom's head was up and looking. I prayed we could make him laugh – or at least feel happy, wherever he was inside there. Igor was wiping his eyes. My sketch was going so well I put my hand to my mouth scared that my play would seem too sad, dull, after such laughter. On the way home maybe people would say that after the intermission it wasn't so good as the first half?

'An encore you'll work out for tomorrow,' Benjamin frowned at Drushki and Pinchas as they came back amazed from their fourth curtain, failing to praise them as always. 'But only a short one; a circus this isn't.'

As we had heard his sniffy views on drama as against the shocking indignity of tumbling and juggling many times already, there was nothing to do but thump the backs of our two non-theatricals, who were equally baffled by their success.

Leah was born dancing, that's what the family said. That Isadora Duncan was trying to say something with her feet, but my sister made you *feel* something with hers. Now Mama wasn't around to argue with her, she had taken weeks and weeks choosing the music, driving Hersch sick sometimes – but when she had what she wanted, she unstitched the movements, climbed inside, sewed them up and put feet on them. Amazing. Extra sadness in her dancing these days – extra gaiety too, mind you. Growing up, is it? Or motherhood, maybe? (Will I ever get the chance to stop being jealous of mothers?) So I watch Leah with love and feel almost like a mother to her myself.

The family; we make happy faces at each other over the off-stage piano we're leaning on to see her and even here, backstage, we're clapping. Pinchas covers her quick in a shawl but even he's pink with pride.

And now, Hersch and Pinchas are pushing the piano on and – when did they decide to do that? Everyone's going nuts laughing again. They're pretending the piano hasn't got wheels and every inch is a big struggle. That's really funny – oh I see, two wheels have really fallen out and are lying here in the wings with us. It's good. Tomorrow the wheels we won't put back. Pinchas comes off, out of puff and coughing and it's jealousy I feel when Leah undoes his stiff collar and he smiles his modest love at her.

Hersch's monologue isn't going well. Last week it sounded funnier. You know what, it isn't funny at all – only twelve he is and in his eyes you can see that he knows the fire's gone out under the samovar. Quick, finish already. It's the time of the evening when the good people who came to our new theatre and paid up their money have been here for two or more hours and bad things from home they're beginning to remember. Maybe tomorrow Hersch could sing some of his own made-up songs instead – oh, poor child. The bit of clapping they're making is only for kindness. Did the kritikers from the newspapers come? How could you tell? Who knows what they look like? The *Stage*, the *Playgoer*, the *Daily Eastern News*, Igor's *Pall Mall* we even sent a free ticket. Well, sometimes someone they send to the little theatres to show how snobs they're not. The Jewish papers, tickets we don't send: they have to come anyway. Igor says in London they only stay the first hour then go home and put their feet up. I was worried as that way they'd miss my play but please G-d they'd missed Hersch tonight. Benjamin's saying something to him as he comes off red with shame. I hope . . . oy, an encore? Who asked him back? The kleinele's sitting at the piano again and . . . goot. He's playing *Roshenkes mit Mandeln* and they're crying and swaying and singing with each last line of the chorus, '*Shloff sie, Yidele, shloff!*' And the four men who aren't singing, they must be the kritikers.

And the audience is shouting more titles at Hersch and he's playing every one and they laugh and clap through the funny songs and when they cry we cry a little too. I know Benjamin thinks all this is vulgar, but so what? They're happy and they're singing their throats so dry much lemonade they're going to buy.

When they let Hersch stop and the shouting stops and we find the lights again, out we go, Pinchas, Drushki, Hersch and me, and shopkeepers we become, selling drinks and oranges and the posh little boxes of chocolates I swore no one would afford, just like at the Pavilion. And how soon before I'm standing with them all, my hands wet, my feet curling with fear, waiting for *Only One Day* to begin.

What a play.

True, Pinchas is not strong enough as the wicked father of the boy they say is a musical genius, but when the boy gets his precious fingers crushed in an accident at the workshop where he is forced to work instead of 'wasting all his hours shpiln pyano' the shock of the accident kills the father nice and early in the play so Pinchas is free to shlep around the scenery and the furniture for the workshop and the parlour and the grand drawing-room of the Great Master. Benjamin plays this fine teacher with such . . . but listen, the story I was telling you. So, the Master not only believes the boy can play brilliantly with the seven fingers that he has left but writes special music for him himself and, happy ending on happy ending, with the Mama falls in love also.

'Der shrayber,' they called and called.

'All writers have to be men?' Drushki sulked as I edged past them all, more willing to be screamed and whistled at for writing this play than anything else I'd ever done.

Somehow it's midnight and everyone's gone home. Only each other to say vunderlekh to and the perfume of achievement is so strong who can smell tiredness. Whilst Drushki and Benjamin sit cross-legged on the stage as if the two tailors in *Di Hoyzn*, counting not stitches but Rubenovska money, Pinchas and Hersch drag the furniture around, change the scenery, pull pulleys and call to each other without interruption, Leah and I take the two best brooms to sweep under the seats.

Benjamin's so excited about the takings – and they're only half way through counting – he starts to 'if' this and 'if' that. We'll see, we'll see. But see or not even after all the place is clean and ready for tomorrow, when the adding's been done and Hersch has argued but gone to bed at last because of school tomorrow, we're still too excited to close up and get to sleep. Frankenberg's won't be open – soon it will, we promise each other – so we start to cook whatever we have and right where we've cleaned it we dirty the stage up again with our party and when a knocking on the doors we hear it's Igor back to join us. After taking Avrom back to the hospital in his motor car, he too couldn't sleep without talking about this evening. Tonight he's a Rubenovska and even my Benjamin has some respect and thanks him for all that he has done.

And when the last 'gei gezint' had been waved to Igor as he backfires off into the dawn, when the last candle has been set in the saucers of our neglected rooms, as my cold toes and shoulders warm in the welcoming wrap of my Benjamin's body, we sigh and wriggle and agree that tomorrow plenty of worries we can find. From the mouths of our first-nighters to the ears of their cousins and friends of their friends will come the good words and the bad words about the Rubenovskas whatever the papers say, whatever we say to one another. So quick it gets around a Yiddishe neighbourhood, tomorrow they could be queuing down as far as the City or Pinchas could be pasting 'Last Two Nights' on his beautiful posters.

'Zee-Zee? Aah, Zee-Zee.'

You should excuse me.

ACT IV

SCENE I

Shabbos, 24 August 1907

Barmitzvah boys, they're a miracle.

Their vulnerable knees covered, sometimes for the first time, by long trousers today. Clean and sombre, varying from up here to down there in size, loved to bits, babies still, solemnly taking upon themselves such vows. Today I am a Man, they squeak and all of a sudden, one day it'll be true.

In the packed synagogue in Tenter Street it was hot. Stifling. A gloriously oppressive August day for our nice new clothes that were too thick, too substantial. And a little bit tight. I whispered to Leah and she nodded her new hat and reached to help me off with my jacket. Better. Then all the women could see I was expecting.

Leah and I had managed to wedge ourselves into the front row of the ladies' gallery but now from this row and every row, from so many faces I'd never seen before, came kind smiles, wise nods, encouraging expressions, even a little budge-up to give us more room. Motherhood is the biggest secret society I ever joined.

The clear Rubenovska voice Hersch used so well did not, of course, have the power to silence the strong tradition of indecorum in the congregation as he chanted the Sedra for the week but when he looked up and smiled at us, Leah and I stopped whispering together for a little and even Drushki, who didn't need religious clap-trap because she was a socialist, blew down a surprising kiss of encouragement from behind us. And through the long rituals Leah and I sniffled and snuffled into our Brussels lace, initialled handkerchiefs as if we were Annie herself seeing him so competent and grown-up in the fine worsted Holborn suit we had finally agreed on from Gamages, the five-button waistcoat just showing the silk tie Igor had added.

The stage – the bimah, I mean – started to clear. The solo performance, the Haftorah, was about to begin. Only three men stayed with Hersch. My Benjamin, standing in for Lev, Pinchas as Hersch's teacher and the resident rabbi to see fair play. A row full of his friends just barmitzvahed themselves or just about to be, jostled and pushed to catch his eye, make him laugh. Benjamin put a quick hugging arm round Hersch for luck just in time. The rabbi took in a breath to call Hersch's Hebrew name out loudly but – just a minute, Pinchas is praying.

The rabbi lifted his eyebrows and shrugged his face. You could see he was thinking that if everyone started praying a morning service could take even longer. At last.

'Chaim ben Levi!'

Hersch, son of Lev, surrounded by the silence always respected round this tuneful party-piece, was making the delicious throat-lumping musical phrases rise and fall in the hushed shul and it was time for Leah and me to cry again in Annie's place. Family is family. And when he was hurrying through the easy last four blessings that we could all join in, I could barely swallow enough to sing I felt such pride and love for this thirteen-year-old so far from his parents. If only we knew if they would approve of how we had loved him.

'Shokoyech!' the whole shul shouted with an enthusiasm reserved for fine singers, good scholars and wealthy sons.

Another few minutes and I'd have to put back on my new shoes that were killing me and shake hands with everyone and our friends would come with us to the wine and food of the Kiddush that was laid out ready under damp cloths on our stage.

'Adon Olom . . .' This last song of the morning sounded out louder and more joyfully on barmitzvah mornings. Hersch had done us proud.

Life getting easier has not, so far, torn us asunder as the rabbis and Pinchas warn us it might. I'm having this precious baby, please G-d, in two months time; I've got my fine bed; from Igor, a bit at a time, we've started to buy the theatre. Terrible it isn't.

The Family Theatre is just sort of catching on. The Zigmans aren't our only regular patriotten any more. We've had to change things. Every week something new we have to have. So Igor has himself a new assistant who doesn't need a drawer for her plays and on the typewriter Igor gave me to take home, plays leak out on to the paper because they're needed – Leah tells me it's the same with milk for babies.

It's the last chorus and I must start fighting with my shoes. If my legs will last out, this is going to be some day.

'. . . Finally, thank you to everyone here for your wonderful presents,' Hersch nodded behind him to the table heaped with things he wanted and things he didn't want, 'and to my cousins Zelda and Ben-Ben and Leah and Pinchas and Drushki who have done everything for me since I left home and have been my family and . . . and today would have been perfect if only my Mama and my Tata and Manny and Katya and . . .'

A fine speechmaker. Look at us all choked with tears. How Annie and Lev must regret having let Hersch go, never to see him again, perhaps, till he's grown. Feeling the baby inside me leap with fear I held it with both hands and promised it never to let it go from my side till it was from choice.

'L'chayim.'

Wineglasses were lifted. To Life, indeed. I drank for me, for my Benjamin, for our baby, for Hersch, for the future and I couldn't speak for tears.

'Zelda?' Leah tucked an escaped black tangle under one of those dreadful scarves Pinchas still makes her wear off-stage. She leaned up and kissed me. 'Something I want to talk to you about.'

'I want to bring in some more food,' I said, eyeing the tables, wondering at the spaces. 'Help me take out the empty plates, then we'll talk.'

163

The fish-balls had long gone, the hot cakes going like hot cakes. Leaning between two of Hersch's school teachers who had wanted to come for his big day, I gathered up the empty greasy platters and took them to the improvised kitchen we had made in the biggest dressing-room, followed by Leah with a big tray full of plates and dirty glasses.

'Zelda. Zelda help me. Take this.' Leah shoved the tray in my hands and ran out past me, past the other dressing-rooms. From the klozet came noises – oh poor Leah.

'Any help you girls need?'

Mrs Zigman and I stood helplessly listening to the painful retching from the klozet. 'A daughter's what I always wanted,' Mrs Zigman sighed, 'but at least my sons can't get pregnant and be in pain like that. Your poor Mama should only be here to see you both like this.'

Leah pregnant again. No wonder she wanted to talk. No wonder she had kept so quiet about it. A second baby and no more Rubenovska, no more theatre, Pinchas had demanded.

'Zelda,' Leah called weakly. 'I've spoilt my dress.'

'You go see to your sister,' Mrs Zigman said. 'Food I can manage. I'll take in more of everything, yes?'

'You're a guest, Mrs Zigman –'

'It's a pleasure. See to Leah.'

'Mrs Zigman – please keep Leah's secret, yes? Even Pinchas doesn't –'

'Leave it to me. And Drushki? Where's Drushki? She can't also help?' Mrs Zigman, like a needle and thread to our torn afternoon started bustling, catering, managing.

'Come to my room, Leah,' I said, helping her up the stairs.

I helped her unhook her dress, soaked a handkerchief in lavender water for her forehead and as she lay back, white and red-eyed, I tried not to mind her crushing our pink-striped dimity quilt. I fetched her another handkerchief to cry on.

'What am I going to do?' she sobbed.

'You'll wear one of my old dresses,' I said.

'No, I mean . . .'

I knew what she meant. We needed Mama now. Too many worries. It was seven months ago we'd been excited that

Mama was coming; sometimes I knew that the delays and the frights, the tightening up of regulations and the wonderfully inventive edicts would finally defeat her and we would never see her again. We hadn't known it was Tata's last wave from the turnip field. Mama's too?

'Don't you cry too, Zelda, or we'll never get back to the party,' Leah sobbed.

I gave her a hug. I'd do what Mama always said. Worry about one thing at a time.

'If you don't want Pinchas to know about the baby yet . . .' Leah shook her head, crying again, '. . . then you'll have to say you spilt herring . . .'

'Don't even *say* herring,' Leah laughed and cried.

'And I'll sew you into this dress, look. I was making it for you for that new play *A Bissel Meshugah*. It's a bit dark but if you'll stitch a lace collar on it and I get out my box . . .'

Since she was a child she could do it. I watched her shoulders come down, her cheeks fill with colour, her chin lift, her eyes clear. She jumped up, chose a white rose for the neck of the dress, caught up some folds at the hem all round like the latest model and was humming and sewing. Me? Three days I'd have been unhappy inside and my face showing it for two.

Arm in arm we slipped back to the still noisy party. How long had we been away with our troubles outside? Not long enough for my Benjamin to miss me.

Pearl Wise, a cousin of the Frankenbergs, the Behrens' young actress, sat looking up at my husband with a sparkle like rainwater. Pearl Wise and her two sisters, Tilly and Roochel, were being told a story by the great story-teller, Benjamin Rubenovska. I sighed. Then I sighed again.

Pretending I hadn't seen them and didn't ache to join them, I picked up two full plates of food to give me something useful to do.

'Thank you, Mrs Zigman,' I said, pushing a plate under her nose.

'For what are you thanking me? Till your Mama comes, you girls are my girls. She's all right, Leah? Good. Sit next to me. Don't worry about your guests. Starving they're not. And at a barmitzvah like this the talking's as good as the eating. If I'd realized that sooner, I maybe wouldn't look like this,' she laughed, spreading her hands to show her spreading body. 'Sit. You're tired, Zelda, for myself I can see it. And why shouldn't you be? All Leah talks about is how much you did for today. The arranging, the thinking, up at five to get all this ready, yes? Up all night too? I know. Only a woman knows.'

'You cooked the fish for us.'

'The fish? That's nothing. That's my job. I'm a mother. A mother feels. This you'll know soon enough,' she said, patting my growing baby with such genuine warmth that the tiny ice-sacks of worry kept frozen long enough to give Leah the strength to face her new problems, finally melted at the unwilling corners of my eyes.

Then Pearl laughed again out loud. It wasn't good for Benjamin to be so adored but – nobody could help themselves; least of all, me. I'd go to him – in a minute.

But suddenly me, secretive me, there I was unlocking one or three of my brassbound trunks of worry. Going on and on about how we fretted because Mama hadn't answered the letter about her date of departure, about Leah and Pinchas and her dread of leaving the stage. About my dreading being put back up there on the stage to replace her, about Drushki, well, look at her, about how strict Pinchas was getting with Hersch, about not knowing how to look after babies, about the pain and the torture everyone said it would be, about . . . and then there was . . .

It had taken some while to notice the strain even on the kindly face of poor Mrs Zigman. I stopped guiltily, a little giddy as though I'd been turning round and round on my toes instead of just in my mind.

'To talk everybody needs,' Mrs Zigman kissed me kindly. 'It helps, yes?'

'It helps,' I nodded dutifully, bitterly aware that it did no such thing, only making you feel worse to hear for yourself how pathetic you were and now someone else knew too.

'You know what they say, my dear. A person lives from day to day but a Jew lives from minute to minute. Every minute as it comes. Time heals all wounds. Things can only get better. Everything's for the best. When one door closes another opens. G-d is good . . .'

Streams of phrases like this have glued Jewish life together for so many centuries it's a wonder none of our oppressors have yet got around to forbidding their use.

And now Mrs Zigman was looking from Benjamin and the Wise girls to me. Did being a mother pull the shutters away from the windows and tell her the worries I hadn't told her?

'A little shmoosing, a little flirting keeps a man healthy,' she said. 'My Sam would be like that if he wasn't so short and had more hair. Now you've rested you'll go and keep an eye on your handsome husband.' She waved me away, smiling, perhaps not as silly as she sometimes sounded.

'Zelda, my dear,' Benjamin said, showing off, taking one of my hands but not seeing me.

'Excuse me,' I said, too proud to stay, tearful with anger and pleased to see Igor across the stage, unattended, sad, watching me.

When I came up to him, nice, he smiled. He was pleased to see me. Soothing it was. I offered him a glass of wine but he didn't want one and went to get two chairs for us.

'Young Hersch is a boy you can really take to,' Igor said, looking round at him with his friends. 'No worries about his future. Except — well of course I'd like to make him a special present — some money for when he's grown, but do I put it in his name? In yours? Who does he belong to until his parents . . .?'

Another worry, Mrs Zigman. I keep putting this off 'until Mama arrives' as I've asked her to speak to Annie and Lev about that.

'You're very kind . . .'

'You're my family, almost,' Igor said looking down at his slim-laced shoes that would look better on my Benjamin's narrow feet. 'I just wish —' sanding the floor with his shoe and looking unhappy, 'I don't want to push myself in, but Zelda it would be good if I could spend more time with you. With you all,' he added miserably.

I looked back at Benjamin who didn't seem to want to waste his farthings of time on me and wondered if Pearl and Igor would perhaps like an introduction.

'I mean, Zelda, you really should see good English plays if you want to write them. I could take you to see the really good shows Up West. There's so much to see and you'll maybe come back with new ideas?'

New ideas I could use.

'That would be lovely, Igor. It's easy to get stale, writing only for the family. Perhaps they'd all take a night off and we could all go?'

Igor talked on kindly, gently, soothingly. A real mensch, Igor. Now, thanks to him, thanks to my classes, always in English we spoke together. Sometimes I forgot it was difficult, it was getting so much easier. Another worry: Benjamin was going to be a foreigner to our children. All of us, even Leah, had been to classes but Benjamin had made up his mind that Yiddish was enough and that was that. So every minute, 'Ich farshtay nit' he's saying and all of us bored with translating for him everywhere but inside our theatre where Yiddish belonged. But in the real world you also have to live.

'So,' Igor was saying. 'We'll sit down with the newspaper and a calendar and we'll work out when you can all come and what we'll see. That'll be nice. Something to look forward to.'

Igor followed my wandering attention.

'Who are the young ladies? Cousins?'

Pearl, Tilly and Roochel were putting their little wraps round themselves and Benjamin was leaning all over them kissing their hands, so at least they were going.

'Come and meet them, Igor. Pearl acts with the Behrens. They are Frankenbergs. When they're older they'll all look like Lily.'

I hoped.

Watching the extra time Benjamin took with the hand of Pearl before she left it's a wonder two holes weren't bored into it. Igor had escorted them back to their home and I put a nearly-forgiving arm through Benjamin's and my weary head on his shoulder.

'You put on a wonderful party for Hersch, Zee-Zee. I'm really proud of you. How are you feeling?'

I look round. Everyone's having a good time. Hersch is laughing. Leah and Pinchas are having a nice talk with a few of their new, quiet, sober friends. Maybe Drushki looks worse than she feels; she's reading a leaflet to someone I don't know. Avrom's asleep where we put him in the corner. And Benjamin is very gently rubbing my back.

I'm feeling all right, that's how I'm feeling.

He's arrived at last. I was ready too early. Igor Lottenstein has arrived outside the Family Theatre with his 1907 Vauxhall Mark II and this one's a four-seater and makes more noise than thunder. It's shiny like a japanned money-box. The whole street of step-sitters of the buildings opposite paused as they fanned their sweaty faces, moving the tight, still London air with fans of corrugated paper, pointing, nudging, shouting, half-heartedly swearing at their barefoot brats to come away from the dangers the motor car's dramatic loud dust seemed to herald.

'Such a lovely summer's night,' Igor says, helping me on with my bolero.

It is? In Wisherodik on a night like this the sweet-smelling jasmine would be yearning for the pruning fingers of pretty young girls, who tuck stolen pieces of scented blossom in their bodices. And here in London? The street muck just smells a little stronger. In Wisherodik on a night like this, Pashka Yankel would put his tables and chairs outside his cafe and laughing families would quick make them sticky with summer yoghourts and plum pastries. And here in London? The restaurants just opened the windows to let in a lot more flies. Why suddenly so homesick tonight? Who knows. Perhaps I'm tired of Benjamin and my family being so difficult. Perhaps a London baby I never expected to have. One thing I know: a Mama I need.

I call out that I'm going to my Binyomin, to anyone. Nobody answers, so I give up and shut the door.

'Lovely, isn't she?' Igor said, stroking the motor car mirror

169

free from summer dust. 'It's more comfortable in the front,' he said shyly, 'but sit where you like, Zelda.'

I got in at the front, sniffing lovingly at the leather and tied a long white scarf over my blue opera-hat.

From the streets the children and their parents shout agreement that these bleddy rich Yids don't arf know 'ow to live, but there's good humour in the joking and waving and more than a hint of admiration too as I turn back to wink and wave at our neighbours.

'Lovely,' I repeated, meaning everything: the motor car, the weather, the company, our destination, being free.

'Shame no one else could come but it's nice to have you to myself,' Igor said, lowering his voice from its shout as he waited for a rag-and-bone cart to get out of the way at a crossing.

Nice? Believe me, Igor, it's a pleasure. The Rubenovskas are, just at the moment, you should pardon me, an ache in a place a young lady doesn't mention.

For once the theatre is closed. Tomorrow too, maybe. Until the builders had put the bulging wall straight, no performances, the inspector said. So a night out at an English theatre Igor had planned for us all.

'I wish I could join you,' Benjamin had said insincerely, his feet up on a footstool as I dressed. 'But someone has to be here or the builders, they'll pull down the wall, not build it up; you know what they are.'

Benjamin had known for weeks about *The Merry Widow* tonight. He could come, but I knew why not. English, that's why.

'If you understood English you'd come,' I muttered quietly enough so he'd be sure not to hear, angry not to be able to share this treat with him tonight.

Pinchas arranged some teaching tonight and won't let his pupil down so Leah must stay with Jacob and Drushki's Sarah and is, in any case, too weary to come out. Drushki, of course, is still in the hospital, and Hersch's cheder class has gone on a seaside holiday to Southend, however much Pinchas didn't like the idea.

Up West the shops were shutting already. Only eight o'clock and outmuster had begun.

In the close hotness of the streets, shop-girls were arm in arm, loosening jackets; the younger girls had taken them off. Ties were rolled, studs and collars flew, the sun caught the shiny silks of waistcoats held over young lads' arms. Staff back doors hung with admirers, alert and lounging. It made me feel quite old as I watched the teasing and the laughter of it all. I hadn't ever been young like them. Shame I still loved Benjamin so much; sometimes I think he's bad for me – like with Leah and strawberries.

The streets were full. And all of us – 'out on the town' the Londoners called it – with our carriages and motor cars and hansom cabs couldn't help wishing all these workers would give us a space or two to get to our theatres on time. Curtain up at 8.30. Already I was worried at our lateness because the staring before it begins is half the joy for me and tonight there would be plenty worth staring at.

At Cambridge Circus I could see the Palace of Varieties had the builders in too. I wonder where they were off to, tonight.

Past the Hicks Theatre and the Apollo, then the Lyric in Shaftesbury Avenue and there: Daly's. We could see it but not move towards it. Later and later.

At last, Igor handed me down from my seat and hurried me towards the grand entrance.

Not only was I fat and awkward, but dowdy and unfashion-able and I felt glum with myself. The mirror in the bedroom had lied. It had spoken of simple dignity and neatness and meant dullness and safety. My head was tired from twisting everywhere. These women were alive with flowers. High-standing tortoiseshell combs and elaborate hair ornaments they didn't know about in the East End. Who would have thought that hair should be like that at the back and so at the sides. And how it matters if you didn't know.

We were no strangers to theatre crowds – didn't they queue every day wet or dry for standing room to see my Benjamin do a new Bar Kokhba in July? But the hugger-mugger here was altogether different. Being at Daly's was almost enough, without seeing any show at all. The women had the air of accomplishment about them, not of having lived through another day but of drawn-threadwork neatness, of arpeggios on a well-tuned piano. The men, careless, carefree, not here to forget for a few hours their needles and their fatigue. Just to be here.

I listened to the dainty laughter, the leisured fanciness. It was enchanting. All in English and me, here, part of it. Hersch says my accent still is terrible, but nearly every word I can understand – even jokes, sometimes in the *Punch* magazine. Igor never spoke Yiddish to me any more; I was proud of that. And with Benjamin not here to translate and think for, English you could even think in.

Look at that fichu, that dress. If Leah were here she could copy it all tomorrow. I tried to hold the details in my head. At least on the stage the Rubenovskas were right up to date in the fashions; our audience demanded it.

We dawdled up the wide steps to the dress circle in the perfumed squash at the pace of the fashionable theatregoers not anxious to be too early in their seats. I had to stop myself from picking my dress up high and rushing through them. Mother-of-pearl opera glasses clutched to jewelled bosoms, opera-hats flattened against well-nourished chests, the show just another ingredient of the tasty dish stewed here.

The woman attendant with corns sticking out of her flat slippers looked distastefully at our tickets, sold Igor two programmes, though I tried to give one back, and took us to our seats, sighing.

'Front row! However did you do that?' I gasped.

'Bribery. So they couldn't understand it when they got the five other seats back to sell again. Your family are the end. So, Zelda dear, what do you think of Daly's?'

What did I think? I unbuttoned my jacket, flicked the ruffled collar of my new blouse out over its edge as I'd rehearsed in my mirror before resting my arms on the plush velvet of the balcony rim to think about it.

Like ours, Daly's theatre had electricity, but here crystal teardrops of glass hung electrified from the gilded, moulded ceilings, and the walls looked as if they wouldn't dare to bulge. And from under the pelmet of the extravagant curtains, thick like a good book on a rainy day, came light I couldn't even understand where it came from. And down there, japanned iron music-stands like bare trees waiting for music-leaves as the musicians in their tailcoats, not one of them under fifty, tried and tried for the right note, rudely drowning out the polite stalls conversation. So even here in the West End theatres weren't always perfect, Benjamin would be pleased to hear.

'You'd think,' I said, pointing to them, 'they'd do that before they came to sit down.'

Igor smiled but said nothing.

The big, beautiful boxes were beginning to fill. A wonder to see so many people wave or bow to one another yet stay in their seats, not visiting. And something else was missing: children. True there were some older girls and boys, slicked and scrubbed and tightly restrained between parents, but no small ones ran, jumped the steps, handed half oranges each to each.

The lights went out all in one go – a hundred lamp-dowsers working together. Then a violinist walked late to his front seat under sudden unexpected applause – for being the last to arrive, presumably. He was followed by a broad hurrying man with a baton for whom the applause was even louder.

I muttered darkly that to make a Jewish audience that enthusiastic you at least had to do something and Igor laughed as the baton brought the drums and the cellos from retirement, the violins sung together like a choir and before my tears of delight had had time to dry a waltz was being played that started the wet joys of music flowing again. And when those curtains went up – up? Sideways isn't good enough? – a thousand beautiful women and gorgeous men in uniforms the Tsar never ordered, waltzed on a stage big enough for a street of houses.

What did I think? I thought the Family Theatre was a lot like a cowshed after all.

'A mel-o-dy in waltz time, dah-dah dee-dee la-la . . .' I couldn't stop humming it, thinking it, even as we drove jerkily, jammed again against all the home-going hansoms and carriages. 'You'll find him at Maxim's, la dee dee dee dee dah.'

'So? *The Merry Widow* you liked?' said Igor, smiling. 'Something like that you could write?'

'Well on the quiet, Igor, a play I've written already I was going to take maybe to one of these big theatres but – well I've got my ideas all wrong. Again I'll have to start.'

I pictured the fat file of papers I'd been working on with scratched out words and grammar that was still a struggle and hated the time I'd wasted. Angry tears leaked and vanished again. Waves of new ideas crashed on to the shores of my play-writing mind and drew back again leaving only a scummy ring; until an idea was so good it didn't need any encouragement, I wouldn't ask for any anyway.

'Singing they don't all have?'

'No, Zelda. It's operetta and it's all the rage, that's all. The plays this year – they're very serious. Now, what have I seen? Well dear, there was one about an anonymous letter . . .'

I listened but the story Igor told me would have been better, altogether, played for full rolling laughs. Through Cheapside to Aldgate High Street, where we turned off into Mansell Street, a hundred old plots came racing in and out again. To make those fancy gentlemen cheer, stamp and whistle like they had tonight, to make so many small lace handkerchiefs wet, in so many dorothys and chatelaines, new it would have to be. New and very funny indeed. Going bump-bump in a car in the dark, with a stomach like a bolster, who can think funny?

As we shook to a stop outside in the alley, the Family Theatre lights still, to my surprise, shone everywhere.

'Oh no,' I sighed. No quiet, relaxed Benjamin who would show me the finished wall and take me, after the moaning I'd put up with, arm-in-arm to bed. No; he'd stay watching over every brick position and drive the builders even slower. I made my resigned face to myself and reached for my glittery little bag.

'So late the builders are still working,' Igor said. 'Zelda –'

He held me back by the arm.

'A million thank yous, Igor,' I said, leaning over and kissing him. 'Vunderlekh it was. If ever again a night off we have, Benjamin and I will take you out somewhere nice, yes?'

'Zelda – being with you tonight has been such a pleasure . . .'

The theatre doors flung inwards and a woman stood there, her bun coming a little unpinned.

'In England,' she said, 'in the middle of the night pregnant women come home, at last, to their husbands? In England other men take them to the teater? So, what did you see? A play you can bake from it, Zeldele, choochele? So big you are! Like next week it looks you're due. You'll introduce me, efsher, to your driver? But first, a kiss, maybe?'

'Mama? Mamele! Oh, Mama!'

INTERLUDE

23 October 1907

Funny thing, a journal. When you read it through again, the most important things you've left out. Who knows why. You maybe have the important things so much in your head you know you'll never forget them. The twenty-third already, and the world just changed and what did I write? Nothing. Not only nothing about Katya, my tiny room-sharer, a long-legged schoolgirl now sent with Mama to live with us, but nothing about Mama settling in, and nothing, not a word about my baby. Eleven days old and I'm sorry I didn't put it down, all the muddled, worried, loving feelings before they begin to fade. Mama keeps on saying my beautiful baby Dovid (named for Tata, olev hashalom) had an easy birth and I heard my Benjamin boast the same to Pinchas. For who, easy? For long the pain I hope I don't remember or brothers Dovid won't play with. But the loving jerking moving blinking mottled living lump who seemed to put his arms out to me, those tears, that moment, I never want to forget. As Drushki joked, in three weeks, when I'm stronger, Dovid will be just right for the baby in *Shlomo's Judgement*, and I should rehearse him for the audition.

She jokes more these days, since she's out of the hospital. Shame she had to get thin that way but her clothes look better now and she uses her stick like a weapon. So proud, she is, you can't feel sorry for her.

'With care a few years you can live yet,' Dr Turiansky said to her.

'And without care, even longer,' she said in her usual bitter way to us.

Maybe. Please G-d.

24 October 1907

Only twelve days and Mrs Levy (she says we're to call her
Mother Levy but though it's only six weeks since she arrived
here, one Mama's quite enough for me, if you know what I
mean) says tomorrow I can go home. I had a walk right down
the passidge yesterday and though my legs were like herring
fillets, my insides stayed inside and didn't fall out like I was
dreading. Dovid feeds quick as quick and I'm holding him nice
like I'm a real mother and know what I'm doing, nearly.

And I've made up my mind, whatever Mama tells me, I'll lie
a little. 'Mother Levy says it the modern way to do it,' I'll say,
or, 'Boys are different, Mama.' I don't want to hurt her, but
right away the moment she got here she started to take over
and . . . am I being terrible? Of course I am. But for three years
we managed; along she comes, just when things are easy and
right away she can do everything better than us. And strangely
enough my Benjamin admires every word she says and
everything she does. And she isn't his – she's my Mama.
Terrible, it is. Leah brought Katya along to see my Dovid this
morning. I love that child. She's not sunny and funny like
Herschele but solemn and loving and homesick and how Leah
and I try to make it up to her. She was disappointed that Dovid
mostly just lies there sleeping but we promised her more fun
with him at home.

Home: there's a pekl of worries. The bassinet I know Leah
and Mama have sewn ready and I long to see it but how can I
be down at the stage and up with Dovid when he gets older?
How can I write when he's running about? Will we ever be
alone again, my Benjamin and I now Mama and Katya have
moved in and Drushki's staying 'just for now' and – oy.
Perhaps I can think more clearly when I'm not so tired. And
who can sleep when they've a baby's breathing to worry
about?

8 November 1907

Mama's a real greener. Compared to her, we're English as
King Edward; except my Benjamin, of course. When the first
Guy Fawkes Day firecracker went off on Tuesday, you'd have

thought it was in Mama's petticoats. And after the next couple of squibs, for all our explanations ('Plot? Shplot? Fire is fire. It reminds me too much.'), she stayed all day inside and was amazed we had nearly a house full that night.

'*Di Freylech Almoneh* is in its second week. Lehar wouldn't recognize it. His waltz we've bettered. It's a Polische peasant dance now, but still the cheerful woman is a widow at least. Leah's Becky of Besserabia has all Lily Elsie's fun without being so naughty. Shame. That Pinchas, the way he fusses over silly things.

My Dovid is putting weight on, you can see it. And except through the night he's so good. I put him on the table where Leah makes up and if there's time we just stare at him and try to think who he looks like. Benjamin's colouring, of course. But such a nose? That shape chin? A complexion like a cold-cream pot? Any baby would have done, I kept telling G-d, but to send such a perfect one? Leah still cries sometimes about that miss when we're together, but what is she? Still only one-and-twenty. Time yet.

19 November 1907

A long talk I had with Mama, yesterday, no, the day before; Sunday. Now we've moved the stage furniture down under the stage – that little ladder of steps down into where the beer barrels used to go is worth a fortune to us – we made a parlour on stage-level before it could quick be filled up again with hat-stands and mirrors and halves of boats. Mama thinks nothing of it but for us, who've been without a place to gather together for three years it's like being normal again, a family again. Somewhere to go when we want to squabble and disagree with each other.

But what I meant to write was what Mama and I talked about on Sunday. It's funny but Mama doesn't really feel easy with me like she does with my Benjamin. It's as though I'm not theatre enough for her. They're performers and me, all I do is give them something to perform. When I'm having a good day, I hum and smile and know that without me silent they'd be but – well, who gets in all the papers? They do. Whose photogravures are all over the theatre? Not mine.

So – about Sunday. I can't stop thinking about it, yet it's as though I don't want to write it down in case I won't get it quite right. Gevalt, it's time to feed Dovid. How long has he been crying? When I'm writing, nothing I hear. And then tickets I'm selling. Another day I'll write about my talk with Mama.

24 *November 1907*
So, a week ago, last Sunday just gone. (Still, crowds we turn away every night for *Di Freylech Almoneh* and we decided last night to keep it going till my first pantomime – a sort of play for children they have here in England to be taken to by kind uncles.)

So, I was saying about Mama. Now we've got our own Dovid, Mama is more of a real person to me, you know? She's only forty-five. That's not so old. She's maybe ten, fifteen years more to live. Longer, in our family. Look at Bubba, olev hashalom. And all of a sudden, Mama's talking to me like I'm a mensch too. Nothing much, just about when she was young and about Tata and how she fell in love with him and what her best parts were when she was Leah's age – stuff I'd heard before, stuff I hadn't heard before but real, honest – as though I was a woman, not a daughter. And I realized very slowly and with terrible pain that I hadn't really loved her before. Tata was always my favourite, so much so, that I didn't see Mama as anything but a walking, talking trouble-machine, who wanted us to sit pretty, stand straight, dance nice, sing loud, speak up and stop sulking. How she must miss Tata. So although she doesn't usually like it, I got up and hugged her. And though her arms didn't move to hug me back, she smiled and smiled gently. Next time, she'd hug me. I could tell. And that's all that happened. But since she came here it's the first time I've been happy.

ACT IV

SCENE II
January 1908

'Everything isn't pantomime!' Mama screamed at Katya. 'For what are you smiling? Dying's funny? You walk on, you see your poor Mama's so ill. You'd smile? Put your head down. Down! See? What do you need to see? Just act.'

So Katya walked off again and on again – this time laughing. That's the stage for you: once something's funny, it's funny.

Mama went mad and Benjamin put his arm round Katya in sympathy. Look, Katya, when you want to look sad, when you want to look like it's the end of the world, it's your Cousin Zelda you should study.

The thing I can't forgive this time is that I didn't guess for myself what was going on. Even though Benjamin started to be so tender to me again, even though he'd been coming later and later back from Frankenberg's, even though a dozen things I should have noticed, it was Drushki who told me bluntly. That Pearl Wise had fallen for Benjamin was her own fault. That Benjamin should be making such a cruel advantage of it must surely be mine. Me, I'm not enough for him; I'm maybe not the right woman for him. We came from such a tiny village that for Benjamin in Wisherodik it wasn't so much that he chose me as that I was nearest. The prize bridegroom I won for myself is all the time looking for a better bride.

Look at him; head down, leaning into his hand. Thinking of Pearl Wise? Remembering how she looked last night in the moonshine after they'd relaxed at Frankenberg's? Remembering her face as he whispered . . . ?

'Ssh!' Mama hissed as my chair scraped noisily back.

'Without you, Mama,' Katya said, draping herself near to the old cane lounger we used for such scenes, 'I'm like a leaf with no tree to cling to.'

The old, old phrase from the old, old plot. But Katya, whose own Mama was a faraway tree, was feeling the words now and we all stopped to hear anew and sob a little inside. The child was blessed (cursed?) with the family gift of holding attention, making you care. Please G-d she'd use it more wisely than – some.

Issy, Leah's new baby, his stomach drum-tight with milk, let out a rehearsal-stopping burb, setting poor Katya off again into laughter and Mama into a fit.

Drushki's Sarah, stocky, sturdy, sensible, stood by with the crocheted blanket, ready to tuck it around the baby when Leah put him back inside the warm Moses basket, gazing at Issy with the blazing interest of the two-and-a-half-year-old cousin-mother.

'How does it look, Zelda?' Leah said, kissing Issy and on her way back to the stage.

'You're taking the dying a bit fast, Leah. She's not so much in pain as weakening. Like – the music's getting slower. Do you know what I'm getting at?'

Leah looked at me with admiration; I noticed because there wasn't much of it about at home and I was hungry for a little attention. I was, to be honest, sorry for myself. Pearl Wise. Pearl Wise.

'Mama should leave the managing to you, Zelda. You can always see these things. Benjamin says so to me, too.'

He does? Well why not? My Benjamin being unable to think for himself, I suppose any woman can push him around. Better it should be me.

Hadn't it always been me who knew what was wrong in play after play, scene after scene? A manager. That's what I'd like to be. All right, none of them would take much notice of what I said to begin with but when they saw that my ideas worked – even Mama would finally listen. And I really must, I yawned, seeing Leah still dying up there a while later, rewrite this scene. Even real tuberkuloz this long doesn't take. Ten different ways they'd shown *La Traviata* in London this last year. But as mine was the first Yiddish one, I made it with children in it, of course. Better like that. They should all do it.

'. . . without you I also don't want to live, Mama,' whispered Katya with such tight control even Drushki stopped folding her leaflets to look up.

'Yes, yes, yes, worse I've heard,' Mama said, meaning it was something better than perfect and kissing the top of Katya's head. 'Shoyn. To school, Katya, bubbele, tell them the ache from your stomach it stopped all of a sudden.'

'That's what I told them yesterday,' Katya said, picking up her school bag and blowing a kiss goodbye to Sarah, her special favourite, who cried to see her go. 'If a letter from my Mama comes, tell Hersch it's my turn to open it.' And she was gone, to learn things an actress didn't need to know.

And for how long could we keep from her that Annie wrote the good news to the children but to us she wrote the bad. Lev was watched every minute; their route out had been found and blocked. Every day, every letter, they cursed themselves that they hadn't let more of the children come here with Mama. One thing – we could stop worrying whether Annie and Lev would be upset that we were taking their children so much from school, taking them, too, from being ordinary children with ordinary lives. So long as they were free. How would Annie and Lev make that journey without the help that we had? How soon before they could try?

'Did you hear Mama's latest, Zelda,' Leah said, breaking in on my thoughts.

Up on stage Mama argues with Benjamin in the repentance scene. Let him go on rehearsing it – he's going to need it at home soon.

'What, Leah? What's Mama's latest?'

I'd pack a big box, take Dovid over my shoulder in a shawl and get on a boat – somewhere. Yes, back to Annie and I'd cry and cry and tell her that despite her help Benjamin didn't turn out to be such a bargain in the end.

'To England Jacob Adler's coming.'

'With his family? He'll close us down. Where did Mama hear?'

'In the paper. Happy he's not. But he's just travelling, here, there, back to Americhky maybe, if the unions will leave him alone, or if there's more trouble perhaps even Russia he'll try again. Look.'

Leah pushed the brown, smudgy, closely-written *Forward* to me, with pictures of Jacob Adler waving, Jacob Adler shrugging, Jacob Adler with a cane, waving a hat, kissing a child. '. . . in England but more than likely to settle in Russia.' Good, we could travel over the water together, maybe.

'And Mama wants him to come here and act with us. Can you imagine?'

He'd go to the Pavilion for certain and say how pleased he is to see so many Yiddish companies playing in London – but come here?

'Mama can ask.'

'No, Zelda. Mama's going to ask *you* to write and see.'

Of course I argued with Mama. But she's got this way and kept saying such a wonderful letter I wrote and if anyone could persuade him it was me and what could we lose, and there I was sitting with my pad and the only pencil I had down here with me asking Jacob Adler himself if he'd prefer to come to our kleinshtetldik playhouse than bother with the chandeliers and enormous stage and floor-traps that the Pavilion has in its velvet, glittery insides.

'Since I was a child, Mr Adler, I have heard of the wonders of your acting . . .' Nothing would be too shmaltzy if he were as easily flattered as that other great actor, Benjamin Rubenovska, the womanizing swine. 'With our own hands, Mr Adler, in the family-theatre tradition like your own, we have made a small Yiddish baby that to a giant could grow if you . . .'

Some scribbling out, some changes and I went up to get my best cream-laid envelopes and notepaper and wrote it over again nice and neat, no ink blobs.

When Igor came, I had to take it out of the carefully stuck down envelope for him to read. Of course he thought it was a brilliant idea; everything Mama did was like that for him. We knew Mama wouldn't be lonely for long.

Pinchas, who had given in only after quoting enough of his wise Talmudic sayings to make me want to wrap his tefillin round his gentle mouth, said that Leah could do 'just this one last play', and I suppose Leah can make him go on saying that for ever.

Drushki didn't answer from the back of the theatre when Mama called her to do over her small party-piece near the end of the play.

'Mama!' Leah called. 'Look at her!'

Drushki didn't try to push us away much as we helped her and covered her over, her hand still clutching an unfolded leaflet full of ideas Charlie Marken had given her instead of a wedding. Again we'd ask Dr Turiansky to come. Again he'd be kind but say there was nothing he could do. And unlike my plays, for Drushki there would be no coming alive again after the curtain went down. But I felt so sorry for the waste of her. Had she been born and lived unhappily just so Sarah could be created for us to love?

We sent off that letter to Mr Adler and a couple of days later another one, almost the same, as much as I could remember, because as Mama said, 'That way one boat or another is bound to deliver it to Americhky.'

And if he gets both, he'll think we're crazy; but this I didn't say.

My *La Traviata* is settling down. Nothing special but not bad, and the audience love it. If Drushki rests all day she can manage. Katya we'll soon have to slap down. A little slapping of her Cousin Ben-Ben might have been a good thing when he was her age. I'm too proud to tell anyone but how comes nobody notices how unhappy I am? Pearl must know what I'm feeling. How comes she doesn't care? So – soon I'll speak to Benjamin. Maybe then all my life I'll be alone. And the tears keep coming even though, if my family were to notice, I'm not peeling any onions.

Eleven o'clock, Mama said, we'd meet on the stage round

the big table and it's long past and we straggle and giggle and sigh and move next to this one and move over to that one.

At the end of the table there's a second chair and Igor's in it to our winking delight. He has his businesslike notebook and sharpened pencil and sits patiently shielding the latecomers from Mama's daggers. Lovely, Igor is. Wonderful to have such a calm, clever man unfussing life as it tangles past. Though it was rather unflattering how quickly he'd forgotten me in his heavy falling for Mama, he'd been so nearly our Tata for so long he just fitted naturally into the chair beside her. But Benjamin he hasn't been able to take to, after the Natalie business – it would be cruel to make the gap wider by spilling out to him about Pearl.

Here's Benjamin – he prefers to enter a room, a perform-ance, a discussion, just as it begins, as though to prove that life doesn't start till he gets there. He brings one apple – one – and without any notion of selfishness, bites into it, happy with himself. Mama permits herself a tut or two, checks the watch around her neck and begins.

Nice and demokratish we're screaming and arguing (well, not Igor, of course and Pinchas is burying someone today and has, in any case, given in about Leah once more) about the rest of the year's programme.

'*The Musicmakers* – how long since we've done that?' Leah said, pushing across a programme from Wisherodik where Pinchas had drawn her dressed as a tattered boy begging in the streets with a bamboo flute.

'*The Truth* is a clever play,' Benjamin urged, 'and cheap.' Very cheap and just one good part – Benjamin simply stood in a courtroom and talked for an hour. Pearl would love it.

Lists were lengthening; a programme of plays so familiar if the family stayed in bed from now to performance they could do them. Must London sit again through *Das Grosse Gevin*, *The Yeshiva Bocher* and *Dybbuk*, yawn, yawn. *Uriel Acosta*, *The Wronged Bride* – even some of my own not-so-good plays they wanted to play again.

And I screamed about the new Teknik where everything's not done for you but you have to think for yourself a bit – more like you're looking through a window at someone else's life and, 'Up West, by the way, in the middle of the play, no matter how good the acting, back they don't come for the cheering. Never. It's altmodische.'

'Altmodische?' Mama's shoulders rose to her reddening ears. I stood by, head down. To accuse Mama of anything about her work being old-fashioned was asking for trouble.

'Yes, Rosa, Zelda's right, it's so.'

Don't mix in, Igor Lottenstein, I murmured, shutting my eyes and waiting for Mama to turn Cossack.

'Mm. Maybe you're right, Igor. Maybe I should see more shows Up West.'

Pardon me, but was that my Mama who spoke? Agreeing with someone? Leah and I smiled like summer at each other; our plans for Mama and Igor were further advanced than we'd realized.

'You don't mind if something I say,' Igor deferred politely.

'Say.'

'In any business, changes you don't make when things are going well,' Igor said, pulling his watch-chain exactly central before leaning back so it jerked to one side again. 'But Rosa, every week a little Yiddish theatre closes down. This one I care about and – you don't mind if I speak honestly? For one thing, there aren't enough of you. I mean, you couldn't even do that new murder play that Zelda wrote that's one of my favourites because – because you need everybody you can get.'

We settled further in our seats and I knew that the thick worrying mud that had blocked up the Rubenovska gutter was to be washed away by Igor's hose of good sense and would shine up lovely.

Borrow actors from other families like our own, he said, and only Benjamin and I didn't nod and agree, our heads full of Pearls. Advertise for actors. Nod, nod. Better, newer style of plays, not just by me. Nod, nod, nod. And in the interludes, like Up West – living pictures. We'd be the first Yiddish Theatre to have them if we were quick and kept quiet – we turned to point a warning finger at poor bored Katya and Hersch who were drawing on a piece of paper and didn't see.

And why, Igor went on, didn't Benjamin try to get into living pictures himself. Americhky was already lying down and dying for these new 'movie stars' and for this who cared if Benjamin could speak English or not.

No more nodding from me. Did I need Benjamin any more idolized than he already was? Enough patriotten already at the stage door. But Benjamin's mouth was a trombone in a bar rest. Not here at the table with us at all, he was seeing 'Benjamin Rubenovska' in bright letters on flickering back sheets.

'And Leah,' Igor said, 'it goes without saying, is made for living pictures, isn't she?'

Poor Leah went on smocking a little dress but I could see her pink, excited, hopeful. Together we'd work on Pinchas, make up a good Talmudic saying or two if necessary. What did the good Lord give us an imagination for if not to pull a tallis or two over a few obdurate eyes?

'And Zelda –' Me? What now? 'Her gift for detail is being wasted. She should be managing the plays.' So Leah had been opening her mouth in the right places, had she? 'Then you, Rosa, would have more time to do what you're best at – acting. And,' he blushed, 'some home life you could also have.'

Poor Mama. She didn't have enough hands to hold her suddenly aching head, beating heart as she needed both of them to wring as well.

'And what,' Igor said, unaware that it was customary to give Mama time to disagree with all that, 'about water-closets?'

One minute we're all in living pictures, the next we're worrying our heads about klozetn. That's the theatre for you.

The dreaded Metropolitan Board of Works, Theatres and Music-Halls had it in for the lot of us. Fire regulations, now that we couldn't agree more about. But now, all of a sudden, water-closets we have to have. Appendix 8, subsection xviii, yet. Who ever complained about such things in darling Wisherodik?

'And you'll be clever,' Igor said. 'You won't wait like all the others for 31 December, you'll do it right away and advertise you're the first. And from the queues you get, you'll pay me back, yes?

'And lastly,' Igor made his final characteristic little cough, 'how do you feel about your seat prices?'

Seat prices. Now at last he's talking Rubenovska. They should go up. They should stay low. Full price for the kinder at night-time. Cheaper seats behind the pillars. Special prices for standing room. Balcony the same. Balcony different. Every meeting ended with seat prices. My family couldn't always be thinking big.

And with all the talking, lunchtime came and went so Leah and I volunteered to go to Frankenberg's to bring back some food.

'Don't bother, Leah,' Benjamin called. 'I'll go with Zelda.'

We all turned to look at him, not just me. Did he maybe feel a little faint to go out into the windy day in daylight? Did he think Pearl Wise might by chance be at her uncle's restaurant? Why the sudden helpfulness? The husbandly companionship? Something there must be behind it.

Even in our hurry and for a six-minute walk, I had to wait while my Benjamin brushed and put on his new black beaver-cloth coat lined with astrakhan that flowed over into a huge roll collar and cuffs. Every actor in London who could afford it was wearing one of those and the big black hat and the silver-topped cane. It was a walking advertisement that our theatre was on the up.

Benjamin courteously put his arm out for me to hold as the doors were locked behind us and even though I knew he was performing for whoever may have been in the streets with us, I still took it, hoping for a glance and a smile.

In the busy streets of the East End we walked past ordinary women, doing ordinary things for ordinary husbands and children who would never miss a day's schooling for a first night and I was jealous of every one of them. Theatre, theatre. All we ever talked about was theatre and me with twenty tragedies bottled up inside me.

'Binyomin – I have to speak. The ache, the pain . . .'

My words, overcooked from being too long simmering, fell

to unpalatable pieces.

'Binyomin – Natalie, well, but Pearl . . .'

My voice wouldn't behave. It deepened, wobbled. Frightened I'd said too much, terrified I'd said too little, cursing myself for saying anything at all.

Stopping at Frankenberg's door, his hands deep in his pockets, Benjamin looked all of a sudden like an ordinary man.

'They butter me up, Zee-Zee. They remember everything I said on the stage and how I said it. They send me little notes and strawberries, maybe, in the interludes. It happens to actors. It's still happening to Maurice Behren; he brags about it. And you know what they say about Adler himself and the others. How old are they? Fifty? More? What can I do? They give you that look . . .'

'You don't have to give them that look back.'

'I'm not that much of an angel, Zee-Zee. Or that strong.'

'It must be me,' I said miserably. 'My own fault. Can you imagine Mama letting Tata, may he rest in peace, play with any actress?'

With one foot up ready to push open the restaurant door, behind which flowed a babble of customers and a stream of busy Frankenbergs, with the shocking honesty I had thought I had wanted, till I got it, Benjamin told me that Pearl he'd give up, but the next ten actresses would probably come and go in the same way; that that was the way it was with him and that me and Dovid he loved more than – more than – quick, I can't breathe till he tells me more than what – more than – ah, more than the theatre.

In Rubenovska language to be loved more than theatre is the most a belovéd could ever hope for and was, in any case, all I was going to get.

All the way home, I held Benjamin's arm very close, choked with love at every new understanding smile he gave me.

INTERLUDE

Wednesday 29 April 1908
Our Dovid is already crawling and Benjamin and I can't get enough of watching him do it. When he sneezes or turns over or laughs out loud it makes us as foolishly happy as if we ourselves had done something clever. But I'll be honest, when Benjamin plays like this with Dovid, I feel safer from Pearl. Does he think I don't know she still writes, sometimes, on that pale blue paper? What about? What good if I find out? Benjamin will always have a woman somewhere to meet with, to walk with, to make up to. What can I do? Only love him and not nag. He's what I want so I'll fight for him.

Igor has been Mama's hero. As soon as we were finally agreed, he took on all the trouble about the water-closets and without us wasting our artistic energies on such unspeakable matters, diggings were dug, drains drained and pipes piped. We almost wore out that linked silver chain that made the clean water flood pulling, pulling it. Sarah and Jacob loved it; nearly crawling in it to see how it worked. Dovid was frightened by it, every new stream of fearful tears down his face making us shriek with loving cruelty, poor baby. The stoutly varnished rosewood seat is better than any of our furniture. Also Igor was right: the *Illustrated London News* and the *Stage* were too grand to mention it but the *Era* made our toilets a little headline. We were certainly sold out every night, who knows whether to see our plays or see their own waters swirl down towards the floor and disappear. And we, who've loved Igor for so long, are sick of hearing him praised by Mama, and sick of him defending her every outrageousness. They'll be, please G-d, married soon and maybe argue a little; it'll be nice.

Wednesday 6 May 1908

Finally, my family, bless them, agreed about the words of the advertisement we're putting in the *Stage*. Plays I've been writing since I was six but even Katya thought she knew better than me what we should print. Amateurs. I hate amateurs. The *Stage* couldn't print it in Yiddish, of course. But I say it's actors we want not Yiddish speechmakers. Leah says when the Behrens want someone for a show they just go to the other Yiddish theatres, pick someone good and take them away with a few promises and a bit more money. Not the Rubenovskas, I said. Fair's fair. Me, I was pleased about the advertisement being in English. So if I *ever* get my own way and we put on English plays, plenty of actors we'll already have. Benjamin? All right, so I'll strike him dumb in my plot. Often I wish I could do that with him anyway.

Thursday 7 May 1908

Such a long letter from Annie and Lev and such good news and such bad news. They are nearly prisoners in their home, all their papers have been burned and to keep the children safe, Lev has done what he said he would never do and he is a clerk for the Government in the Yemolsk area. A spy against the other workers, that is. Drushki can say all she likes but with a knife to your children's throat anything you'll do.

But it must have done some good Tsar Nicholas meeting King Edward after all, because the Tsar, may he be blessed just a little, says Yiddish Theatre in Russia can come out of the cowsheds. And what plays are they doing? Plays by Sholem Aleichem, Sholem Asch, Jacob Gordin and – Zelda Rubenovska. Annie saw it on the posters. Mama went mad. The Rubenovska cousins still living there near Vilna would raise a troupe again; Rubenovskas would sweep the Marinsky Theatre and all Russia would thrill to Yiddish theatre again. Yes, Mama. Of course, Mama. One day the rest of the world will love Jews better than themselves. But quietly, secretly, the day of the letter, for me it was vunderlekh to be the most important Rubenovska of them all.

Friday 15 May 1908

From the noises I heard as my eyes opened, I was sure that there must again be a rowdy strike of some workers and I hoped Drushki was well enough for it. (Her doctor, such smart advice he gives her, says whatever pleases her she should do – is that different from usual? – and I know she always feels wrong not having in her hands at these times maybe a broken bottle and a couple of bricks.) But what does the gevalt turn out to be? A shouting, pushing queue of want-to-work actors.

When I woke my Benjamin to tell him in wonder what I could see from the awkward high angle of our attic and he'd climbed out to see it for himself, he released one of his rare, relaxed swamps of excitement and pleasure so generous that far from hurrying to get dressed and go down to the multitudes I was swept up, kissed and tendered back to my old belief that Benjamin was perfect sometimes. Then we were dressing and singing and hand in hand and when the family were all in the theatre ready for the queue, all the time he's winking over at me and asking what I think and listening to what I answer, even. Every husband isn't perfect, and Benjamin simply has too big a personality to be satisfied with just one woman being crazy for him. So women I have to put up with. Did he leave me for Natalie? For Pearl? For the others whose names I don't know but whose perfumes I've had to smell? Maybe if he was a drunkard or a gambler I'd wish he was only a woman-krieker? (Maybe not.)

In the end, in the street such a tumult these actors were making, we let them in to also be an audience for each other. Benjamin gave me such instructions, I took a big notebook to impress him with my seriousness as I was to be his scribe for the trials. It said in the paper 'Yiddish speakers only' but in London, even for actors, things must be bad and plenty didn't know Yiddish from Polish. So the ones who couldn't speak Yiddish we threw out right away except for the ones who stayed hoping we just wouldn't find out.

In London there were more actors than acting jobs. (A new field of despair for Drushki.) Back in Wisherodik the Ruben-ovska experience had been very different; for bit parts we waited till someone not too ugly passed the cowshed and rushed them into a costume before they could say no. So it was no surprise that Benjamin, who like the rest of us, didn't know what it was to be anything but a boss, who had never been out of work, who had never been hungry, listened to their grim autobiographies restlessly, only tight with attention when they came centre stage and began their auditions. Mama, who thought she was in charge of the choosing, wore her best silk guipure shirtwaister and her most frozen expression of distaste. It was a relief when Pinchas had to leave for a lesson he was giving and stopped clucking at every overdressed or ankle-showing woman. We sent Drushki off to the market and promised to give out her still-wet leaflets about actors' unions to everyone – everyone we didn't hire, that is. Thank G-d for Leah (or at least Leah when Pinchas wasn't around). She swelled out to normal naughtiness and the two of us were soon crippled with laughter at mistakes, mis-starts and mishandlings up there on our Rubenovska altar. Hersch did his best for them on the piano but the first time we took today for anything but a waste of time was when Danny Klug announced himself.

If you wanted to pick someone off the streets and say 'this is an ordinary-looking man of 1908' it would be Danny Klug you'd choose. There's no describing him. If he did a robbery and you walked right in on him with the swag by his side and talked to him for half an hour, later you'd tell the police he was middle height, middle weight – I don't know what you'd say. But he stood there and instead of a great chunk of *Kuni Lemel* or *Live a Little Longer*, or sighing choruses of *Roshinkes mit Mandeln*, he just stood there telling jokes. Some I'd heard, some we'd all heard and a few even my Dovid must have known by now; sometimes it wasn't jokes, just talk. About families, about being in London, about being poor, about – I don't know. He was just funny, and very real. He, as Mama leaned over and said to us, like we needed telling, was a definite. Me, I felt sorry for the three prawbas after him as we were so excited about Danny we hardly listened. And how can he be nearly thirty and seem like a cheder-pupil in comparison with my Benjamin who's maybe a year or two younger. Before,

Danny was glueing raincoats for a family. For two years, just glueing. But they left to glue up in Manchester where they say the rain's better for business and Danny, he said, doesn't have a family to . . . Before another word came from his mouth, a family he had. Danny Klug, today you're a Rubenovska.

Then we all settle down and make up our minds who to take on from the seven others we're nisht-ahere-and-nisht-athereing about. Soon enough news of Danny Klug will get around. Family being family, no one could be flattered or bribed away by Behren or any of the others, but Danny and the others we hire? Suddenly Drushki's union rules for actors start to make sense. Rules we'll have to have to suit both sides. Benjamin – ah of course, jealous he could be – says the first rustle of a little more money and rules or no rules Danny will run. So, clever we'll have to be. I knew one day Drushki, even, would come in useful.

Wednesday 20 May 1908
Drushki's Birthday. We couldn't go out and organize her a nice march on the government, so instead a nice summer suit we bought her. She'll take it back but just to see her in that pink even once was a kind of triumph.

Pearl – now a bigger triumph altogether this is; she'd seen our advertisement and when she heard we'd taken on four new actors and Benjamin never once asked for her or her sisters she went, Benjamin said, batty. 'I've never seen such a temper.' Good. 'Such words she knew.' Excellent. And when she found out it was Benjamin himself who had chosen Anna Feinstein . . . he had to run somewhere for comfort, and me, I happened to be free.

Anna I like. From the third row her squint scarcely shows. Her devoted husband, Joseph, is older by years and years and not full of imagination but what a memory he has. Words he never forgets and never since Tata has anyone been better at recalling everyone's decided moves for every line. Remember I was supposed to be the new manager? A good idea they all said. But will Mama let me? Not yet she won't. But I'm not going to lose my temper with her. Temper never solved anything.

Sunday 24 May 1908
On the other hand, sometimes you can't help yourself. And isn't a cross word supposed to clear the air? Tuesday we open. Oy, Tuesday. Speak to me again soon, Mama, or how can I tell you you're overacting? Eight people in a play we haven't had since we got here and four of them being my own awkward family sulky from being rewritten for a big cast and losing some of their big speeches – well it isn't easy. *La Traviata* is very Jewish, really. *In Every Family a Trouble-Maker* I wanted to call it but long titles they don't use these days. Two, three words is all they can afford the sign-writer to write. So up the ladder Pinchas is writing *Libshaft un Tsorus*, and up on the stage, amongst this huge cast, love and troubles enough I've got for taking up the manager's chair. Mama, please speak to me.

ACT V

SCENE I
Monday 25 May 1908

But Mama never did break her word and speak to me first. She just opened her mouth and screamed, flying towards me as I gripped some stale bread in the asbestos toasting frame and held it over the flame. Her flyaway hair not yet up in its coiling knot, the lines round her small mouth spread out with happiness, one hand holding a bunch of twill dressing-gown, the other a blue letter.

Jacob Adler's pages and pages of slanting tiny letters were debated and sucked on like colour-changing gob-stoppers. Details were picked on, like in a peace treaty, lists were headed, committees nearly formed. Between the demands and the anxieties, the maybes and the what-ifs, lay the easy grease of the flattery and the shmoos, the shmoos and the flattery. Wonderful, vunderlekh, Jacob Adler was doing the Ruben-ovskas a favour. Jacob Adler was coming to us. For definite, for sure, for . . . The blackened bread choked out the little kitchen and woke Benjamin whose bad temper evaporated in the Adler letter all over again.

'It was the way you wrote to him that did it, my bubbele,' Mama praised me, smoothing out this quarrel and starting us again on the road that must, in our lifelong struggle, lead to the next one.

'Your idea of the two letters, Mama,' I kissed her, generous in the glow of our luck.

'My two wonderful women,' Benjamin hugged us, careless as ever with his words.

196

'Of course they say Adler's a dreadful man,' Mama said casually, chewing the toast I had finally made, golden brown and barely touched with butter, just as she liked it. Now she tells us. 'Or he was. Women, women, women, it's all he thought about.' I snorted to myself. That did not – who knew better than me? – make you dreadful. 'Your Tata wouldn't have him mentioned. And you know he says how he and his friends – friends? low-lifes, all of them – started Yiddish Theatre as early as 1880? The Rubenovskas were all over the north fifty years before that, performing in tents and gardens. You tell him in the next letter. Odessa! Much he knows! Down south there, strangers off the street they took – singers from bathtubs they stole. Immoral, they were. Dreadful. And fought like cats on a summer night; liars, all of them; for two roubles they'd buy and sell their daughters, for . . .'

'How can you say all that, Mama?' One minute Mama's writing to Mr Adler as if he's some great man, then the moment he says he's coming to us, right away he's a no-goodnik.

'Because it's true, that's why I can say it. And worse. Too bad for your ears.'

'Then why ask him here?'

'Because he's fifty-three, fifty-four, the way he lives maybe old he won't get, and he's the biggest Yiddish actor in the world and with the Rubenovskas he should act. Even some of us,' she said doubtfully, 'could maybe a little learn.'

Adler's eyes shone a bright light on everything we had stopped seeing with familiarity. Before we could start today's *Libshaft un Tsorus* rehearsal, I walked through our little family theatre with Benjamin holding my arm and Hersch, trailing behind us, our scribe and straight man. Nothing wrong with it, you could say. Except that it was too plain, too ordinary; like me – too safe. The trapdoor hadn't been used – clear it, unbolt it – write something for it. Our plays were safe, too. All comings-on and goings-off and stories clearly told.

Adler wrote carelessly about the biggest worry of all – what play? What play he asks us? '*Koenig Lear* you will like me to do?' he says. 'Or maybe some favourite play you have?' So casual – as if at the last minute such things could be arranged.

They say he's a master of the spur-of-the-moment and it's all that kept him alive in the old days but – no, it's not the Rubenovska way. The Rubenovska way is clever; all night you lay awake and worry, weeks you can't eat, nobody to anybody in the family can speak, minds every minute are changing, and when we've decided, thank the Lord, it's anyway the wrong choice we'll have made. All right, make it *Koenig Lear*. My Benjamin is, after all, a great fool.

By eleven the next morning, Drushki and Pinchas had finished painting and displaying the ribbons all over our posters and boards outside to announce that 'Jacob Adler Will Appear In Person In August' and by the time we were fidgety and longing to stop rehearsing at 12.30, the knock at the door I'd been expecting, happened.

They were rattling the outside bar loudly enough so anyone could tell it was no passing schoolboys nor any of our regular beggars hoping for a pair of boots or the price of a bowl of soup at Frankenberg's. The very clattering had a proud and demanding shake to it. Yet not in any great hurry I went myself to open up.

Smiling, like two thin slivers of underripe watermelon, Maurice and Natalie Behren stepped, as if they were welcome, into our theatre for the very first time.

'Umm.'

Is that it? We build a theatre from nothing, fill it every night, a whole family can live from it and Maurice Behren, the knucker, says 'umm'?

'Very nice,' he glances round, his feet staying in the same place near the back of the hall, with a little pleasure that it's so plain, maybe; amusement at its smallness, I'm sure. 'Isn't it, Natalie dear?'

Two smiling nods and a profile.

Benjamin, who'd been the most excited by Adler's letter and had been devastatingly easy to manage this morning, had gone quiet.

'At exactly the right moment, you've come,' I said, honestly triumphant because I knew they had had to come. 'For lunch we'll send out and you'll join us?'

They nodded politely, unable to be too strong or too grand. These were good moments to be enjoyed afterwards.

Much bustling began. Hersch was sent off for the food, Drushki and Leah to prepare the table in our living-room, though myself I'd like to have seen us on the stage eating, it all seemed so unreal.

'Benjamin? Zelda? You'll excuse me.' Mama had been watching everything from her last position in the scene where she sings the song about faithfulness that makes tears drop down my face no matter how often I hear it. 'Forgive my rudeness,' Mama said, 'but a theatre it's like a shop. When we're working, friends we can't kibitz with, you know? So if you'll excuse me, you'll maybe come another time to see your friends? Some tickets they can maybe give you and after the show a little something you can have with us?'

A dozen times Mama had peered and spat at pictures of Natalie and Maurice Behren in the papers. A dozen times she'd heard our stories about them. She knew who they were. Lovely chutzpah, Mama. The indignation rose in them from their Paris shoes to the tops of their raised-up eyebrows like air in two brown paperbags ready to pop.

'Theatres we know about, Madam. We are Maurice and Natalie Behren. Of Behren's Theatre.'

Mama, gliding forward to the front of the stage as though wearing Hersch's skates, smiled just a tiny bit. 'Very nice,' she said.

Such rudeness, of course, though afterwards so wonderful in the family retellings, comes expensive.

'From the streets we took them and a home we gave them,' Natalie said quietly. 'But for that, gratitude we don't expect.'

And the dignity of her made me, even, ashamed for a moment. Mama, too, it seemed, for she suddenly, like a mensch, introduced herself and held out her hand in amazing graciousness. And Benjamin? He'd only nodded a greeting to them and spoken not a word but now, jumping down from the stage he lifted Dovid from where he was quietly propped with his two favourite wood blocks against a pile of cushions, threw him in the air and caught him, squealing when he squealed, laughing when he laughed, then hiding his face with a big handkerchief and peeping from behind it till Dovid was limp with joy and Natalie was wild with jealousy.

Fatherhood, he had demonstrated to Natalie as he preened himself, putting Dovid down now he'd made the point, is what real love is all about. Dovid, wet from his excitement and irritable now that the fun was over, began to cry. I sighed and picked him up. Motherhood also.

Benjamin, feeling better for his bit of revenge, took them over our theatre from balcony to klozet and it was this they were discussing when I brought my nice clean Dovidl to share lunch on my knee. Cisterns, they were talking about. And chains and Maurice writing down builders' names and nodding at the wisdom of best quality wooden seats. At our table.

Then Natalie wiped delicately at the corners of her mouth – were those tiny lines I could see? I hoped so – and putting on the look I remembered of concentrated interest in the smallest change of the face, she turned to Benjamin with a rehearsed conversation.

'So, Jacob Adler is coming. Vunderlekh. Such an honour. Jacob Adler knows your family? He is perhaps related to you? The Rubenovskas acted, efsher, in Odessa? Your father, olev hashalom, was an old friend?'

Straight in with the questions, straight out with the answers and a straight goodbye.

Benjamin folded his arms over his wonderfully flat stomach I loved to smooth in the good times and pushed his plate away for some woman to clear and wash.

'No, Natalie, that's not why he's coming at all. It's a miracle. All the way from Americhky he heard of us and begged us – demanded – to let him play here. You've the letter there, Zeldele?'

I acted one of my finest roles looking for that imaginery letter whilst Leah kept Pinchas's honest open mouth closed with her glances.

'Yes,' Benjamin sighed contentedly, 'over an ocean even that wide, news can travel. T, t, t, I wonder who? Well, people have seen us, people remember – a bit of luck like that can make or break a family, no?'

You can search all the dictionaries in Whitechapel Library, even the big one that the man with the side-whiskers helps you get down with the three-step ladder and still not a word would you find better for what Natalie and Maurice were doing than the vunderlekh Yiddish word 'plotzing'. It's like you're making fists; boiling from the eyes; clenching with the jawbones; swelling the face with burstings of jealousy; angry from the shoulders. All that and none of it showing, you hope. For all that there is one English word? Of course not.

Nibbling on the edge of one of my more successful almond biscuits in that way greedy women have who try to fool you and themselves that eating your food is merely a courtesy, Natalie stopped plotzing long enough to give us problems.

'Mr Adler, *Koenig Lear* he'll do?' she said.

'Yes.'

'A pity.'

She knows we wait, desperate for her to explain herself but we cling tightly together dawdling her advantage away in our incuriosity.

'It's a pity because . . .', in her dramatic pause we allowed ourselves two raised eyebrows each, '. . . when Adler is Lear who remembers anyone else?'

Natalie has dangled a huge dead rat in the soup of our certainty leaving us thirsty and anxious. Duets, trios and ensembles blended and groaned from the opposite banks of she's-right to she's-wrong with stepping stones, lily-pads and crocodiles of maybes in between.

A shame such an important idea had to come from Natalie and such a good one. I should have seen it for myself: all of us, what were we, day-dreaming?

'You know what?' Mama said, calling for silence in a very quiet voice, as if she were a dayan with the final speech at the Bes Din. 'Mrs Behren, you've said a very clever thing.'

Not just Mama calling somebody else clever but Natalie,

even. It made us silent like for a Cossack house-search. Even the saltspoon I always fidget with until it's snatched out of my hand by someone, I put down.

'The way they speak of him, whatever he plays they'll only see him, but Lear is Lear, I know exactly what you mean.'

They beamed at each other. Well, better she's friendly with Mama than my Benjamin. (More her age, too.)

'Lear isn't a play I like anyway,' Mama said.

'Me neither,' Natalie agreed.

Then Mama and Igor whisper together and suggested that we ask Mr and Mrs Behren to do us the honour of joining our company for the duration of Mr Adler's visit. The Behrens are declining for two seconds, ponder for one more and accept all in the same breath trying to look as if this hadn't been their object in shlepping over from Thacker Close to Hooper Street in the first place.

'You, Zeldele,' Mama says affectionately, 'back you write to Mr Adler and you tell him a new play we have like he's never played before and a script you'll send him right away.'

'What play, Mama?'

'Am I a playwriter? Something where everyone has a good part, that sort of a play.'

'Mama, there isn't enough time, it's . . .'

'Think about it. Tomorrow again we'll talk. Now, if you'll excuse, Natalie, my dear, Maurice, for tonight we must rehearse, you know how it is?'

She even saw them out herself, leaned back against the door and nodded at us, all back in our places, Pinchas and Drushki in charge of clearing up the lunch outside.

'So.' For Mama this meant everything was satisfactorily settled and worries were over. For her, maybe. Tomorrow we'd talk and, you know me, in the end I'd agree.

But it was *Libshaft un Tsorus* we should be concentrating on. Tomorrow wasn't just its first night; the world would be coming to see why all of a sudden we were Adler's chosen few.

'How did he know about them?' they'd whisper. 'Good meat travels well,' they'd whisper back. 'Didn't I always say they were the best?' Our regulars led by loyal Mr and Mrs

Zigman would gloat to the patriotten of the other acting families.

All the time my responsibilities were getting more serious. All the time I was being pushed nearer to the bull's-eye of the Rubenovskas and isn't that where poisoned arrows and blunderbusses are aimed?

Our rehearsals were still full of rewriting and argument all the way between Mama and me.

'If changes every minute you're still making,' she sighed, 'tomorrow's first night will also be a rehearsal. All right, Zelda, bubbele, we'll do it your way but listen, tonight, later another letter you'll write for me?'

'Who this time, Mama? Boris Thomashevsky you want also to come from Americhky and with him he should bring David Kessler and Keni Liptzin?'

'Talk sense! I was thinking, a letter you must write to the Behrens with a contract like Drushki invented and in it you'll say how much we agreed to pay them.'

'All right, Mama.'

'Wait, and also you'll say for this play only we want them and then goodbye, and shut the door after them. You'll know how to write it aydel.'

People who don't write personal letters think it's easy. Aydel? Unpleasant is unpleasant however polite. Goodbye is sei gezint in any language. Sure, Mama. I'll know how to put it. Me, I'm the one who knows what's what. When I've finished the letter I'll write a little play for Jacob Adler the whole of London will talk about. That's also easy. They're waiting for me. Look at them. All of a sudden without me they can't manage.

'So, Mama, you stand further over – no even further, so Benjamin can rush in like this,' I said decisively.

'Or like that, maybe?'

ACT V

SCENE II

27 May 1908

'Good girl, Katya,' I said, kissing her carefully where her 'all by her own' make-up tonight wasn't so thick. I smoothed out one cheek a little to match the other and pointed to a little chair in the wings. 'Lift your dress up at the back, choochele, and stay right where I can see you. You're the only one ready. If no one else comes, you can do the whole play by yourself.'

Katya laughed and started reciting the first scene just as it had been written by me. I had finally done it: a script they were sticking to, at last. Same words, more or less, every time.

'You know, Katya, if they like you, you ought to have a curtain-calling all of your own,' I said rashly. 'A Rubenovska prize for good acting.'

Hersch, still too slight to fill out the waiter's suit, put his jacket behind Katya's shoulders and tried to heave the huge table with Pinchas but it scarcely moved. Two weeds and the groaning was so loud, I shushed them. 'Get Joseph,' I hissed, smiling to think what would happen if I suggested Benjamin coming to help.

I could walk up and down, I could check the props again, I could do nothing to make the time pass. Down in the corner, Drushki was bent over in a funny way and I gasped, dreading her death messing up this special opening. No, she was all right, just printing on stiff card with the block letters she had – not to be too sweet about it – stolen from Charlie Marken. The pot of black paint she was dipping them into was awkwardly placed on a towel on a low chair, in the middle of everything.

That black stuff would get everywhere. Tactfully, I set up a barricade of chairs round her and raised my chin to fight with her if she argued.

'You could do that, perhaps, tomorrow?'

Drushki pointed. 'Sold Out', it said. In Yiddish even better that looks. 'Advance tickets, queue here.'

'Already? Good. But it's because of Adler coming, I suppose.'

'Maybe' Drushki nodded, stopping only to cough and spit a little. Since Dr Turiansky had told her she'd live longer than any of us, she'd coughed less and worried not at all.

'Standing room only, I was going to put, but its too long and anyway, when I've finished there won't be any standing room.'

'You're pleased?' I said, to pass the time. She took time, herself, off from her dipping to look at me like rotting cauliflower.

'I shouldn't be pleased? Family I'm not? What are you trying to . . . ?'

'I only meant theatre. You're pleased even though it's only theatre.'

'It's a living, a business. Money we're making so now I can be pleased and the family treat the workers good and that's all right so pleased I shouldn't be?' Drushki dipped on and me, I was an angel, the drips down the back of the chair I didn't even mention.

Joseph and two friends of Hersch's heaved and Pinchas pushed a little. The table moved, tearing our best rug right through the middle.

'Get Leah,' I shrieked whispering, 'and strong needles and tell Benjamin when he runs in in the scene about the letter he shouldn't trip and tell Hersch . . . Where's Katya gone?' I said limply, seeing the empty chair and wanting to burst into tears and lie down somewhere dark. Manager, who made me a manager? What do I know? 'Mama. Get Mama.'

But Mama didn't come and you know what? I managed.

When my Benjamin, himself and no seraphim, brought me out

to that stamping shouting applause, at that moment I had been too wild with conceit to worry why this *Libshaft un Tsorus* was such a mad success. A wonderful play, I had thought then. Great management, I had thought then. Fine actors, I had thought then.

But now there was time to worry that it was because Adler was coming to us that the audience took us to their souls.

'What matter?' Drushki shrugged.

To me it mattered.

'You know I made a mistake,' I said, fitting into the beautiful curves of Benjamin's favourite sleeping position after I'd cleaned my teeth and winked back at a couple of stars through the skylight. 'The play's not bad but the title should be the other way round: *Tsorus un Libshaft*. Did you notice? It makes it sound like as soon as there is love there's trouble instead of . . .'

'Zeldele, I'm tired. In the morning you'll get on a ladder, you'll print your title backwards or upside-down, you'll paint new programmes and posters and tickets or, better, you'll leave well alone. I can sleep now? Acting is exhausting, Zeldele. This you've never understood.'

Lifshaft un Tsorus.

Benjamin can't sit still.

So? We all feel the same. How come my Binyomin, may the good Lord keep him, makes you feel guilty and responsible for him being restless or anxious or emotional? Is it our fault these dockers are on strike? The boat's docked. Adler's here. We're sure we can see his white hair now – though I suppose other men also bring white hair from Americhky. The trunks, the baggage, the cargo – this, all of a sudden, they won't unload on a Sunday.

Drushki, who didn't want to come with us to meet Mr Adler and only came to please her Sarah, brightens and glows in the conflict, spending her time with the union leaders down near the huge side of the boat, leaving poor Sarah to us. Drushki has to be separated from her brother when she returns breathless from the shovings she'd endured to push through the rumpus to explain the dockers' rights to us like a curtain speech.

Rights or wrongs, I'm ready to go down and agree they should get extra – double, triple for all I care – pay for their sabbath work even if they would spend it in the public houses. Anything so we can get the children out from this crush and home.

Nearly midday before they settled it.

The crowds cleared slowly, slowly. A different brand of passenger from Americhky, I noticed, than the hopeless hopefuls from Wisherodik; prosperous, shaven, healthy.

There's quite a crowd here for Adler. The minor actors of the Pavilion Theatre have brought a banner – why didn't we think of that? – and try to keep it readable in the sudden wind of this open area. Their patriotten are everywhere. But we've our own loyal little crowd too, headed, of course, by our faithful Zigmans. Never a play without them, in the seats we call 'theirs'. 'Very nice,' they say every time. Critics they're not. And Sadie Zigman's feet hurt and still she stands there for us as if we matter.

Photographers from the London papers and the stage papers wait more patiently than we do for the long ritual of the customs shed to finish. They're setting up their tripods – oh wouldn't you know Mama couldn't be upstaged even by Jacob P. Adler. She's broken the news to them. Igor is being dragged reluctantly under the shade of Mama's new exceedingly large Merry Widow hat for the newsworthy picture and story that not only are they to be married but Jacob P. Adler is to be asked to have the honour of being unterfehrer for them during his visit here. And with Mama asking, a fat chance he'll have of refusing. So this second wedding will be a theatrical triumph. To tell you the truth, I feel a little sorry for Igor. Of course, nobody wants Mama to be lonely and everyone, except perhaps Drushki, likes Igor and we'll never forget how much he's done for us. But me? I love him. So maybe a bit jealous I am because I see his tenderness, reliability, soothing calmness to be better than Benjamin's swinging from perfection to moody selfishness. Two husbands they don't let you have if you're Jewish. But any tribe I'd join where you can have two;

one for loving and one for loving you.

At least this time for the celebration we don't have to go mad cooking, like for the barmitzvah. Frankenberg's are cooking everything for us and after the wedding they're closing the shop to everyone but us and our guests. A good thing we can afford it now. Mr Adler wouldn't expect anything less.

The Behrens have arrived, I notice. I smile and wave to them. Her I'll never like. How could I? But they were really useful the day Mr Adler's letter came back about my new play. 'Nothing new under the sun,' he says casually, like it doesn't matter. Othello he's already done with David Kessler, no less, and good business it hadn't been.

Of course Othello's about marrying out and that's what I've called my new play so from outside the theatre, even, they know what story they're getting. It's also about how if you're too clever, too good and too successful, even your best friend will be too jealous to love you. It is a real Yiddishe play with a good part for everyone in the company and even when Adler's finished with us and leaves, I've got it all fixed up. In rehearsal, when my Benjamin gets to play Adler's part, he's so good I often say I don't know why we're bothering with Adler at all. Mama says that's being narrow and probably that's right – but love it also is. So my *Marrying Out* works like a dream and Mr Adler, who only uses the best playwrights in Americhky, will really know if I'm good, won't he? (And would I believe him if he said I wasn't?)

No more thinking. Katya's brought a crying Dovid to me. I kiss the little bump on his poor forehead better ten, twenty times and he's laughing into my face and clutching at my new hair-style. Has he really only been mine for ten months? Don't go on the stage, my Dovidl.

He's coming!

'That's him! It is! Tallish. Squarish. Dandyish. Such white hair can't be real. Those hooded, loving eyes – no wonder women yearn for him.

We push and shove – me too; I'm holding Dovid up to see and be seen, how foolish – to get closer, to tell him who we are, to be noticed. Silly.

Half-way through Natalie's explanation of who she is, Mr Adler politely interrupts her to ask if she knows Zelda Rubenovska and her husband, Benjamin.

He couldn't have asked anyone who knew us better.

'So young, Mrs Rubenovska,' he shmoosed me, kissing my hand. 'Such beautiful red hair and such a playwright; Mr Rubenovska, the whole of London must be kneeling at her feet.'

Poor Mr Rubenovska was too astonished to look astonished but he gave a half-proud bow in my direction which gave him time to think.

'The Rubenovska family welcome you to London, sir,' Benjamin said, having apparently decided to overlook Adler's lapse from good sense. 'Mr King and Mr Gordon of the Pavilion await you to take you to luncheon and after you have rested may we expect you for some dinner with us?' he said, failing to consult with us slaves of the kitchen first.

Adler's still-thick eyebrows went up. 'My good sir, I shall rehearse early afternoon at the Pavilion and with you at four this afternoon. There's no time to spare.'

The black-bunned Annie Ehrenbaum, star of the Pavilion, pushed towards us and was reluctantly introduced to Adler by Benjamin.

'So young, Miss Ehrenbaum and such black hair, the whole of London . . .'

Danny and Benjamin were so funny being Adler as we walked quickly back through the quiet Sunday streets wheeling Dovid's perambulator. Adler shmoosing all the women, Adler not knowing a line of his part and making it up, Adler playing Lear to our Othello, Adler trying to make up to Mama – we were in pain laughing and for ten minutes I stopped worrying about this all too sudden rehearsal with such a grand visitor let alone what we would have for such a quick lunch.

Such a day. A day like this we should be taking the children to Victoria Park. Leah, Drushki and me ought to be dressed in muslin, carrying lace parasols and taking our time, stopping on the way to nod nicely to other young mothers and their kinder.

Benjamin unlocked the doors. It was hot and stuffy in there. Don't go on the stage, Dovid, I beg you.

INTERLUDE

Sunday 16 August 1908

Mr Adler didn't come at four in the afternoon, of course, though we were ready. We were so nervous by six that we started rehearsing without him and then in he comes when we're dropping and he's had a nap and is as bright as tomorrow's sun and – what an experience. The Rubenovskas may have been actors years before the Adlers but maybe we've stayed too close to one another to pick up from the outside those acting jewels that sparkled on other stages. When we came up to bed, at last, having watched my Binyomin rise like a steamed pudding in the warmth of Adler's new pot of know-how, he was so golden with the delight of tonight and made me feel so miraculous, who wouldn't love him? I've just covered him over, now the night is finally cooling off, but me, I couldn't sleep if the Tsar was in the room himself commanding me.

How Jacob Adler acted, how he made you look at him, how he wore his clothes, when he made what he was doing 'big' and when 'small'. It's all feeling and timing and leaving gaps round words and empty spaces one side of the stage with everybody in a bunch on the other that used to be wrong until he did it. Tomorrow in rehearsal I'll see for myself what Benjamin has 'stolen' from Mr Adler – but soon he'll unpick it and make it into a new pair of breeches for himself and when he does, that I'll write down. Where did he learn it? Where did Katya who never even lived with us in Wisherodik? And even the Behrens had sniffed and blowed after Leah's heart-stopping speech swearing her faithfulness and Danny had said we should, along with the lemonade and the chocolates, sell handker-chiefs.

Mr Adler started talking about some Russian actors he'd known. He was young when he met them and he said they made him ashamed of Yiddish theatre the way he and his friends were playing it. And these Russians – how I don't know – seeing how great he could be, made him start again and play only good parts. He was wonderful to listen to – less boastful than my Benjamin, but maybe he was just more used to success.

He'd asked, of course, dozens of questions about our fire precautions – that we'd expected. When I was first learning to curtsey at the Wisherodik cowshed, he was having his hideous fire right here in London, seventeen or more dead and it had perhaps made him run to Americhky in the first place. He was still fire-crazy and the family put up with it patiently. Not so patiently, with his walk around the theatre, downstairs and up in the balcony and his 'With such a small theatre a fortune you won't make.' Unless he was offering to buy us a bigger one, where's the sense in saying that? Then in the last part, when we started again, Adler showed how you thought not only of yourself but the actor-wall you were bouncing your feelings off, the comedy sharpened into points you never dreamed of and – there's no explaining it. Sometimes, for no reason, lockshen soup tastes better than other times.

Then the talking began again. This time about Mama and Igor's wedding. Adler was, or pretended to be, moved by their request for him to unterfehr and was really quite silly with joy at their marriage for a man who'd been bridegroom at three weddings and best man in so many bedrooms. We talked theatre, we talked Americhky, we talked nonsense; Danny started the jokes and then Maurice Behren turned out our new lights and lit a candle to tell one of his famous ghost-stories.

It's a shame to waste tonight. I think I'll wake my Binyomin and tell him a fairy-story.

Friday 21 August 1908
You know what it's like Friday lunchtime, you can't think what to cook that's quick so you can get on with the Shabbos meals and on top of that it's the wedding this weekend – a thousand jobs for us all to do. Again eggs we ran out of and a few bits and pieces so while the girls go on baking I'm running

down the Lane early with my Dovid in my arms as today, of all days, he just wouldn't let me leave him, and he's beginning to weigh like a set of entsiklopedye books because this one and that one I'm bumping into who want to stop and talk and then I met Sadie Zigman. At least while we're talking Dovid goes to her and she holds him for me and makes him laugh while I put the eggs better in my string bag and the onions underneath and only the matzo meal and the black olives to get. And out comes the whole story I've come up here to write although the girls would kill me if they knew. In a minute I'll go down and cook.

The Zigmans went to the Pavilion last night to see Adler and punkt, suddenly, before the last act, someone comes on and says, 'The Pavilion management regrets . . .' but nobody actually says why someone else will be Lear for the end of the play and everyone's murmuring to everyone else that he's maybe dead and then after the not-so-hot clapping had finished, out comes Mr Adler without his make-up and talks, Mrs Zigman says, all about me. Well, of course, she's exaggerating but it was really about Avrom Goldfaden and he's dead. Not only was he Mr Adler's best playwright and the Yiddish world's best playwright but he was Adler's best friend too and when the news came he was too upset to go on and then, from what Mrs Zigman told me in a great rush, he said good playwrights are hard to find, even in the Goldene Medina and now he must look to new young writers like someone the name she can't remember because she wasn't listening and Zelda Rubenovska here in London. The rest of what she's saying I'm also not listening and I forget the matzo meal and the olives and I run back through the crowded Friday streets, forgetting how heavy Dovid's getting, and I want to brag about it to Benjamin first and maybe start to pack for Americhky but he's not there. Not there. Nobody to tell but my journal.

Monday 24 August 1908
What a wedding. Mama used her eyes so prettily and was so happy you could nearly, except for the softening under her chin, forget she was forty-six. She made such a performance of

213

this second wedding I'm glad we weren't at her first. This quiet wedding they were having – right from Hooper Street, through all the little roads, crowds stood and cheered as if this private occasion were a show. Free, as well.

'There are no people in the world,' Mama kept saying, 'like the Rubenovska patriotten.'

That the great Jacob P. Adler was at the wedding makes also a bit of a difference; this she forgot to mention. He stood by the iron gates of the shul in a mass of his own patriotten and they screamed when he kissed Mama's hand and held it up as if she had won some contest like in his much talked-about youthful boxing career. The whole day was Adler's really. When he was sitting eating, later, the picture they took of a Frankenberg lutka between the Adler teeth would curl in the restaurant window for a decade. But looking back at yesterday, I'll always hear laughter – the day seemed full of it. Different, I whispered to my Benjamin, from that secret, hurried double wedding Leah and me had to have. But Benjamin, gloriously funny and happy himself, frowned as if he could barely remember such a thing, whispering something so pretty in my ear I wanted to block it with cottonwool so it couldn't get out. After that warm, loving wedding-lunch that went on till four in the afternoon, Mama and Igor we waved off in the motor car to Igor's house that she had 'made over' so that all Igor's years there had vanished. Mr Adler raised his hat to us and said how much he was looking forward to next week in our theatre, but as he didn't mention how marvellous *Marrying Out* was, it didn't seem a good time to ask him about his praising of me at the Pavilion. Plenty of time – for a fortnight we'd all be together.

Saturday 12 September 1908
And there we stood outside Frankenberg's again tonight, after the last glorious performance of *Marrying Out*; Morry, shutting the door after us and locking up, was barely awake enough to grovel anymore. Outside in the light rain, the talking threatened to start all over again but I think we were all sick of so much praising, them to him, him to him, me to him,

him to her, her to her, us to them – like a river of syrup. It was almost a pleasure to see Igor and Mama drive Adler off in their motor car, we kissed goodbye to each other, even kissed the Behrens and in minutes Benjamin and I were flat out in the Gardiner's bed that I would demand to take wherever and in whichever country our new big theatre would be built. Every night, Jacob Adler praised me on and off the stage for writing *Marrying Out* and begged to be first with my next one, but – I think he's a man you take with that lovely English thing, a pinch of salt. We'll see. He told me he writes a journal, too, every day. Wonder what he writes about us. Anyway, plays I'll send him and when the tickets arrive for the whole family to come as his guests to Americhky, as he promised, then I'll apologize for not believing him. One play, I keep telling the family, isn't a garantye.

One thing he said I do believe though: every day he warned us, begged us, nagged us to get in quick with the moving films. Didn't Igor say that too? Here it's nothing yet – an interlude extra – but in Americhky already every actor is rushing for it, even Adler himself. Katya and Hersch know more about it than we do, going to see every session at the Bioscope. They tell us it's easy – you just overact. Maybe, but for me there's nothing. Writers they don't need. But the idea has excited Mama and Leah and Benjamin. And even me, I'm curious now. There was, I have to admit, something lovely about Jacob Adler but I don't feel like shlepping tomorrow with the rest of the family to Victoria to see him off on the boat-train to Paris. Dovid'll be a good excuse. I feel he'll have forgotten us before the boat docks – can you blame him? How could you carry all that favour on your shoulders without getting bent? I reached out and held hands with Benjamin who was thinking his own thoughts over there. He was still only successful in a very small circle. So – tomorrow while they are at the boats I'll start writing the changes for the play without Adler. To have him here was good for business and something to tell our grandchildren, but a disturbance like that has to be smoothed over. I held Benjamin tightly. The Rubenovskas will always survive.

November 1908
What for? Annie, Lev, Manny, the babies, the whole of
Yemolsk. What for? Wiped out. Shooting now, not just
burning.

I can't

ACT V

SCENE III
October 1912

When our Dreadnought cinematograph ('the finest show-man's bioscope on the market') caught fire, it seemed like a message to me personally from the Almighty.

It took with it the flimsy table it was standing on, the new curtains, the pelmet-curtaining Leah and I had pleated, sweated over, stuck up and draped, scorched some floorboards and completely destroyed my set of red books that I'd kept as journals for – worse than I thought, when there was time to check such things – nothing, right back to the end of 1908.

Nobody was hurt, nothing was new about such a fire; the Behrens had it happen twice this year, the stuff's so inflam-mable. Insurance will pay for most of it, the safety curtain came down nice and fast and Benjamin and Danny were out in front doing fire jokes before three screams hit the roof from our new dress circle and gallery. We had them all filing out nicely, holding their free tickets for the next night's show and before their footsteps had faded away, Hersch and Pinchas were scraping away at the scorchings, borrowing varnish, and tearing down the last hanging smoulders of drape, while Leah and I changed in a moment to mop up the extinguishing water and sooty puddles to save the wetness seeping into the floor.

But I couldn't stop my own sadness wetting my face; slow hot separate despairing tears, one for every page I had lost. Whenever it was that we started this animated picture-show – when? Two years ago? Less? Where can I look up such details now? We were only copying what all the other theatres had been doing much longer than us. Despite what Igor and Mr Adler had said, we had never got around to it sooner.

Maybe a dozen machines we've hired and none of them seem to tilt the right angle for the screen. They're always propped carelessly up with books and quite often the only books around are my precious journals I always carry for quiet times backstage, where I sit altering, polishing, adding, sometimes just reading and remembering. How careless this was it's too late to realize. The family don't understand. Jacob Adler would. Samuel Pepys would. Even if Bubba hadn't made me begin the journals I know I'd have come to it. Those who keep them are the ones who like the past. It's safer there. It can't come out of the woods and take a bite out of you like the wolves of the future whose tiny barkings you can barely hear. You can lie awake at night, with the past, wishing you had, wishing you hadn't, about a million things but wishing's all you can do. And it's enchanting to look back and see what you used to think and feel before this year's brambles had pricked and hurt you or this year's bramble jelly pleased and delighted you.

'So you'll write them again,' Benjamin said, impatient with me later when I couldn't stop grieving and mourning for a few scraps of paper.

I tried for a bit. It's hopeless. Without the feelings, it's all just a stream of distant events seen from up on a cliff with field-glasses on a foggy day.

What happened in all that time?

If I say that the theatre's bigger now, will that bring back those six wild months with the builders — the mumsers — promising, promising. Everything so unfinished at the end we were back with the brushes and the putty and the sandpaper just like when we were burying the Sheep and Shearer forever.

To tell again the story of how we sat shiva for Annie and Lev and their babies — our lovely Katya and Hersch on low chairs — I couldn't write again the pages and pages of the dreadful times those children had. They are really our children now: Benjamin and I adopted them properly last year at the same time as —

where is it written that Drushki died? See? No journal and right away, nothing is important. Drushki just died, that's all. Up there she's head of Rights for the Dead. And Benjamin, who had scarcely spoken to her in six years like a real brother, never spent time with her even as a child and certainly never expressed real love for her, isn't really over the shock yet. Guilt, maybe? I don't know. We still only talk about Drushki carefully, briefly, unwillingly. So when Pinchas and Leah announced they would like to adopt Drushki's Sarah, we asked Hersch and Katya if they'd like to be ours and there was much weeping and sentimental sorrowing and . . . I'll never be able to recapture that the way I wrote it as it was happening. It seems easy and inevitable now, but then it was all soul-tearing and not-wanting-to-wake-up-in-the-morning-unhappiness and doubts. Were there ever more doubts and difficulties?

And Mimi. My Miriam. Where did she go? Our baby girl was born on the night before Erev Rosh Hashanah, Danny's benefit night, the audience streaming in in their best clothes. Miriam was too quick for any hospital; backstage, like any good Rubenovska, Mimi made her first appearance in a great hurry and, unlike her Tata, with very little fuss. Eighteen — nineteen months she is now, and everyone's favourite, I'm afraid. And her first walking, her first words, Dovid's first day at the bright cheerful little kindergortn at Stepney, so much laughter — we'll remember, I suppose, but not with the clear brightness of the journals. Ach, Benjamin's right. This moaning must stop. What's gone is gone.

Another of the things smoothed over by the years, jumped over with the burning of the journals, is the miracle of this house in Forest Gate. With a bit of help from Igor and because the theatre's nearly double the size, we bought this house before Mimi's first birthday. Though it isn't very pretty, the rooms are enormous, so we persuaded Leah and Pinchas to leave the Zigman's smelly fishshop and take the upstairs. In a few words like that it sounds easy.

But it was just as good as I'd dreamed, playing house away from the theatre, like any other house-proud woman. But — it's also not so good. It happened like this. A couple of years ago,

Leah, our Rubenovska baby-factory, was expecting again – a third boy she had to call Abi, of course, for the full set, and finally she gave in to Pinchas and left our theatre. She's Mother Goose to her three goslings, Pinchas is so meshugah frum sometimes that G-d's thinking He should maybe retire.

So, we had to replace Leah and finally we hired Bella Grossman, may she lose all her teeth but one. Bella is a very beautiful young lady (the rest of the story do I need to tell?) with a sweet soprano voice, a flair for comedy, a nice restraint in melodrama, a quick study – did I say enough in her favour? She can probably cook and sew, too – this I don't know.

All I know is, since she came, though our Gardiner's bed looks even better here in this big bedroom with the French windows out to the tiny piece of garden, though I've propped Bubba's little glass souvenir nicely dusted on the mantelshelf to remind Benjamin that his destiny lies with me, I don't have to tell you who he's rented our theatre rooms to and well, well, well, Benjamin has to stay later and later most nights at the theatre though believe me he must be word-perfect in his love-scenes by now.

During the worst of the Bella Grossman time, I wrote three plays – was it four? – about unfaithful husbands making them come to terrifyingly nasty ends but it didn't help, except in my heart, so something else I tried: a magnificent comedy that we put on called *The Shop Assistant*. Benjamin plays seven of the twelve parts and is, by the end of every performance, like a lettuce left too long in the sun. But my idea wasn't that clever; Benjamin started to say that after it he was too tired to come home at all and would sleep at the theatre.

It has to be the wife's fault if a man is all the time looking somewhere for somebody else. It makes no difference to remind me that Benjamin's maybe unjust, selfish, cruel and plenty of other words, because all that hasn't stopped me loving him. How I wish it had.

The girl who comes in Tuesdays and Fridays is playing nicely with our little ones; the big ones are at school – so many wonderful first days at school, first this and first that gone with the burnt missing journals. Such a shame.

At last, Leah. Not one of us can shout at her though we've been waiting so impatiently. What a beauty. What courage to take off her sheitel and put on a dress like that. You can see she's trembling and has been daring herself to come out of her room.

Igor's taking us to meet Benjamin in Mile End Road at this place and to say the least of it there's no time to spare. Pinchas would go crazy if he knew what Leah was doing.

Igor pulled up outside the big messy push-back doors, rusty grilles over the high, dirty windows. It didn't look right, but it was the only old tram-shed around and outside it paced an impatient Benjamin, and Danny smiling and waving.

A small door set inside the left-hand front opened at once to Igor's knock and with our various degrees of caution and excitement we stepped over the high bottom of this doorway and stood awkwardly, pulling down waistcoats and shirt-waists.

The electric lights switched on abruptly, unbearably and we all put our hands to our faces before we could blink. Men everywhere, all shouting to? at? each other, a big painted scene of snowy mountains and a small stage made on the floor by sticks of wood like we used to make for Purim-Spiel in Wisherodik when we went to cheder.

Two photographers knelt behind two cameras either side of the stage and shouted, 'No, no no,' to someone who couldn't possibly have heard them.

A different world.

A megaphone mellowed a scream and the lights went off again and there was silence. Now it seemed dark, colder, lonely.

The snowy mountains creaked up into the high ceiling with a ratcheting noise that wedged your teeth together and a small wide man in a jacket cut for a tall wide man came over to us with a long pad of lined paper.

'Rubenovskas? Right. Title, *The Shop Assistant*? Right. First timers?'

'Yes, indeed,' Igor said proudly. 'Our company are launching into the cinematograph . . .'

'Thousand footer?'

'Well, we did think a thousand feet would mean extensively shortening the action but it seems this length is the most . . .'

'New 'uns,' the wide man called. 'Thousander. Send 'Arry. 'Arry'll do.' He smiled at us without moving his mouth for more than an inch. ''Arry'll tell yer. 'Seasy once you get the 'ang. What d'yer want?' he asked. jerking his head up to the roof. 'Big shop? Little shop? Shelves? Counters? Yer not sure? Eight, fifteen, sixteen and two, maybe, Ted!' he shouted to the empty roof.

Enormous black and white flats of various shops came winding down and jerking up. The fourth one was gone and still none of us had spoken.

''Arry'll know. Where's the rest on yer? Only six?'

'Only four of us are actors,' I said, 'but he', I pointed in wonder at my Benjamin, 'plays seven parts.'

''Snot new,' he said mildly, like I didn't know. ''Arry'll 'elp you.'

'Arry helped a lot when he turned up but as it was nearly an hour later, Mama's face looked hot as horseradish, Benjamin was icy with boredom and all the lunch sandwiches I'd made were gone and it wasn't eleven yet.

Benjamin didn't like it. We were only renting this outfit and it wasn't up to him to call for silence, say when and where he was going to rehearse – and those wooden sticks!

'Keep inside the STAGE!' 'Arry bawled again, unaware that my Benjamin had to be handled with quiet dignity and blatant flattery.

'Take it slower! What does he say for slower, luv? Pamelech, Mr Rubenivski, pamelech!'

'Rubenovska,' Benjamin said politely. 'A fire in his kishkers; would you ask him not to spit when he speaks? Pamelech,' he nodded.

'Turn!' 'Arry called and into the dazzling brightness of the big bareness, a buzzing and whirring began. In surprise, Leah and Benjamin didn't begin at all.

'Stop!'

The noise stopped. You could tell this had happened before.

'That is the sound the handles on the cameras will make. You will ignore it. Tell him,' 'Arry said in a flat voice.

'TURN!'

All morning it took to do what was the first act of our play in the theatre. Five minutes it would be up on the screen, 'Arry said.

Depressing.

The days of rehearsal and filming passed annoyingly – every morning the snowy mountains were wound up to the ceiling and our shop (we had chosen number sixteen reluctantly) was wound down and when we left sharp at one o'clock each day, up went the shop and down came a public house. Three new films a week they pushed out. A good business, if you could stand it.

As the week went on and it was nearly completed, Leah and Benjamin and Mama and Danny got happier and happier. Not me. It had made mincemeat of my story. All that was left was the wrapping of the story; they'd made up the rest. Black and white mime it was, that's all. Glorified mime. And for mime, writers you don't need; it's what I've said all along.

Depressing.

'Arry showed us roughly how it would look when it was completed. To me it seemed some of it would be just the same put in backwards.

'Needs cleaning up a bit, mind, needs shuftying abaht a bit, but it's come up nice,' he said. 'Funny it is. Even made the blokes 'ere laugh.'

It didn't make me so much as smile. Not a shmerchel. If I privately thought one would be plenty, I still nodded wisely when we all agreed ten copies for now would be enough – the children could maybe juggle with the other nine spools. But I'd never let Igor waste his money like this again.

And that was that. At least we were the first Yiddish family in London to have their own film in the intermission. Up it went on our posters and in our programmes and it must have given the Behrens and the others a krank.

And during the week we filmed it I made sure Benjamin knew that black shadows under the eyes show up shocking on a silver screen, whether it was true or not, and had my Gardiner's bed occupied on both sides as it should be. And whilst he was there I spoiled him with all the welcome that there was. And as Danny's fiancée had broken off their engagement and left him to go to her family in Americhky and he was more than a little upset, I told him Bella Grossman, too, was lonely, here's some money, take her out somewhere lovely and he did and . . .

If the world was run by writers there'd be more happily-ever-afters.

EPILOGUE

Tuesday 31 December 1912

I'm not so superstitious that I won't walk under a ladder but when my journals got burned I really did think it was maybe enough of an evil eye to put me off ever keeping one again. But in England they have a good thing: New Year resolutions. You make up your mind that in the New Year you'll do something and you start on 1 January. So tonight I bought a Straker's notebook. They aren't quite the same size or thickness as they used to be – cheaper looking altogether – but the red outside's the same and already I feel at home just starting this.

I'm making a party tonight and we'll listen to all the bells and dance around in the streets a bit though we don't know so many of the neighbours yet. Everyone's coming. And even though Pinchas and Leah will be here, Mama's promised to keep quiet and make no trouble tonight. At least, not much. It was that first film we made that spoiled everything, if you ask me. I was so wrong, wronger I couldn't be. It's true that year it happened that most of the films were weepies or tragedies; it's also true that 'Arry – Mr Bennett, we call him now – put his knees and elbows into making the best of it. What I'm saying is that those ten copies had disappeared as soon as the embarrassingly good review was in the *Bioscope* magazine and the next fifty went as well. Offers came from everywhere – Jacob Adler wrote and invited us to Americhky all expenses paid – and this time I believed him – and he wasn't the only one from out there.

Somewhere in the Bible it is – Pinchas could tell you where – is all that stuff, 'a time to sing and a time to dance, a time to speak and a time to keep shtumm' – something like that. Pinchas must know it if I do, yet right in the middle of the week

225

when Danny and Bella Grossman tell us they're getting married and leaving us for Americhky where her famous cousins have two grand theatres out there, Pinchas chooses a terrible moment and interrupts a difficult rehearsal with a short lecture on graven images and announces *he*'s taking our Leah, Sarah – whether she wants to go or not – and the three lovely little Rottmans to Palestine. Since Igor soothed and smoothed her into a bride I haven't heard Mama give a yell like that. She screamed new inventive curses, was so unfair, hurtful and discouraging that any self-respecting son-in-law would have pointed out that Palestine wasn't far enough to get away from such a mouth. But it's Pinchas we're talking about; Pinchas the angel; and angels don't put their hands on their hips and hate you with their eyes. Leah – the angel's wife – was doing just that. Meanwhile Pinchas was, quick, trying to repair the family net before all the Rubenovska fish got out. A little quiet talking, a bit of advice he was asking Mama – shmoosing now, 'And who else would have given me a home with your family and even given me your daughter for my wife in those difficult days, like you did?'

Mama made the familiar sound that clearly indicates that anyone can make a mistake.

'So, in Palestine, Leah and I have decided to take in some forgotten child like I was, Tante Rosa, in gratitude for what you did for me.'

And look, the shmoos had worked – doesn't it always? – Mama was wiping her eyes, Igor was polishing, polishing the face of his watch rather than look up, even Benjamin, a man who never jumps until he's seated on his horse and glued to the saddle, was nodding sympathetically. But say what Pinchas likes, he was breaking our family up for the second time and this time, noch, for choice. How would I bear it without my Leah, my friend, who told me everything and never minded that I told her nothing? Well – what would we do without new problems to fill up the yearning wadis that solving the old ones left?

'They need us there in Palestine, Mama,' Leah said, tears starting every minute down her lovely face. 'Our friends Yudit and Daniel are going too and we're going to start a new place right in the desert and . . .' Mama interrupted her. 'Palestine's got malaria, black death, ten plagues at least; my grandchildren will love it out there.'

It was an all crying day. I need a friend like buttons need buttonholes and there she was – gone. I shouldn't cry now. To Leah it isn't fair. Like me, where her husband goes, she goes.

'Forgive me, forgive me,' Leah said, kneeling and calling out like the youngest daughter of Koenig Lear and making everyone feel much worse.

That day passed and plenty more, but since then Mama treats Leah like an enemy. There will be so few of us left. Five – six and me are in ganz the whole company.

But the moving pictures have changed many things. No, tonight isn't for worrying about business. Tonight is for New Year resolutions. Me, I've already done mine: I'm writing my journal; Mama's never going to argue again; Pinchas is going to make jokes; Leah's going to be on time and my darling Benjamin is going to give up actresses.

I'm running from the kitchen to our bedroom, which is the biggest, loveliest room, and finally Leah comes down from upstairs bringing a couple of chairs. And she's amazed that everything's done, the bed's pushed back and the gate-leg table set up and all my chairs and the table's laid nice. She pops up again for the plates of food that she's made – lovely. Then Leah helps me set up the projector we borrowed from Mr Bennett. When everyone's back, we'll wake the children and show them themselves on the screen. I know we'll have to show it again and again tonight. The children didn't realize when they were playing 'moving pictures' at the warehouse that Mr Bennett was using the cameras. He says it was so funny and good, them pretending to be us, he thinks it'll make a sweet little filler. Sarah's going to surprise everyone tonight. A shame – in Palestine, moving pictures she won't have time to make. Dovid, of course, everyone can see he's turning into an acrobat and a clown and a show-off. You too, Dovid, can have a New Year resolution: be a schoolmaster; go home every day for tea and read, nights, like your Tata should.

Good. Mama's back with Katya. When the machine cools down and our men have counted up and locked up Igor will drive them here, Mama said, sitting down and looking suddenly very tired. I went to put on the kettle and heard Mama kiss Leah and start again to nag her not to go. So quick I made the lemon teas for us and put them on my little papier mâché tray and put a little table for them.

'Bubba must have known something,' Leah said. 'She said I'd take you across the water, didn't she, Mama? And to the Promised Land. And look at me, I'm going. And the moving pictures, they'll take you all to Americhky, won't they, Zeldele?'

'Tea,' I said stiffly, not looking at her. 'For you Leah, very strong. Mama? So-so with plenty of lemon. Katya? Just as it comes? And mine . . .'

Poor Katya. She can't understand why suddenly we're all staring at the mantelshelf and crying.